I WAS THERE WHEN THE GIANT FELL

Adam Nitz

ISBN: 1502774429
ISBN 13: 9781502774422

ABOUT THE SERIES

Each book in the *I Was There...* series takes a character who is very briefly mentioned in Scripture and imagines what his or her life might have been like. I want readers to experience a pivotal moment of Bible history and see it from a new perspective. In God's story, no one is a minor character—including you and me! We all have a wonderful role to play. My prayer is that these stories remind you that your life is important to God. I want you to get excited about God's Word and the story of *your* salvation. May God use these books to glorify his name, draw people ever deeper into his word, and there, open blind eyes to see the bright reality of God's undeserved love expressed in his Son and the world's only Savior— Jesus Christ.

NOTES TO THE READER

The Bible mentions Benaiah of Pirathon in only three verses. In 2 Samuel 23:30 and 1 Chronicles 11:31 he is simply a name listed among David's thirty mighty men. In 1 Chronicles 27:14 we are told that Benaiah of Pirathon was one of David's top army commanders and that he lead 24,000 men in his division. Other than these references we know nothing about Benaiah of Pirathon. (Please note that the Benaiah in this book is not to be confused with the more famous Benaiah son of Jehoiada who was also one of David's mighty men.)

Since there is so little known about Benaiah of Pirathon, it leaves much for the imagination. This account of his life is a work of historical fiction. Please read it as such. However, whenever the story crosses over into scenes mentioned in the Bible, I have done my best to remain true to the biblical portrayal of those actual, historical events. If you would like to read the biblical accounts that are mentioned or portrayed in the book, please see the "Bible References" section in the back of the book.

I have chosen to make the dialogue in the novel sound familiar to modern ears, while still being respectful of the time period. I have also done my best to thoroughly research the historical background to this period of Bible history. Not everything is known, and on some debatable points I had to make an educated choice.

I pray that you enjoy the book and are blessed by it!
Adam

1

SERVANT OF SAUL

I step through the doorway. The calm quiet of the storeroom gives way to the flurry of activity. Loud voices fill the chambers. Robes swish wide, billowing above the stone floor as several elders cross my path. A cluster of army officers stand in the corner—straight-backed and posture-perfect with bearded faces bobbing in animated conversation. A portly merchant totters past me toward the adjacent storerooms under the weight of a bulging basket.

My arms ache, full with a heavy load of freshly made robes. I weave my way along the corridor and into the antechamber just off the throne room, heading for the king's private chambers. As the king's chief attendant, I have a long list of things to do. My feet carry me as fast as they can.

As I walk, I think through the king's schedule for today. It has filled up quickly: Two merchants have requested an audience with him this morning, and they are already waiting outside. A group of Benjamites have come to petition him about some tribal matter. A thief was caught stealing from the palace treasury the other day—a serious offense!—and his case will go before the king today…or tomorrow, if necessary—

—*Whack!*

A deafening noise shatters my stream of thoughts. My feet stop moving. My heart stops beating. I stand still, swaying under the weight of the stack of robes. Are the Philistines attacking? There's been no advance warning! I don't hear war drums or watchmen shouting!

The activity in the once bustling throne room has stopped, and the noise has melted into an eerie, uneasy silence. Servants have stopped what they were doing, and they listen tensely. I set the robes down carefully on a low bench along the wall and start to walk gingerly forward in the direction of the king's chambers.

Suddenly, it comes again—an unearthly crashing sound, followed by several violent clattering bangs, and a gruff, roaring curse that is muffled by a wall. I stop moving again. Another dramatic moment of silence hangs in the room. It's that awful pause between knowing and not knowing. What is it? What's coming next?

With no warning at all, King Saul explodes out into the throne room. His tunic is torn, his heavy armor hangs disheveled, and his long hair flings around behind him, tangled and undone. His empty scabbard scrapes along the ground, dragging from his loose belt. Startled servants and officials scatter in every direction. I step back, sucking in my breath. It's happening again! It's only been a week! At least he's not wearing his sword this time. It took three of us to wrestle it away from him last week, and I have a nasty scar on my leg from the struggle.

I recover from the initial shock and snap back into reality. Getting down to business, I gesture to other attendants and whisper words of command while keeping a wary eye on the king. Fortunately, I am in the small anteroom off to the side which opens out into the throne room, and Saul hasn't noticed me yet. Instead, he is roaring at three attendants who are frozen in fear in the throne room. He stands next to his throne and stares at them with that barren, frightening expression on his face. He slams the palm of his hand violently on the back of his throne—once, twice, three times—and the bangs resound loudly through the stone chambers. Each echoing sound makes me cringe. Somehow, the sturdy wood never cracks. His face glows beet red, and his veins are arching like ropes out of his head. His eyes roam the room with a wild light glimmering in their depths.

I gesture to Elmar, and he nods, understanding the normal protocol for the situation. Elmar's sandals swish on the stone pavement as he sweeps out of the throne room and into the rest of the fortress-like palace to do whatever damage control needs to be done. He is excellent at explaining these outbursts and calming all who witness them. He will also cancel all of today's scheduled appointments for the king. Shamra and Hoshan follow behind him and quietly shut the large sliding doors to Saul's throne room so that only his closest attendants remain within.

Now the real work will begin. We try our best to keep these outbursts as private as possible. When the king goes into a rage like this, or his infamous melancholy settles down on him like a black cloud, there is no telling what damage it might do to his reputation among the people. It's also impossible to gauge how long it will last. Sometimes it only takes an hour or so, and sometimes it takes days for him to calm down and return to normal. Even more important, we have to make sure that no Philistine spy gets word of Saul's weaknesses. His enemies must always see him as the fierce, military genius that he usually is.

Today, judging by his eyes, the evil spirit is on him stronger than ever, torturing his mind and driving him insane. Anger blows through me like a violent wind at the injustice of it.

I curse under my breath. *Why, God?*

As the chief attendant, I feel most responsible for keeping yet another outburst in check. I continue trying to issue orders to the others from the shelter of the anteroom. There is a side entrance to the rest of the palace behind me and to my right. Only Saul's closest servants are allowed access there. If need be, I can slip through there unnoticed and go get reinforcements.

Shamra finishes shutting the door and scurries in my direction.

Saul roars at him from next to his throne. "Where are *you* going? Conspiracy! Is it you? Or you?" He points ominously in the room at several of his other servants with his meaty finger, and his words hang in the air, trembling. Spit is dribbling down his beard, pooling on his expensive red tunic. Suddenly, his back arches as if some invisible tormentor has just jabbed his back with a needle. An unearthly scream erupts from his lips.

Several of the newly hired servants stand transfixed, staring wide-eyed at their king, hands hanging limp at their sides. Even for those of us who are more seasoned attendants, we never get used to it. How many months has it been since this terrible spirit began to torment him? Sometimes, like now, he is out of his mind with violent rage, and other times he wallows in a deep sadness.

I never dreamed things would turn out this way. Years ago, when I became the king's attendant, I was so excited and proud! It was like I lived in a dream. I had prayed my whole life for Israel to have a king, and now my greatest hopes had come true—and I would be *his servant*. How I looked up to King Saul, as if he could do no wrong! I just knew he would unite our fractured people, unify all the tribes, make us the most powerful nation in the world, and spread Yahweh's fame to the ends of the earth. And *I* would be part of it all. And he started out so well! He was doing everything I had hoped he would do, and our nation was becoming stronger and stronger.

Yet, he kept disobeying God's great prophet Samuel and taking matters into his own hands. He had some great military successes, but also many setbacks and problems. Despite it all, I know Yahweh will bless him. I continue to store those same hopes for the future in my heart, even now as I see him in such a terrible state.

Shamra comes up beside me, his breathing frightened and raspy. I take him aside and whisper in his ear, "Hurry—go and get that young man. You know—the youth from Bethlehem that plays the harp. He is one of the king's armor-bearers."

Shamra looks at me blankly. He stammers, "Which one is he again? Harp player…a court musician? An armor-bearer, though? There's so many of them…I get them all confused!" He is blabbering in his fear.

I scowl at him. "How can you forget him? His name is David. The king favors him, so he comes and goes from the palace when we call for him…"

Shamra's blank stare continues. He blinks at me like a confused sheep.

"Don't you remember? He's a good-looking, strong young man. His playing is the only thing that can settle the king when he gets this bad. He is probably at home with his father's sheep in Bethlehem."

A light of understanding finally dawns, erasing Shamra's mindless expression. "Oh, that boy! Yes. It's been a while since we've had him come. Forgive me. Whose son is he again? Where does he live?"

"Beth-le-hem." I pronounce the word slowly for him this time. I shouldn't be so short with him, but I am frustrated. "His father is some inconsequential man. Let's see…he's of the tribe of Judah…older man…what's his name again? Jora? Jubin? Josiah? I don't remember. Ask Hoshan—he's from Bethlehem. He knows the boy's father and where he lives. He's the one who suggested him to the king. Go get directions from him."

"Why doesn't Hoshan go, then?" Shamra turns and looks back nervously.

I pierce him with my sternest gaze. "Are you questioning my decision?"

"No…I just…"

"I need Hoshan here to help me control the king. He's invaluable to me. I need you to do this. Now!"

I watch as Shamra stumbles away and ventures along the wall, cringing as Saul's voice booms through the chambers. He steps haltingly back out into the throne room and approaches Hoshan. Hoshan stands on the dais, desperately fanning the king with a frond and trying to speak calming words to him as he continues to roar and carry on.

Shamra reaches Hoshan and touches his back. Hoshan pauses, the frond wavering in the air as he bends down to listen. Shamra whispers to him. Warily, Hoshan keeps one eye on the erratic king. He whispers the answer into his ear and then quickly turns back to the king and resumes fanning him with the frond. Shamra scampers back to me and jumps midway as Saul roars at him from the throne.

"What? I saw you whispering! Don't think I don't know what you are trying to do!"

I squeeze my eyes shut, wishing with all my might that the king would just be silent. The words that come out of his mouth when he is like this shake my confidence in him. I cringe as he rants on and on.

His voice gets louder as he suddenly switches topics. "Samuel! Where is Samuel? I need God's prophet! I command him to come to me *now!*" He slams his fist on the throne. "The longer he stays away, the more the people whisper. Doesn't he know he's destroying my reputation? How am I supposed to lead these people without God's prophet? Besides, I didn't do anything wrong!" His eyes scan the room. "It was the men—the *men!* They didn't listen. *They* disobeyed God, not *me!* Where is God, anyway? Why won't he *listen?* I'm his *anointed!*"

Suddenly, tears stream from Saul's eyes. He whimpers like a small child and collapses backward into his throne. His head drops into his hands. "Why? Why? Why?" he repeats in a broken voice, his final words fading into a bitter silence. His head now slumps down over his knees, and his long unruly hair drapes over his lap as several violent sobs shake his entire body. He looks like a child having a fit.

I turn and see Shamra staring senselessly back into the chambers at the king.

"Go! What are you waiting for? Go on! Fetch that boy and bring him back here!" I say.

He almost falls over himself as he runs for the servants' door.

I turn back to the king. It is as if his body has turned to wax; he has melted all the way off of his throne and now lies on the floor in front of the dais. I have never seen him so out of his mind, and it scares me. I watch with bated breath as Hoshan bends closer to him.

"My lord king, perhaps you would like something to eat? A bath? A brief rest in your chambers?" he asks.

At the sound of the word "king," Saul's whole body goes stiff like a log. He lifts himself up on his hands and knees and roars again. "*King*! Yes! Yahweh's *anointed*!" He spits out the last word like it's a sour grape. He throws his head back, and bitter laughter echoes through the chambers.

I shake my head sadly. These tirades can last for hours. His mood will swing from delirious rage to unhinged terror to helpless sadness. Then he will be perfectly normal for days, weeks, or even months. The strong, intelligent King Saul will return. He will lead his people with strength once more.

I pray that this episode is over soon. When it is, I'll have to gather the servants together and threaten them with death if they breathe a word of this to anyone. There are enough rumors of the king's instability out there. No need for one of his trusted servants to add more fuel to the fire.

After several excruciating hours, Shamra finally returns with the boy. I am one of five attendants holding the king down as he struggles against us—his eyes desperately wild, his chest rising and falling, and his whole body trembling with fury. My muscles are strained to the breaking point. Saul's strength is legendary. He is using all of it to break free from our grip.

I glance back and see Shamra guiding the young man into the main throne room where there is a low bench behind a folded wooden screen. We try to shield even the musicians from seeing their king in this state, though no one could prevent them from hearing the sounds that reverberate through the chambers. We do the best we can.

"Hurry up! Play! *Play!*" I shout as I struggle hard to hold the king's arm down against his throne. He is trying to kill himself again. He yells out that he's going to his private chambers to fall on his sword. Then, desperate silence fills the air again as he strains with all his might against us.

From behind the screen I hear a rustle as David lifts the instrument. Suddenly, the king changes positions in his struggle, and I brace myself rigid against his mighty arm. My head feels like it will burst with the energy.

And then, the most enchanting melody wafts into the air of the chambers. I feel the king's arm stop struggling, pulse with latent power, and then begin to relax beneath me. Another one of the king's shouts chokes off midway and dies on his lips. His mouth hangs open, and his eyes stare out into space. Slowly, ever so slowly, he begins to sink back into his throne as his body shudders, and he draws a few deep, wavering breaths. Tentatively, I release my firm grip on the king. I can see his mind just barely starting to return as his chest slows to a steady heaving. He keeps blinking his eyes and shaking his head.

Suddenly, the rich, sweet sound of David's youthful voice fills the room. He is singing a song about Yahweh and his mercy, his words rising like fragrant incense. The whole mood in the room is instantly transformed. I smile weakly at the other attendants as King Saul closes his weary eyes and rests his head on his hand. It is the only thing that works, when he gets this bad. His violence and depression are getting more serious each time.

As David continues to play and sing, Saul sits quietly, still as a stone, and the beautiful song fills all of our souls. Like a man waking up from a bad dream, color begins to return to his cheeks. New life flows through him as the evil spirit leaves him and his sanity returns.

A warm ball of hope and relief wells up in my throat. Rare tears form in the corners of my eyes. It is an unrefined peasant song, like a shepherd might sing to his sheep—humble words of God's love sung to a simple melody. Yet, there is something about these words that lodges in my heart. The cold and stony places within me begin to melt. Maybe it is the sudden transition from struggling with all my might against an unreasonable king to sudden peace and a tender melody, but it seems deeper than that. It is a holy moment. The future is frightening and uncertain, but in this instant all is right with the world. I know Yahweh will get us through. He will protect this crumbling nation. Perhaps he will return to Saul and empower him again. Silently, wordlessly, I pray for it with all my heart.

2

SERAH

The heat wraps around me as I bend over the fire. The pot sizzles. I breathe in deeply. Earthy fragrances—onions, carrots, lentils, fresh herbs—fill me with pleasing warmth. I stir the mixture, blowing at the rising steam. It's almost ready. It's almost time. My palms grow sweaty. That familiar tightness seizes me inside my throat. That familiar panic rises like the chaos of the seas inside my heart. Tonight I eat alone with Piram, my husband. Breath escapes from my lips in a soft, trembling sigh. I finish stirring the stew, tap the wooden mixing rod against the side of the pot, and set it aside. I rub my hands together, warm skin twisting against warm skin—a physical symbol of the twisting nervousness and panic rubbing together in my mind.

This is how it always feels when I know that we will be alone together. Last night I cringed beneath his rough embrace. I did not sleep well. He has been so unstable lately, more so than normal. His mood changes like the weather—so unpredictably!

I am not often left alone with my husband. My son Arah and his wife Jadia are usually here, but they left this morning with our youngest son, Joel, and set out to visit my brother Shem's household in the nearby town of Arumah. They will bring back some supplies that we need from a trader there, but the main reason they left is to help my brother with his work. Shem is almost as poor as we are, and two of his sons were tangled with their oxen last week. They will live, but their broken bones and bruises prevent them from helping in the fields at such a busy time.

I look around the small courtyard in the center of our house. It is my favorite place because there is no roof overhead, and the lighting is better than anywhere else in the house. While I cook, I am still just a few steps away from the storerooms or the back room where we eat and sleep. Many of my neighbors don't have that luxury. Their fire and oven are outside. The rooms in the front of our house off of the courtyard often serve as shelter for our animals, especially when the weather is cold. Today those rooms are empty, except for a few supplies. I've left the front door open so I can see when Piram is coming home. I turn in that direction for a moment and look out through the doorway to the distant hills. A bird circles beneath the lowering sun. The hills are bathed in the gentle light of evening. Benaiah, my first born, is still out there with my husband. Since there is extra work with Arah and Joel gone, he must be working the fields late. I am sure Piram is working him to death.

Sadness descends like a dark cloud on my soul. Poor Benaiah!

When he was a tiny boy he used to toddle around naked in this courtyard, throwing stones and digging in the dirt. How he would giggle as he played. His dark, round eyes would fill with mischief and laughter when he played with his friend Berechiah. They would pretend to be champion soldiers hunting Philistines in our garden or around our olive trees. I would stand at the entrance to our home and laugh as I watched them creep around and throw rocks at imaginary enemies.

His childhood was certainly not easy, though. My brief smile melts away as painful memories cross my mind. I can still hear the songs the children would sing about him in the village streets. The names they called him stabbed my heart! I would rub oil on his cuts and bruises after the fights. His eyes were shot through with pain as he asked endless questions about why the villagers antagonized and hated him.

And the hatred goes on to this day. Lately I have seen the resignation, the resentment, and the bitter anger that broods over him. I am frustrated by my utter helplessness to change it at all.

My eye catches movement along the path outside our house. It is my husband, Piram, coming home, and Benaiah is not with him. It is just as I feared. Benaiah will not be home for the evening meal. I will be alone with Piram. It saddens me and scares me. Benaiah likes to be alone. He stays out late in the fields and avoids the house. While other young men look forward to the evening meal with their families, Benaiah is often absent. He and Piram do not get along. I am sure the long day together has not gone well.

Piram saunters behind our donkey. His robes are loose and surprisingly clean after a long day's work. They are still tucked into his belt. I cringe as I watch the large muscles in his arm flex and release as he beats the donkey onward with a stick. *Swap! Swap!* The animal surges forward the last few steps, and Piram ties it up outside. The wind catches Piram's wild mat of hair as he bends down, pouring water from the outdoor jar into his hands and splashing it onto his thick, black beard.

"Serah!" he bellows.

I jump.

"Serah!"

I run to the entryway. My heart is leaping. "Yes, my lord, what is it?"

"The water jar is getting low. Did you fill it this morning?" His black eyes bore into me.

"Yes, of course. I do it every morning."

"I can't believe it would be this low already! Fill two jars tomorrow! This is not enough."

"Yes, my lord." I keep my eyes down, avoiding his look.

"Is the meal almost ready? I'm starving!"

"It will be ready very soon!" I assure him.

"Hurry it up, then!" he barks.

I hurry back inside and check the food. My hands are trembling and damp with sweat. I wipe them several times on a rough cloth. The flatbread is ready, fresh from the oven, sizzling and steaming on its hot stone slab. It is warm and moist—perfect. I bend close and breathe in deeply. Fresh bread is one of my favorite fragrances—one I smell every day. It is strange to me that even though this smell can bring back my most painful memories, I still enjoy it.

Piram brushes past without acknowledging me. I hear him rustling around in the back room where we eat. Fortunately, I already have the blanket spread out for the meal. I will give him a few moments to relax. The cool shade will help him calm down after his hot day in the field. Hopefully he will be in better spirits when I bring in the food.

I try to gather my confidence. I made a delicious meal. What could go wrong? He is not drunk tonight—at least not yet. He will probably busy himself with his wine after the meal. Then, perhaps, I will slip out of the house later and get away on some pretense. I might go to my friend Ruba, the midwife, on the other side of the village. Her husband is one of the most respected elders of Pirathon. She is an older woman—wise in the ways of the world and deeply compassionate. She helped me birth all of my babies. She cared for me and comforted me after my miscarriages. Our bond is strong. Maybe tonight we can sit and talk, or I can help her finish her evening chores. I will be long gone when Piram's wine begins to take effect.

The stew is ready. It smells delicious. I can't leave it on the fire too long—burning it would be absolutely disastrous. Using a bit of goatskin over my hand, I lift the heavy pot off of the open fire and use my ladle to spoon some out. The steaming mixture pops and sizzles as it slides into the bowl. Spicy aromas make my mouth water. Gently I blow on it-- once, twice, three times—swishing it back and forth, relishing the smell. I permit myself to feel a rare taste of pride. A tiny bit of confidence trickles into my soul. I pour a little water from another bowl and mix it with the hot stew. I touch some to my tongue, and flavors explode in my mouth—rich, earthy, delicious flavors. More confidence flows through my thoughts. It will all work out! I will be okay tonight! Good food is one sure way to pacify my husband.

A loud shout makes me jump and shatters my thoughts into fear again.

Piram calls from the other room. "Serah! Serah!"

I resent the way he spits my name.

"What's taking so long? Bring in my food!"

Anger rises in my throat, mixed with fear, but I put out its fire. "Just a moment!" I call. I take another deep breath and pick up the warm bread in one hand and the pot of stew in the other. The serving dish is heavy, but I have done it many times. I whisper a quick prayer as I walk. *O God of my fathers, be with me tonight. Protect me! Give me strength!*

I turn the corner from the courtyard and enter the main room slowly, as quietly as I can, my feet brushing soft on the stone floor. Piram sits on the blanket that is spread out for the meal. His wicked scowl confirms his bad mood. A flicker of fear dances in my eyes, but I quickly blink it away. I notice that the wineskin sits open next to him, and a familiar smell fills the room. He is already deep into some of our strongest wine! My heart sinks, and my hands grow cold and clammy despite the heat coming off the dish. This changes everything! For now I must do the best I can. I smile at him, mustering the sweetest, most demure, most accommodating look I can. Perhaps he sees that it is a bit forced—I don't know.

He shifts his large frame and leans forward as I set the meal down between us. A trace of a smile steals across his lips as he breathes in the fragrance of fresh food. I made his favorite yogurt drink tonight, so I hurry back into the courtyard to fetch it for him. I reenter the room and take my place. We sit across from each other in an awkward silence. He seems fine with it. He says nothing and barely even looks at me.

I say my prayer, mouthing the words silently so that only Yahweh can hear them. Piram rarely prays before the meals anymore, like he used to when we were first married. Sometimes, if he is in good spirits, I might gently ask him to lead us in prayer—as the head of the household ought to do. He sometimes does, but it is a fearfully rare occurrence.

I know he has strange notions of God. He worships Yahweh, but he worships many other gods as well. He often goes to the high place, the Bamah, and sacrifices there. He used to ask me to make cakes for the Queen of Heaven or perform other rituals for Asherah or Astarte. I will not join him in such things. I cannot. Where does he get such ideas? I am a descendant of the great leader Abdon who followed the only true God! How can Piram forsake the God of Abraham—the God of our fathers? Yet he's not the only one in the village. Sadly, there is a great mix of beliefs in Pirathon.

It was not always so. When Abdon ruled, the idols were all broken, and the high place near town was destroyed. Over time, his reforms have been ignored. Our great prophet Samuel led a great reform not long ago, yet many of my people cling to idols still.

I shake my head and try to return my focus to my prayer. My mind is flitting about so nervously! I must keep it under control tonight! If Piram sees any sign of negativity on my face, or if he senses a moment when my attention wanders away from him, he'll raise his voice at me—or worse. Focus, Serah. Focus!

I look up at my husband. Piram already has some of the bread in his hand and is dipping it into the olive oil. I watch him gnaw at the bread. Wet, oily crumbs slide down his face and stick in his beard. How sloppy and disgusting! There is a coldness in his eyes as he looks at me tonight—a coldness and yet…a fire. He takes another swig of his wine. I can't read his thoughts right now, and it frightens me all the more.

"How was your day in the fields?" I venture.

"Hot," he says curtly. "Maybe tomorrow you can help me in the fields. We're behind."

Silence again.

The last thing I want to do is work in the fields with Piram. I will have just as much to do when I get home as any other day.

"That dog of yours is still out there," he says between mouthfuls of bread. "He'd better finish that ditch before he comes home tonight or I'll bury him in it."

I bite my tongue. It frustrates me that Piram thinks so little of my Benaiah, even though Benaiah works like a slave for him.

My nervousness grows during the long silence that follows. He chews loudly, lips smacking a little as he takes another bite of the bread. His robe rustles against itself as he reaches out and rips more bread off the flat loaf.

I take my turn and drink some of the yogurt drink. This meal is one of my favorites as well. My mother taught me how to make it so long ago. I can still hear her kind voice and feel the touch of her gentle skin as she directed my hands and taught me her methods. She was so kind. Why did I ever have to leave Father's house to marry a man like *this*? Why did God have to take my parents away from me so soon? Both of them died in the great plague several years ago. Many villagers got sick and died. Not many of the older ones survived. They are with Yawheh now. How I long for the old days!

Piram takes some more of his bread and reaches for the steaming dish of stew that I set before him. He scoops some out with the bread and lifts it to his mouth. I allow myself to study his reaction. I know he secretly looks forward to this meal every time I prepare it. His approval would mean that I might finally be able to relax and enjoy this meal. I smile as the savory mixture touches his lips, but my anticipation melts at the change in his expression. He recoils, spitting and spluttering, wiping his face with his hand.

"Hot! Too hot!" he roars. "You fool! I saw your smile! You wanted me to burn my lips off, didn't you?"

My mind reels in panic as the rage boils out of him. He does not know how to make it stop. Why didn't he blow on it? Instant fear freezes my body rigid.

My lips mumble apologies over and over again—phrases well-worn by much use. The words come to me so naturally I barely have to think to produce the sounds. "I'm sorry, my lord. I should have cooled it with some water. It was very foolish. Please forgive me." I desperately hope my stream of apologies will make a difference this time.

I run to get him a bowl of water from the water jar. I fear for my life. As if I'm living with a savage bear, I walk gingerly around him. I try to appease and appeal to him, but I still never feel safe. I can never be sure everything will be okay. If I were perfect, maybe he wouldn't get so angry—maybe I would be safe. But how can anyone be perfect? The stew is far from perfect. I know that now.

He violently grabs the bowl of water from my hands, spilling a large portion of it all over our meal. "Look what you did!" he roars, gesturing erratically over the meal. He lifts the water to his lips and spills it down his beard, drenching his robe.

Why is he acting so wildly? Is he already drunk with wine? He hasn't been home long enough! Has he been drinking in the fields again?

He throws down the bowl and rubs at his beard with his hand, trying to wipe the water away. In the process, he bumps the pot of stew, causing some to slurp out and splatter on the blanket.

"Look at this mess, now!" he roars. His black eyes are radiating like red hot furnaces. Violent curses stream from his mouth as his rage deepens in intensity.

I feel myself begin to shut down. My soul crawls into its shell, created for times like this. I bend down like a beaten creature, wordless, desperately trying to clean up the mess. I cringe in expectation of his touch. Still, it shocks me out of my senses when his hard grip digs into my arm and he yanks me toward him. Awash with fear, I stand on shaking feet as he hisses cutting words in my face. The alcohol on his breath is nauseating. How much has he had already? A whole skin of wine?

I apologize again and again. "My lord, please—I am so sorry, my lord. I was so foolish. I should have tasted it first." My stomach sickens as he drags me out of the room and into the courtyard. It really is my fault. I should have added some cool water to it before he tried to eat it. I know better. I was so sure he would like it. I forgot. I wasn't thinking.

He shoves me hard onto the stone bench along the far wall. I sense that he wants to slap me across the face. I know he will not. He finds other ways to unleash his fury on me. He tries not to leave marks on my face where others might see them and suspect what he does to me. The elders of Pirathon are good, upstanding men. If the elders find out what he does to his wife, they will not be merciful to him. Such things are not permitted in our village, even though they happen.

Instead, he spins me around and holds my neck down with the rigid palm of his hand. My cheek presses down on the rough, cold stone. He screams into my ear as he pushes his hand down hard, harder, harder... His words are just angry sounds, unintelligible to my frightened ears. I feel like my head is going to burst.

I begin to struggle with the rest of my body—a wild, desperate struggle. I know I shouldn't. I know it might make it worse—but what if he kills me this time? What if his rage takes control? He stops pushing my face into the bench. He stops screaming in my ear. I feel his intolerable weight shifting behind me as I whimper and plead into his stony silence.

Suddenly, I feel his full weight settle down as he sits on top of me, as if I am some beast for him to ride. His awful heaviness presses my body in an unnatural position. He is killing off my struggle. I give it up and lie limp like an empty wineskin. He grabs my hair, pulls my head back toward him, and bends in close to my ear. It feels like my neck might snap if he pulls any further. A thousand needles are piercing my scalp. I feel his rough beard against the side of my face. His lips press right against my ear, and another explosion of sound erases all my thoughts as he hisses unmentionable words—names that tear the humanity out of my soul.

Tears of pain blur my vision as I try to focus on something, *anything*, else. I try to break free in my mind and escape the terror I feel. I look out through the open door, out to the hills and the setting sun. Perhaps I can focus on their beauty and leave the ugliness of this room.

I blink, surprised, as a strange shadow fills the open doorway of the house. The figure looks like an avenging angel aglow with the blinding light of the setting sun. From my vantage point—pressed down on the stone bench, head hanging from my hair, hot tears stinging my eyes—only I can see him. He steps through the door, taking in the scene before him. The evening sun touches his curly black hair, his face emerging from the light. I see the fullness of his shocked expression, both tender and hard. His eyes that are often faraway and pained are now blazing like coals pulled from a fire. It is my son—Benaiah!

3

BENAIAH

Sweat stings my eyes. I slam the shovel into the ground and feel the satisfying bite as it cuts hard into the earth one last time. I heave it up and dump another shovelful of earth onto the pile. Good enough!

Piram wanted this ditch to reach the tree by tonight. I've got twenty or so cubits left to go, but I'm done. I'm tired and I don't want to do this anymore. We could have finished it if he would have helped more. Instead he spent all day criticizing my work and cursing me out. Of course, if my half-brother, Arah, were doing this, Piram would have treated him differently. He's the favorite, and Piram hardly ever criticizes him.

Frustration boils inside me. It's been a hot, miserable day in the field. The last thing I want to do tonight is eat the evening meal with my stepfather. It must have been nice—sitting in the shade and drinking from his little personal water jar all day. Ha! Like he actually had water in there anyway! Judging by the glaze in his eyes, his jar was full of strong drink. His laziness and

22

drunkenness will be the death of our family—especially now that we are shorthanded for a few days!

I squint into the setting sun, annoyed by the sweat that drips down my face. I scratch my beard, which itches intolerably, and I run my fingers along the back of my neck and through my hair. My whole head is wet! I use my arm to wipe the sweat from my face and eyes. Stooping down, I gather the tools together in a pile, wrap the cloth around them, and heave them up onto my back. I feel their weight settle on my shoulder. Of course Piram took the donkey home before I could load my tools on its back. It's just like him. He wants me to carry them myself, like a slave. I should leave them here and let them be stolen! I can't, though—Piram is not the only one who relies on these tools.

I set out on the path to town, swaying a little at first as I get used to the weight of the tools. I don't want to go home, but where else can I go? Anger courses through my blood. No matter what, I need to go back to the house to drop off the tools. And if I'm home, I might as well eat there too. I *am* famished and dying of thirst, and I know my mother is making a tasty stew tonight.

The thought of being anywhere near Piram again grates on my nerves. Isn't there somewhere else I could go? Who might lend me some food tonight? My friend Berechiah and his family are good to me, but they are busy with visiting relatives tonight. My other friend Mahlo might help me, but his family doesn't like me. Hannah's father, maybe? He respects me, but he keeps me at arm's length. I doubt he would appreciate me dropping by tonight. I shake my head. I could try my hand at hunting for my evening meal, but how long would that take? Finding game, let alone roasting it on a fire… I guess I just have to go home and endure another few hours with Piram. I spit on the ground in frustration. I need to calm myself down before I get there.

My feet crunch on the path as I walk homeward. I pass a young boy as he leads his father's sheep just off the trail. He glances my way and then quickly turns his head, pretending not to see me. His name is Miclah. I don't know him that well, but he certainly knows me. His head is down. He calls to the sheep and turns the small flock slightly away from the path. He does not look at me. He does not talk to me.

Pirathon sits proudly atop the hill. Sun glints off the side of the stone wall and the mudbrick homes. A few other young men are coming in from the fields with their fathers. Hooves clatter on the ground as they lead their animals back to shelter or pasture. Shamgar and his four sons pass me on the path. They don't say a word to me, but they don't have to. The frowns that wrinkle their faces when they recognize me communicate their feelings clearly. There is a hardness in their eyes that I have grown accustomed to. Most families greet each other on the road, but I rarely get a nod of recognition from those who pass me.

My mood worsens.

I pass through the town gate. Several elders are debating heatedly amongst themselves as I walk by. I catch bits and pieces of the conversation.

"Are you certain he moved the boundary stone?"

"How can anyone be sure?"

"What's the punishment for such a violation?"

Their voices fade as I turn down the long street. Piram's house is on the other side of the village. The distance from the fields to the house makes for a long walk. The houses are spaced out with areas for gardens and some fig and olive trees. I pass the large olive press near the center of town. Its wide beam casts a shadow that flicks over my face as I walk beneath it. No one is pressing olives this time of year.

I take a short detour through town that takes me past the household of Eliezer, Hannah's father. Maybe I can catch a glimpse of Hannah working outside their home at the oven. That would definitely improve my mood! I stretch my neck from side to side and shift the tools slightly on my shoulder. I can feel the ache in my muscles after another long day. I can't wait to sit down and relax.

Soon I see Eliezer's house in the distance. I quicken my step, despite the tiredness. Two women are gathered about the oven outside the home. Hannah's mother, Miriam, shades her eyes and looks off in my direction, trying to figure out who I am. She's a sickly woman, easily one of the thinnest I've ever seen. I'm surprised to see her working tonight. I wave my hand. She does not return the favor. I follow her gaze as she looks to a woman who is facing away from me on the other side of the oven. My heart beats a bit faster as the woman turns—it's Hannah! A smile flashes across my face. At least *something* is going right today. Maybe I'll be able to talk to her a little as she finishes helping with the evening meal.

If I have my way, Hannah will be my wife someday. Her father has made it clear that he disapproves of the match, but I will not give up. I see the sparks in her eyes when she catches my glance. A fire blazes inside me at the mention of her name or sight of her. She's the only woman who seems to have any interest in me, and talking with her feels like sunshine after rain. It's been a little while since I've helped her father in his fields. Often she comes out to bring us water and bread. Thinking of her gets me through the long grueling days of monotonous work. Talking with her tonight is just what I need to lift my spirits.

Miriam takes a few steps toward Hannah. She seems upset. She points at me and then points inside the house. Hannah's head comes up and around as she glances in my direction. My breath stops. Her beauty captivates me. I can't read her expression when she recognizes me. I smile and hold my hand up in greeting. Is that a trace of a smile on her lips? Her hand begins to come up to return my wave but stops as Miriam commands her full attention. I walk even faster, trying to close the distance between us. Hannah's mother is speaking sharply to her now—ordering her to do something. Hannah's face twists in anger. She gestures wildly with her arms at her mother, who then raises her voice even more.

I catch a few words—"...not good...get inside...I feel faint..."

Hannah's hair flips sideways as she turns abruptly and heads for the house. Just before she opens the door, she turns toward me again. Her large, dark eyes find mine and pause. I sense a slight longing in her look, a gentle glow in her eyes—or am I just imagining it? I get a fleeting glimpse of her, and she's gone, swallowed by the darkness of her home.

My heart sinks. When I reach the house, Miriam sits calmly near the oven, her face pale. She looks shaken, tired, and sickly, but she wears an icy expression as I draw near.

I nod to her. "Good evening to you, Miriam, and to the whole house of Eliezer."

"Good evening, son of Serah." Her tone is restrained.

"May I speak with Hannah for a moment?"

"No, Benaiah. Tonight is not a good night. She's very busy. We all are."

I swallow my frustration hard. "May I come by later, after the evening meal? It's been a while since I've talked with her."

"Not tonight. I do not feel well. Surely you understand, Benaiah. Please be on your way. Give my regards to your mother."

"Sorry to disturb you. I will." It is difficult to hide the defeat in my voice.

As I walk away from the house, bitterness rises within me. The raw beauty of the setting sun splitting a cloud with orange light does little to lift my heart. The large fig tree near their house casts a shadow that matches my mood. The tools press hard against my shoulder. I just want today to be over.

Finally I arrive at our house and lift the tools off my shoulder, setting them on the ground. I stretch my shoulder and rub at the soreness with my other hand. It feels good to be free of the weight. I lean forward against the rough bark of a tree and take a deep breath. I need a moment to gather my wits before I go inside. I must calm down before I face Piram again. The last thing I need is a beating from him tonight. Not that I couldn't handle a beating. I just don't care to deal with the consequences of losing my temper and fighting him.

I can already hear his voice, dark and thick with disdain. He's going to ask me if I finished the ditch, too. What will I tell him? I let out a deep sigh before gathering a long pull of air back into my lungs. The fragrance of my mother's cooking is undeniably tempting. It's been too long since I've tasted her delicious stew. My stomach rumbles at the thought. I sigh again. I might as well get it in there and get it over with.

I head over to wash my face and hands at the water jar outside the door. A noise from within stops me in my tracks. I listen—senses on high alert. Again, I hear it—a muffled scream, a grunt, and a desperate shuffling sound. What is going on? I rush to the door and stop just inside. I look through the courtyard and squint into the dim shadowy place beyond.

My eyes take in the scene and then grow wide with shock. Piram is on top of my mother, forcing her down onto a stone bench. He has a fistful of her hair, and he's pulling back, stretching her neck in a gross, unnatural position. His mouth is next to her head, and he's hissing violent, hateful, demeaning words into her ear. It's not the first time I've seen his violence toward my mother, but I've never seen it quite like this. Her lip is bloody, and tears stream from her eyes. She looks broken and crushed. He's going to kill her this time!

Something snaps inside me. Hatred explodes in my brain, and all my senses burn to life with intense heat. My thoughts go blank. I must end this once and for all! I rush at Piram, my muscles bunching in readiness. I unleash years of pent-up fury as my elbow connects hard with the side of his head. He reels backward off of my mother and down to the dust where he belongs. Hateful worm! How dare he treat her like this! I'll kill him with my bare hands!

4

SERAH

My head bobs up from the bench, and I gasp desperately for air as if I have just escaped drowning in rushing waters. I rub my scalp, breathing through the pain that throbs in my head, and I watch—eyes wide and wild with fear. Piram falls backward, narrowly missing the oven. I hear the smack as his head hits the hard stone floor. He bellows with pain and surprise. It only stuns him momentarily, though. He suddenly comes up from the ground like a madman and lunges toward my Benaiah, roaring with all his might. I am in a dreamy daze of shock. It is like watching two male bears—one old and experienced, the other young and strong—fighting to the death. I sob uncontrollably as they slam into each other—I feel like I am outside of my body.

Years of rage and resentment are boiling out of my son. When I try pulling them apart, Piram shoves me off to the side, and the cold earthen wall slams into my body. New pain shoots through me. I stand flat up against the wall, sobbing and screaming for them to stop. My voice sounds like it comes from a distant place, not from my own throat. Oblivious to my cries, they continue to wrestle. Their feet scuffle against the floor as they strike each other, grunting with effort. It lasts only a few moments, but it feels much longer. At first, I fear Piram will kill my son instantly. I know all too well the power behind those meaty hands. Yes, he is older, but he is not weak—not yet. He is a strong man, and his grip is as hard as bronze. Most men in the village fear my husband for his sheer physical size and strength. He grabs at Benaiah again and tries to throw him against the wall, but Benaiah twists around, uses Piram's momentum against him, and once more slams his stepfather hard to the ground. Once there, he kicks him brutally in the side. Piram bellows and thrashes around, trying to regain a better position.

I have never seen Benaiah like this! He is a starving, enraged animal released from a cage. His face glistens, tight and intense. There is a fury and strength about him that unsettles me. It's like I do not even know my own son. As he rains blows down on his stepfather, I realize he is stronger than anyone knows. He might actually kill Piram with his bare hands. The thought is so shocking to me that it takes a moment for me to recover.

Piram's blood smears on the floor as he twists about, desperately trying to ward off this wild, furious attack. He grunts in pain as blow after blow connects with his body. I have to step in. I have to stop this. The elders will punish Benaiah heartlessly for this. He is disrespecting his stepfather, the head of the house. They will never believe Benaiah's version of this story over my husband's. They will have no mercy. I grab at Benaiah's arm, and it drags me along on its way to batter Piram again.

In response to my touch, though, Benaiah's arm soon slows, and he lets it fall. He takes a step back. Hate is still radiating out of every part of him—his chest heaving, eyes blazing, body trembling, and jaw clenching. He stands there looking down at his stepfather who has been knocked unconscious.

My touch has always had a calming effect on him. When he was a small boy and the villagers picked on him, he would come home trembling with bitter sobs that shuddered out of him. Without saying a thing, I would put my arms gently around him and feel his body relax in my embrace. The sobs would slow and the trembling grow less. I thank God that my touch still calms him today. The hate is still burning in his eyes, but it has drained away from the muscles in his arms. I can feel his body relaxing and his breathing becoming less intense.

Piram sits slumped sideways, his head rolled back against the wall. There is a gruesome cut above his eye and blood trickling from his lips. What if he wakes again? Piram's eyes are closed for now, but during the fight those black orbs were lit with the brightest hate I'd ever seen.

The terrifying realization strikes me: Piram will kill my Benaiah. I saw it in his eyes. I know it in my soul. This chilling fear has always lived hidden inside me, and now it breaks free and floods my heart. This has changed everything. Our lives will never be the same.

Benaiah turns to me with troubled, tender eyes. "Mother, are you okay?"

He gathers me into his warm, gentle, and strong arms—so much like a grown man. There are real, honest tears in his eyes. It shocks me. I have rarely seen him cry since he's grown to manhood. Maybe his tears now are brought on by the sudden rush of emotion after the unexpected struggle. Perhaps they come because he has seen me so humiliated and shamed. I do not know. His eyes are hot with pain as he looks down at me.

The compassion on his face melts my heart. I look down at his hands, stained with Piram's blood. The sight shocks me back to reality. My body trembles like a leaf as I step back and sit down on the stone bench.

What will Piram do now? He will be furious with me when he wakes up! He is beaten and bloody. My son is cut and hurt. What am I to do? What will happen next? My mind is a flock of birds that cannot land, startled by predators at every possible landing spot. Should I send Benaiah away? What will happen if the elders find out? Will Benaiah be punished? Will I lose everything? It is all my fault! My son could be stoned to death for this!

I know the painful choice I have to make. I know I have to be the good wife, as much as it pains me. I have to attend to my beaten husband and send my dear son out of the house, for his own good as well as my own. I turn to him. His expression full of compassion and concern is also marred and bruised. I whisper loudly, "Go! Now! Before he wakes up and sees you again."

"Where would I go, Mother? What did you want me to do? Let him kill you?" His voice is breathless, but still strong and assertive. "Mother, I'm not leaving you here with him. He could kill you. He's a brutal monster. You should leave him."

"Go, Benaiah! If you love me, leave! Please!" I plead. "He'll go to the elders. He'll have you killed! I'll calm him down. I'll make him happy and beg for your life." I desperately grab his arm. "Go to your uncle Shem, or hide out in the hills. I'll send word with Berechiah when it's safe to come home!"

I see the concern lining his face and the struggle raging in his young mind. He hesitates for several moments. I rush about the house, gathering whatever supplies I can find—a few morsels of food, some of his extra robes, some olive oil, and a few other necessities for his journey.

He stands there, a hard look in his eyes, unsure if he should follow my words or follow his own heart. "I should just kill him now and get it over with."

I am shocked and angry. "Benaiah! Don't you dare talk like that! I've taught you better! Kill your stepfather? God's wrath would follow you all your life! You would be cursed like Cain! God forbid you do such a thing!"

"Mother, come with me, then. You are not safe with him!"

"I am fine. I will tell Ruba. Her husband is an elder. They will help protect me. But you need to go! Now! If your father wakes up, he will kill you or have you killed!"

Benaiah's eyes blaze hot with anger. "He is *not* my father!"

"Go, Benaiah. If you love me, you will leave. If you stay, you will die. I know it in my soul!" I push him toward the door, panic searing through my body.

"If he wakes, I will hit him again, Mother!"

"No, Benaiah! You've done enough. I need to clean this up. I need to make this better now." "Mother, he might have killed you this time! Yet you go back to him?"

"I must, Benaiah. I must!"

Benaiah breaks free from my arms that are pushing him, and he turns to face me. "No! If Yahweh is a god of love, he would not want you beaten by your husband! Come away, and we will find sanctuary together in some other town. We'll take our case before the elders."

"No, Benaiah, it isn't that bad. It isn't worth the trouble. He is usually fine. It's just when he drinks."

"Mother, he drinks all the time!"

"I will not leave him!" I shout at my son. I regret it immediately.

He shoots me a withering look, and my heart fills with pain.

"I know nothing else," I whisper. "I will not live like a fugitive, cast off without a family or a village. I cannot bear the thought of losing my family. Do not ask me to leave. I will be okay. Yahweh will see me through."

Benaiah shakes his head in disbelief. His anger is simmering beneath the surface. "Fine. If you are so set on dying, I guess no one will stop you."

His words sting, but I feel relief as he turns to leave. I follow him out of the house and touch his arm. He stops and looks at me. I can tell he is disappointed and hurt.

"I will send Berechiah to find you when it is safe and your father is pacified," I say.

"He is not my father," Benaiah says flatly, as a sad resignation. "I love you, Mother." He softly kisses my cheek, and he is gone.

I lean my back against the outside wall of our house and watch him walk away. Every footstep stabs my heart as the distance between us grows. I don't know if I'll ever see my son again. Small tears form in the corners of my eyes. Something about Benaiah always touches that softer, weaker place within me—the place I've tried to bury for years.

5

BENAIAH

Heat radiates off my face. My rapid footsteps fall solid and sure. I can't get away from that house fast enough. The coppery taste of blood sits uncomfortably in my mouth. The pulse of a thousand drums rings in my head. A lost, gaping void has filled my heart. Where am I even going now? I don't know. I don't care. The black of night hovers overhead like a heavy tent. My thoughts tumble like stones rattling down a steep cliff and fall into nothing. I should have killed him. I should have ended the misery once and for all!

I still feel the warmth on my arm where I last felt my mother's touch. I don't know if I'll ever see her again. How could she stay there with that beast? I sigh in exasperation and trudge on into the black.

The evening breeze lifts a few rebellious strands of my hair and brushes cool against my burning skin. I wander about town for a while, angry and confused. I pass houses filled with happy families who are relaxing together in comfort, closeness, and warmth after a long day of work. It sours my mood to think of it. I pace beside the village wall and then lean up against the rough stone. Where am I going to go? I must leave Pirathon tonight—the only home I've ever known. The only people I love are inside these walls. Yes, I am lonely and disrespected in this town, but at least I have the support of my mother, Hannah, and Berechiah. Outside these walls, I have no one.

Before I leave, I must find Berechiah and tell him the news. I make my way across town. Insects are whirring around me and small animals scurry for shelter as I walk down the path.

When I reach Berechiah's house, there's no lamp lit within. All is dark and still. I creep toward the door and call in a sharp whisper, "Berechiah! Berechiah!"

After a few moments, his father, Lamich, comes to the door. I barely make out his bearded face in the black of the doorway.

"Benaiah? Is that you? Are you okay?" His face is furrowed with concern.

"There's been some trouble at the house," I reply. "I need to talk to you and Berechiah. Is he awake?"

"Do you need a place to stay tonight? We have room."

I'm thankful that he knows the situation at my household well enough that I don't have to go into details. I shake my head. "No, there's no time. I need to be gone by the morning. Thank you, though. I just need to talk to Berechiah."

Berechiah appears behind his father. "Benaiah? What is it?"

"I fought with Piram tonight, and I hurt him badly. My mother fears for my life, so she sent me out of the house."

He gasps. "You struck your stepfather? If he goes to the elders with that, you...you could be stoned!"

"I know, I know. That's why my mother sent me away. She wants time to pacify him, and she'll call me home when he has calmed down."

Berechiah looks at his father, his eyes filled with concern.

Trying to ease his mind, I continue. "Don't worry—you know how he is when he's crossed. He flies into a rage for a few days, but then he settles down and things go on as normal." I pause, wondering if that is how it will happen this time. This isn't the same thing—I've never hit him before. This time it's... different. "I must go now," I say abruptly.

Berechiah nods in sad agreement. "Where will you go? Do you need any supplies?"

"Yes. What can we give you? How can we help?" Berechiah's father asks.

"I'll go up to the hills and find some caves or make a shelter somewhere," I reply. "I have plenty of food in my bag right now, and I'll hunt and gather what I can when it runs out." I pause for a moment, herding my scattered thoughts together and re-gaining focus. "That isn't why I'm here, though." I lock eyes with Berechiah. "I need you to promise me that you will watch over my mother—protect her if that dog tries to hurt her again." I quickly tell them what I saw when I came home.

Their eyes widen with surprise, and they exchange a sad, knowing look.

Berechiah's voice is soft. "I will guard her with my life, as much as I can. If I notice anything, I'll report him to the elders. They will listen to me, and my father will testify as well."

Berechiah's father nods in agreement. "I'll send my wife over to be with her as much as possible," he adds. "We'll all make sure she's okay. You don't have to worry. Just go, and may God watch over your steps!"

Relief comes over me like a warm light. I couldn't leave knowing she might still be in danger. I can trust Berechiah and his family. They have been so good to me! Both of them embrace me in turn and wish me well. Berechiah is unlike anyone I know. He's the brother of my soul.

I tear myself away from them and set out for the edge of town and the barren hills beyond. I feel lost and alone as I wrap my cloak tighter around me to keep out the chill of the night. Soon the darkness swallows me, and the noises of the night surround me. I know a hidden cave where I can spend the night, and it isn't far. Perhaps tomorrow I can go farther out, but tonight I need to rest and recover. I trudge on into the night, thinking of Berechiah.

I'll never forget the first time we met each other. I was seven years old and having an especially humiliating day.

Piram was upset about the unusually heavy rain which had just flooded his field. He had been drinking strong wine all day, and toward evening he was especially angry and sullen. He got upset with my mother about something insignificant that she'd done to annoy him, so he went looking for me. He had learned long ago that the best way to hurt her was to hurt me.

I felt his rough hand grip my arm and yank me close to him. I yelped as he picked me up and forcefully set me outside of the house. He shut the door in my face. The rain was coming down in sheets. I was screaming and crying in shame and desperation. My mother was yelling at him inside the house, and then I heard a crash. I waited, half-expecting him to kick her out into the rain too. He did not.

Wet and shivering, I tried to shelter myself by squeezing up close to the wall of the house, but the rain kept hitting me. Just to stay warm, I started to move. I wandered through the streets of Pirathon with no hope and nowhere to go. Water streamed down my face, and my robes were sopping wet. I knew no one would take me in. I had no friends—no one who understood me or wanted to help an outcast like me. Several homes had their doors standing wide open, and I could see families gathered around eating their meals, talking and laughing. A few people noticed me and shook their heads sadly, turning back to their meals as if they had not seen me.

I kept walking until I was on the other end of town. I passed another wide-open door. It startled me to see a boy about my age sitting in the doorway and staring out into the rainy evening. His brown hair was tussled and wet as if he too had just come in from the rain. His eyes were brimming over with happiness and wonder, and when he saw me, he smiled.

He beckoned to me with his hand and whispered, "Come here!"

I recognized him as a boy I had seen around town. His father had a good herd of sheep and goats. Many families bought animals from him, either to start their own flocks or to eat on special occasions. I was ashamed that I did not know his name. I had heard it before, but I couldn't remember it.

As if answering my thoughts, he said, "I'm Berechiah. Why are you out in the rain?"

I shrugged my shoulders. I couldn't think of a lie that would make much sense, so I told him what had happened at my house.

His brow wrinkled a little. "Maybe I can ask Father if you can stay with us tonight."

His offer shocked me. I didn't know how to respond, so I frowned and started to turn away. Under my breath, I muttered, "Don't bother. I'm sure he won't want me to."

He ignored that possibility and called, "Father! Father!"

After a moment, Berechiah's father loomed in the doorway—a large, powerful man with wide shoulders. He wore an incredibly inviting smile on his face. He stooped down so he could be at eye level with the two of us. "I am Lamich," he said in a deep, soft voice.

I nodded politely. "My name is Benaiah." My voice sounded so small and unnatural to me.

Berechiah immediately told him why I was out in the rain. Lamich shook his head, and his eyes filled with pity. He invited me in and helped me dry off near their fire. Berechiah's mother, Ardaliah, brought me a tasty bowl of soup, and they shared their evening meal with me. It was one of the best meals I'd ever eaten, not because my mother's meals are bad, but because everyone there was so generous, kind, and happy.

A strange, thrilling warmth overcame me as I spent the rest of the evening with them. Berechiah showed me a toy he had fashioned with a couple of sticks, a string of goat tendon, and some rocks. There was a simple, joyful exuberance about him. He bounced the rocks about and laughed when I tried to do it. It wasn't the same as the laughter I was used to hearing, the kind that cut at my heart and made me small. This was a joyful laughter that filled me with a rare feeling of happiness.

The warmth in my soul lasted all night long as I slept in some extra bedding they had in their storeroom. Berechiah and I talked well into the night, despite the fact that we knew we would be sleepy for the early morning chores. It was strange to feel welcomed. I did not really know how to react. Later Berechiah would talk about how I was like a stray animal that night—shy, wet, and confused.

After that night, we became the best of friends. When the chores were done, we'd run out into the fields and play. One of our favorite games was "Philistine and Israelite." We would throw small rocks at each other and use broken pottery as shields.

Sticks would serve as swords as we sparred. We would shout and run and laugh every day—our hearts entwined together.

Berechiah is still my closest friend. To this day, he'll occasionally call me a stray, wet goat.

My memories have made the time fly by during my travels tonight. Now I stand at the mouth of a cave, peering into the black, gaping hole. I find a rock on the ground and throw it inside. It clatters about, echoing loudly. No animal runs out, and I hear no growl or grunt, so I bend down and crawl in. I find a relatively soft spot of dirt, mostly free of rocks, good enough to lie down on for the night. I wrap my outer cloak around me, put my supplies between me and the rough wall of rock, and finally drift into a restless, painful sleep.

6

SERAH

I clean up the mess as best I can. The blanket we sit on for meals is rumpled and filthy. The pot is cracked, and the stew that I worked on all afternoon is wasted. Pieces of shattered clay are everywhere. Piram is still unconscious. When I finish cleaning, I reluctantly tend to his wounds by applying oils and wrapping bandages around the worst ones. His chest feels unnaturally soft, so I know he's broken a few ribs. His leg is badly injured too. He will be laid up for days. With Benaiah and Arah gone, who will tend our fields?

As I work, Benaiah's words keep replaying in my ear. I feel like a coward and a fool. I am too accustomed to my life here. I cannot change my situation. I will not violate the law by leaving my husband—I would become an outcast! I would rather be beaten every day than face my future with uncertainty, needing to beg for bread in some foreign land. I will not leave Pirathon—the only place I've ever known as home. Besides, I cannot leave my other children! My youngest son, Joel, still needs my instruction and training, and Arah and his wife need me as well.

Piram really isn't that bad. When the other family members are around, his abuse is much milder. His abuse only gets physical when he is very upset or very drunk. Almost every day his words belittle me and cut at my heart, but at least I can cope with that. There are even rare moments when I see glimpses of kindness from him. If he would have been successful and influential, like his father, maybe he would be a different man. And maybe he will change...someday. Maybe Yahweh will bless us, and he will help Piram fight his temptations to drink. I must hold on to some shred of hope.

I feel hollow and weary.

Piram groans, startling me from my thoughts. He looks around, his eyes groggy, and his voice a rough mumble. "Serah... Serah...get me some wine. Agh! My head!"

I bring him the skin of wine I had already been using to clean his wounds. He lifts himself up slightly and takes a generous swig.

"Ahh. That's better."

I turn to go back into the courtyard. I don't want to be in the same room as him right now.

His voice hisses out hate. *"Where is that wild she-ass bastard son of yours?"* His voice breaks into a nasty cough with the effort. "Send him in here...*now*! I'll rip him apart right before your eyes. I'll use my words to do it, if I have to!"

I stop as ice fills my veins. I've never heard his voice so alive with hatred. I force myself to turn back and look at him. I shudder at the intense fury in his eyes and the blood frothing on his lip. My voice wavers, but I get the words out. "He's...gone, my lord. I...I sent him away."

"I'll bet you did! You always try to protect that ungrateful pig! I should've taken him to the elders and had him stoned years ago! If I *ever* see his face again, I'll tear his skin off his bones!

I cringe as his voice rises and say nothing. I don't want to talk to him. I'm tired of pretending to agree with him.

"When I'm teaching my woman a lesson, nobody gets in my way!" Piram roars at the wall and then falls back, exhausted from the effort and the pain.

I go out into the courtyard, lean against the far wall, and let my body slide to the ground. I work my fingers back into my hair and try to rub the pain out of my scalp. I know in the next few hours and days I'll have to scurry about, attending to Piram's every need and desire. I have to do this for Benaiah's sake. I'll give him more wine. I'll make him comfortable. I'll even agree with his angry tirades about Benaiah and me. I already feel like a traitor, but I fear for my son's life as never before. I just need Piram to calm down and agree to spare Benaiah's life and allow him back home. I have to make this better again!

I try to pray again, but the words don't come. Why has Yahweh made my life so miserable? Have I upset him or failed to sacrifice enough? I close my eyes and take a deep breath. My parents taught me to trust Yahweh at all times—but what if Yahweh has rejected me? He allows Piram to beat me. He allows Benaiah to suffer. Now my son is gone—the one I love and rely on most. Bitterness creeps into my heart, but I fight it down and force myself to pray. It usually makes me feel better to pour out my thoughts to Yahweh, but when I finish praying tonight, he still seems distant. I feel all alone.

It is late into the night when Piram sends me out into the darkness to find his friend Jobal. I rarely go out of doors so late! Whatever can he want with Jobal at this hour? I hope he simply wants to ask Jobal to take over our fieldwork, now that Benaiah is gone and Piram is in no shape to do it himself.

I stumble along as fast as I can in the dark. Jobal lives on the other side of town, and I must cross the entire village to get there. My heart is thumping with fear and exertion when I reach the house. Jobal comes out at my first call. His large, stooped frame bulges in the doorway. He holds a lamp up to see me. As the small light glows close to his face, I draw back at his disfigured face. He barely looks human. They say he was burned in a house fire long ago. He usually keeps to himself, so it's been a long time since I've seen him.

I force myself to look at him as I quietly tell him that Piram has been hurt. I leave out the details. Jobal's eyes grow wide and curious. I urge him to come quickly, and he comes without a word. His large feet crunch loudly on the stony path as he leads the way through the dark of night.

When we reach our house, I bring him in by Piram. Piram has managed to prop himself up on his sleeping mat. He is staring hard at the wall opposite his bed. The oil lamp hisses and spits, casting eerie shadows about the dim room.

He looks up as we enter. "Serah, go outside and sit by the large fig tree. I'll send Jobal for you when I want you back again."

I bow low and go back out into the blackness, wrapping my robe around me. The night air is not the only reason I feel cold. I sit down, exhausted, my back against the great fig tree.

Fear plays at my heart. What is he planning? Why does he want to talk to Jobal in private? My worried thoughts swirl inside my brain and blend together as my exhaustion takes over. My head starts to slump down against my chest as my eyes grow heavy with sleep.

A rough tap on my shoulder startles me. It is Jobal. He grunts and gestures toward the house and then leaves the same way he came.

I blink the sleep from my eyes and get up slowly. At first, I am confused. Why am I outside? Why is Jobal here? Then reality crushes back upon me. I lean against the tree and stare out into the night for a few moments. My son is out there somewhere, alone. "O Yahweh, protect my Benaiah!" I whisper. "Be his rock and shelter. Oh, bring him home to me, alive and well!" I feel a tear squeeze itself free from the corner of my eye and roll down my cheek. I wipe it off with the corner of my robe, suck in my breath, and venture back into the house.

Piram lies on his sleeping mat, a cold, stern look in his eyes. "That son of yours is a dog. He is no longer welcome in my house." He says it simply, no emotion in his voice. "I have sent Jobal to find some men who will get vengeance for me. They will be here tomorrow afternoon. You will prepare a young goat and a great feast for them—none of your usual slop—and make sure they don't burn their mouths on it."

Hot anger rises like steam inside me, but my face is emotionless like a stone. With much practice, I have perfected the art of appearing one way while feeling another. I nod obediently and bow, sick inside with self-hatred and smallness.

"Serah," he says again, his voice thick with anger.

I turn and look into his black, bottomless eyes.

"That bastard son of yours does not have long to live. You'd better learn to love me more than
him."

I cannot hide my emotion this time. My heart melts and my eyes betray me, revealing to Piram the terror in my soul. He smiles wickedly when he sees it. My greatest fear has come upon me like a wild, savage beast. The walls of our house seem to crowd me in. I feel faint. Despite how late it is, I rush outside and fill my panicking lungs with fresh, cool air while looking up at the cloudless sky, lit with a trillion twinkling lights. I fall to my knees and lift my palms to the heavens, once more pouring out my soul to God in prayer. This time the words come out in a rush of desperation. My head hangs down, and tears stream from my eyes.

They arrive the next day—a day cold and wet with rain. One is tall with dark skin and a jumble of black curly hair piling just above his neck. He wears professional armor—a rare sight in Israel. The bronze scales of the armor are worn down and dull from much use. A wide curved sword is slung over his back, the blade thin and sharp. He is a head taller than most men, and he walks with the confidence—or rather, the arrogance—of a man who has killed many and will kill many more. The other is shorter, but his muscles bulge from beneath his tunic. He too wears professional armor, and his robes are obviously expensive, made with tight-woven black and red cloth. He carries a large spiked club, and a bow and quiver of arrows are slung over his back.

My heart is a caged dove fluttering hard against my ribs. Even though he still lies injured on his bed, Piram seems powerful and in control again. He plans to pay Benaiah back for each wound. He has a defiant gleam in his eyes, and his manner is all cocky ease. He looks at me, daring me to do something to stop him. I have been begging him for hours, making my throat dry and my tongue weary, and he has enjoyed watching me squirm and grovel. He has hated my Benaiah from the moment he was born. I have always feared that he will kill my son. I am forced to serve these killers as if they are our honored guests. It sickens my stomach to the core.

Piram welcomes them grandly, according to custom. He holds out his arms, as best as he is able with his injuries. "I am your servant! Please, sit down and make yourselves comfortable. My wife has prepared meat for us to eat today, and then we will talk business."

They bow politely.

Piram sends me off to get water to wash their feet. They sit and talk of the weather and the latest news from the trade route as I set a bowl of water down, wrap my robe about me, and kneel to wash their feet. It is not the stench or sand on their feet that makes me nauseous. My hands tremble as I touch the feet of the men who seek to kill my son. When I finish, I wipe their feet with a clean cloth and get up to bring in the meal.

They sit down to the feast I've made, and then Piram sends me out of the room. Fear is knifing through me as I dare to eavesdrop from behind the goatskin curtain, catching a glimpse of them through the crack.

Piram curses my son by several gods. He spits on the ground and then explains why he wants Benaiah dead. He describes Benaiah as a wicked and ungrateful stepson who refused to follow his orders. He claims that Benaiah was trying to steal some of his property, and when he was caught in the act, he flew into a rage and attacked Piram.

Outrage and disgust pulses through me as I hear the lies streaming out of his mouth. Part of me wants to burst through the curtain and contradict everything he is saying. The truth is burning on my tongue, but I shut my lips tightly and restrain myself with all my might. To contradict my husband in front of our guests would get me in grave trouble with the elders. I might even be put to death.

He pulls out several old family treasures: jeweled earrings his mother once wore, a golden bangle, and several other valuable trinkets that I have never seen. I am shocked! What else has he been hiding all these years?

His family was very wealthy years ago. In fact, they were one of the most influential and powerful households in this town. When Piram's father died, all of that began to slowly crumble. Piram became the head of the house and squandered its wealth. Several bad years hurt our fields. Piram destroyed business and trade relationships that his father had worked his whole life to build. This family's influence and reputation have practically dwindled to nothing. Our fellow villagers look at us with pity and disdain. Now we barely etch out a living with our fields and animals. Our supplies are low again, and we don't have the means to purchase much.

Now the men who will kill my son are feasting on our goat while accepting my husband's precious heirlooms as payment for their crime.

He promises them more when they bring proof of Benaiah's death and orders them to report back to him in six days whether they have found him or not.

The thought of these men handing Piram some bloody proof of my son's death turns my stomach. I tremble now, physically shaking with helpless rage, but I have to fight it down. I have to appear calm and unemotional or else Piram might kill me next.

7

HANNAH

A bird chatters at my feet as I walk down the path. The water jar perched on my head feels rather light, despite being made of stone. I don't mind going to the well today. It gives me a chance to get away from my mother. I love her, but she can be difficult to live with. She is a very kind and wise woman, but ever since she became sick, she's been especially bitter and needy. Her mood swings make me dizzy!

I hum a happy tune as I walk, feeling the first warmth of the sun glowing on my skin. It looks like it will be a fantastic day! I draw in the smells of the wild flowers and vegetation growing along the path. The cool earth crumbles beneath my bare feet as I stroll along. I only wear sandals when I absolutely have to. They are so restricting! I'd much rather go barefoot on the paths and even the rocks, if they aren't too hot.

The sun glints on a potsherd jutting out of the ground just off the path. The sight jogs my memory.

I was a young girl, just learning to balance the large jar on my head. How awkward it was! My mother watched closely as I first placed a round fragment of cloth on my head, and then I gingerly set the large stone jar on top of that. Trying to balance under its weight was such a strange feeling. I had watched Mother do it a hundred times, and she made it look so easy! I practiced over and over with large stones and an old cracked jar until the day my mother handed me the good jar and said I was ready. I was so proud, yet nervous!

It was a hot day, and my skin was slick with sweat under my robe. I set that stone jar on my head and began to pick my way down the path toward the well. Mother followed close behind me, ready to catch the precious jar if I stumbled. At first, I made her job easy, balancing the empty jar very accurately all the way down to the well. On the way back up, though, when the jar was full of water, I stepped on a stone that slipped out from under me. I lost my balance, and the whole jar came crashing down, shattering on the rocks and splashing cold water all over Mother and me. It was the first time I'd heard my mother curse. She angrily pulled me along the path with violent force, scolding me all the way home. She later sent me back with a goatskin bag to collect the broken pieces. We used the shards as tools for different tasks, such as carrying coals.

When Father came home, he was so gentle and forgiving. He joked that I made a poor donkey and that he would have to find a replacement so he could keep me as his girl.

I was so relieved, but Mother began scolding him like an irate bird. "You're not helping! That was our last good jar! We can't afford to let her carry another one!"

He smiled gently at her and said in his softest voice, "Miriam, just last week you dropped the small jar of flour in the back room, remember?"

Mother's face went white with fury at the memory and the implication of my father's words. "That was an accident!" she practically shouted.

"Exactly," he said quietly.

She stared at him for a moment, her eyes cloudy and fuming. "Mercy, Miriam. Mercy is the greatest of Yahweh's gifts."

She stood quietly as the anger drained from her face. She nodded to him and turned to me. Her embrace was a rare gift, but I relished the hug she gave me that day. It was so real, so fervent, so intimate. I knew my mother loved me.

A stick breaks with a loud crack as someone steps on it, and my memory vanishes. I notice several other women just ahead of me on the path. They are also holding stone jars, and several have skin bags for carrying water. One steadies a jar on her head and glances back to see who is following. She whispers to the other women, and they pick up the pace to increase the distance between us. I roll my eyes. It stings a little, but I'm used to it. I'm the odd one in the village. I know how they see me: a beautiful, quirky girl who, for some reason, still has yet to be married. Rumor has it that my father has tried to marry me off several times and I fought him on every betrothal. It is not my place, they say. I am being a fool, they say. I can't help but smile at the thought. The rumors are true, of course.

Honestly, most of the men in Pirathon simply have not held my interest. My father loves me almost too much, and he tries so hard to find a match for me. I love him dearly, but I won't marry just anyone. My heart is set on only one man, even though my father is completely against it. He hates my wish and refuses to try to make the arrangements that I want him to make. He thinks the match is not good for me. I'm afraid he's going to force me to marry one of these other men someday. So far, he's been kind to me and respects my heart's decisions. How long will that last?

A wonderful morning breeze tickles the leaves in the trees by the path, and they shimmer in the fresh morning light. I reach the well just behind the group of women. They eye me suspiciously but say nothing. I watch them work as they take turns filling the water vessels. The goat-hair rope rustles against the hanger above the well as the jar drops down into the watery depths. They help each other pull the rope up each time, pouring the water into their own water jars. I'll be doing it alone, as usual. It is hard work, but I live for hard work. Besides, I'm in much too good a mood for them to spoil it with their coldness.

A young woman, Shaloma, finishes filling her jar and glances up, piercing me with her fiery eyes. I return her hostile glare with a cheerful, indomitable smile. She scowls at me. Her prettyish face is wrinkled up, and her long dark hair is slightly askew from her work at the well.

She turns to one of her companions and asks in a loud voice, "Have you heard the latest news from Piram's household?" She sends a sidelong glance in my direction.

I feel a slight uneasiness creep up my spine, but I don't let it affect the happy expression on my face.

One of her companions responds, "No. Who cares about Piram anyway?"

"Well, did you hear he finally banished that bastard Benaiah from his household?" She turns, fully facing me, and her eyes pin me in place as she continues talking to the other women.

ADAM NITZ

"Rumor has it Piram caught him stealing some of the family treasures, and they got in a fight! He hurt his stepfather badly."

Her companion raises an eyebrow in disbelief. "What a disgrace! So he's gone for good?"

"I should hope so! He's been a troublesome youth in this town for as long as I can remember! Good riddance, I say!"

My good mood has evaporated.

Shaloma's snake-like smile grows larger as she watches mine disappear. Bitter triumph gleams from her eyes. "They say he's joined a band of robbers, attacking poor innocent victims and merchants on the roads nearby!"

"I always knew he was trouble, but I can't believe he turned out so badly!"

"Dear Serah always tried to defend him and stand up for him, but I always knew he had bad blood in him. How could he not, being half-heathen and all!" Shaloma says with a sneer.

The heat that suddenly rises up on my face is intolerable. The fear in my heart is a living thing, tearing me up inside, ripping the hope out of my soul. I turn my face away from the well, away from the hateful women who delight in my displeasure. My eyes reach out into the distant hills. Benaiah gone? Where would he go? My heart is gone with him. How could I live without the hope of a life with him? Will he be back? Will I ever see him again?

Shaloma finishes filling her jar and sighs loudly. "Ah, well, he was not a fit match for any woman in our village anyway—despite his good looks." She laughs and smiles again in my direction. "There you go, Hannah. The well is all yours! Take some cool water back to your sick mother. It's the least you can do for her."

I stand silent, still stunned by the sudden news that plunges my happy day into sadness.

"Hannah, are you well? Lose your tongue on the road somewhere?" She suppresses a wicked giggle. "Come along, Shariza. Let's get this water home. We may have to make another trip. Have a great day, daughter of Eliezer!" She allows herself one more self-satisfying laugh, and the women move away, carrying their water vessels on their shoulders.

I ease myself down by the side of the well, relieved to be alone for a moment until others arrive. I stare into the murky depths of the well, dark like the mood that has settled down on my soul. Just yesterday I had seen Benaiah. Just yesterday he had approached the house and wanted to talk to me. Anger flashes out of me at my mother. Why had she sent me inside? Why had I listened to her? If I had known it would be the last time I saw Benaiah, I would have disobeyed every command and done whatever it took to have a few moments alone with him. Oh, how I want those moments back!

I grab the rough rope and let it slide through my fingertips. The jar plummets down into the well and lands with a splash. Helpless anger courses through me and drives me to work faster than normal. I pull the rope taut, brace myself, and begin to draw the first heavy jarful up from the well.

8

SERAH

I stare blindly into the nothing of the night. My head hurts from lack of sleep. Piram lies beside me, his chest rising and falling as he breathes. Every once in a while he moves and grunts. I listen to the steady sound of his breathing. How many times have I prayed tonight? A hundred? I have not slept well in weeks. Every night since the mercenaries left, my thoughts have been filled with worry. I pray and pray that Yahweh will protect my Benaiah and that Piram will calm down and call off this manhunt. I wonder if Yahweh even listens to my prayers. I have tried everything to soften Piram's hard heart. I've even resorted to groveling! I do anything and everything he wants without any delay or fuss. I have to. I have to help my Benaiah in any way I can. I also have to be extremely careful, not just for Benaiah's life, but for mine as well. It has taken all of my patience having Piram confined to the house because of his injuries. His wounds are slowly healing, and he has been moving about a little more. Several nights in a row Piram has gotten drunk to cope with the pain. He scares me when he drinks. I close my eyes tightly just thinking of his frustrated bellowing and the slurred, cutting words that pour from his mouth when he is drunk.

Arah, Jadia, and Joel came home from Arumah yesterday, and they did much to calm Piram down and ease his rage. I was so glad to have them home again. Jadia helped me with my daily chores today and also helped me care for Piram's wounds. What a relief to have some help!

Berechiah has also stopped by to see me several times. He told me that Benaiah was worried about me the night he left. Seeing him has made me miss Benaiah all the more.

I hear a noise outside in the dark—a tiny scuffling sound. My eyes pop open, and my body goes rigid. What—or *who*—is it? After a moment, I let myself breathe. It must just be a small animal outside.

I can't imagine living out in the caves in the hills, like my Benaiah is now—if he's still alive! How is he going to survive? Where is he right now? *Is he still alive?*

Every time I hear feet crunch on the path outside, I fear it is the hateful mercenaries returning with Benaiah's head as a trophy. The waiting is killing me as I long for word of my son. I smell his sleeping mat just to get the scent of him. Perhaps it is all I have left of him!

The daily chores grind on and on. With Piram laid up as his broken ribs heal, even more work falls on my shoulders. Tomorrow I will have to go out and work the fields with Arah and then come home and do my other chores as well. Jobal has been helping when he can, but the fields are not doing well. So much work still needs to be done. We do not have the means to hire workers to tend our fields and trees.

I wish I could silence the constant chatter in my brain tonight and fall asleep. Thoughtlessness would be a welcome relief. Today was a good day, though. Better than most, anyway. Piram made an interesting comment today, one that I will hang all my hope on. He was propped up on his sleeping mat, and I had just brought in the evening meal for him to eat. I could tell he was tired and at his wits' end.

A bitter sigh escaped his lips, and his words tumbled out. "I don't know how Arah is going to do all the work we need done. We can't afford to get behind. If the cursed villagers would just lend a hand…" He stared through the open doorway for a long time, his lips drawn in a firm hard line and after a moment, shook his head bitterly. "I wonder if that dog of yours is still alive. I wouldn't mind squeezing a little more work out of his worthless hide."

Perhaps after two weeks, my begging is finally beginning to work. I allow myself to hope as never before. Benaiah may be dead already, but I can still pray. Perhaps Yahweh has been merciful and has protected him. The deadline that Piram set with the mercenaries has long since passed. Either Benaiah is dead or the mercenaries have simply given up and gone home. Piram keeps muttering on and on about trusting uncircumcised, heathen fools with his precious family treasures. Benaiah is not a skilled fighter. He has no chance if those men find him. I will continue to beg for his life and his return.

My mind races on into the night, but somehow I drift into a restless, fitful sleep.

I wake, as always, before the morning light. I slip out from under my cloak, which I often use to cover me at night. I gather it up and wrap it around me to keep out the chill. My feet move soundlessly across the floor as I enter the courtyard. A tiny tendril of smoke curls upward from last night's fire. I sift through the ashes with metal tongs, grab a glowing coal, and touch it to the wick of my clay lamp. My nose fills with the ever-familiar smell of olive oil burning. The lamp gives off its tiny glow, and the room dances with eerie shadows. I gather fuel for the fire and work the ashes with a stick to expose the glowing embers beneath.

I hear the rustle of cloth. Jadia enters the room. I nod to her and smile, and without a word we begin to make the morning meal before the men wake up. The routine is so ingrained in my life that my fingers move without thought while my mind continues wandering to my missing son.

The day goes on, as every other day has gone on. I gather water. I work in the garden. I bake bread. I go with Arah to the fields for a long portion of the day. The work is hot and grueling. By the end of the day, dirt has found every crevice of my sore and filthy fingers.

Now I work to prepare the evening meal over the hot coals. I am frustrated because Piram has been constantly taking my attention away from my work throughout these long days. I change his bandages. I dress his wounds with oil and spices. I bring him all the little things he asks for. His demands are endless.

Exhausted, I feel faint when we finally begin to eat. I sit and stare at the food for several moments, watching the steam rise. My mind is filled with fog.

Piram's voice comes to me distantly through the haze. "Serah! What is wrong with you?"

I blink and try to recover. I look up at my husband. His frown is filled with curiosity, not concern for my well-being.

"I am just tired. I will feel better after I've eaten something."

"Good. Eat something. I have some things to say to you."

I lift a bit of bread to my mouth and gesture for him to continue speaking.

"Have you heard anything from your bastard son?"

Despite my weariness, shock courses through my blood. "Heard from my Benaiah?" I gasp.

Piram stares off at the far wall intensely, as if trying to see through it. His voice is quiet but firm. "If he is alive—I pray to Baal he's not—but if he is, he may…return."

I freeze, looking at him with disbelief, yet hope is bursting alive within me.

A moment passes in tense silence. Piram has resumed staring at the wall. Suddenly, he lets out an angry roar and slams his fist down hard.

I jump, startled and afraid.

He turns to me, his eyes alive with frustration and anger. "You're probably hiding him somewhere, anyway!" He hisses through clenched teeth.

My eyes focus on him, but I remain still, leading him to no conclusion.

His voice calms down. "I can't afford to hire anyone this year, and my fields won't make it without his work. I don't want to see him again, but I need his back to carry my loads and his arms to work in my fields. If I allow him back into this house, though, there will have to be some changes. I have rules that he must follow."

I struggle to keep my face emotionless, to hide the tears of joy that are welling up in the corners of my eyes. "Will you really let my Benaiah return?"

"Actually, I hope he's dead! If he's dead, I'll be sure you see his body." He snorts. "If he's alive, I'll let him back." He holds up a warning finger. "But here are my terms: He is no longer allowed at any of our evening meals or any of our festivals or family feasts. He may sleep in this house, but no longer in the family area—he must sleep with the animals or in the storeroom. He will get absolutely nothing of our inheritance—nothing! Don't even think about trying to hide some scrap of wealth for him." He shoots me a sharp glance before continuing. "We will feed him enough food to survive. In turn he shall work for us his whole life. He will be like a slave to me. I refuse to find him a wife. The only time I want to see his face is when he is in the field, and if he doesn't listen to me there, I will make sure he is punished severely by the elders. You know how much I would relish watching that!"

The hope in my heart dims at Piram's harsh terms. I realize with a tinge of sadness that I am losing my son either way. He is either a lifeless pile of bones in the wilderness and I have already lost him, or he will return to me but I will rarely be allowed to see him. He will be worse than a slave in his own house! It will break him, after he has already suffered so much. It is all my fault!

That night, I break away from my final chores of the day and walk across the village. I find Berechiah and tell him the news. I explain Piram's change of heart and his harsh terms.

Berechiah shakes his head sadly. "I have been looking for him this whole time. I have not heard from him since the night he left. I fear for his life. The rumors have traveled around town, each version more outlandish than the next. According to some, Benaiah has stolen from your husband's household and fled in disgrace. Others claim Benaiah has left home and joined a band of robbers, killing and robbing victims along the trade routes."

I can see his pain. I know he misses Benaiah almost as much as I do. "Can you please try to find him again? Please tell him it is safe for him to return home."

Berechiah nods. "I'll do my best."

A full week passes. I wait in endless suspense. For days I have not heard anything or even been able to find Berechiah to ask him for news.

As I am grinding grain in the late afternoon, a movement catches my eye. I look up to see a man walking the path to our house. My heart skips a beat. I squint off into the sun, every fiber of my body alive with hope. He sees me and breaks into a run. It is him! He is alive! My heart jumps for joy as he wraps his arms around me. His face is lined with deep concern and love, but his eyes are dancing with joy at the sight of me.

"Berechiah found me last night and told me it was safe to return. Is it true?"

I nod in silent joy. I look up at his face. How my Benaiah has changed! He is haggard and worn with a hardness and wildness about his eyes that I have never seen before. He looks like he hasn't eaten in days. Concern fills me, and I am afraid to tell him about Piram's harsh conditions.

Benaiah sees the change in my face. "What is it, Mother?"

I try to be as gentle as possible as I tell him Piram's terms for his return. I watch his eyes grow cold and hard. He starts to turn away.

I grab hold of his tunic and plead with him to stay. "Benaiah, please! If you go, I'll never see you. I can't live without you! I love you more than anyone in this world—even more than Arah and Joel. I will make this better—I promise. Please, don't go."

He hesitates at the uncharacteristic desperation in my voice. He turns back to me like a man facing a death sentence. I can see the soft glow of love in his eyes despite the deep sadness and anger. His shoulders sag as the weight settles down on him. He has nowhere else to go. I feel guilty, like I am caging a wild animal that wants only to roam the hills.

"I'll stay. For you, Mother, I'll stay. I've missed you terribly... and Berechiah and Hannah."

Relief floods my body. "Where have you been? What happened to you while you were away?" He looks away, unsettled.

"Many things, Mother—many things you'll never know."

He seems suddenly cold, distant, and aloof. It is strange. We have always talked openly with one another. I realize with a pang of sadness that I have lost some part of him in those hills, and I don't know if I will ever get it back.

9

HANNAH

Grinding grain is a daily, endless task. I do it mindlessly, dropping kernels into the hollowed stone and wrapping my fingers around the smooth, worn grinding pestle. My wrist dances in the daily routine—up and down, shift and turn, up and down—feeling the satisfying crunch as the grain is pulverized between the two stones.

Father is out in the fields. Mother is in the back room, lying on her mat, probably asleep. She's been especially sick and weak these days. Most of her work will be on my shoulders today, as usual. For now, though, my thoughts are far away as my memories carry me back to a day four years ago.

I was barely thirteen. Father sent me to take the sheep to water and then pasture. I hated herding sheep alone, and I was upset with father for making me do it. I had already watered the sheep, which had taken such a long time because I had to wait for several flocks that were already there ahead of me. Then I had to draw water for all of them without any help. The sun came out from behind a cloud and started beating down hot and torturous. As I led them to pasture, the sheep became feisty and unruly. I was having a hard time with one particular sheep that constantly strayed from the path, bucked the other sheep, and caused general mayhem. I was so frustrated! My hair had come undone and strands kept getting into my eyes. Suddenly, the problem sheep made another break for it, plowing through several other ewes. Hooves scurried and scuffed. Sheep bellowed and scattered. I lunged forward, trying to bring the stray back into the fold with my staff. My foot struck hard on a rock, and I fell headlong in the dust. Startled sheep scurried away in every direction. I just sat there and sobbed. My toe was throbbing. I was frustrated and frightened because I had lost Father's sheep. I was ready to give up and go home.

"You look like you need some help!" His voice was kind and soft. Startled, I looked up, brushing the hair out of my eyes and squinting in the bright sun. He stood there smiling, his eyes alive with a tinge of laughter. His arm was strong, lithe with muscle—I felt it as he helped me up to me feet. "Would you like a drink?" he asked, as he unstrapped a skin full of water from his back and lifted it to my lips. The cool water rushed in, refreshing my parched, dusty mouth.

"Thank you!" I whispered.

"No problem. Let's see if we can get your stubborn sheep back in line," he said with a laugh. I watched him as he expertly herded the sheep back into the fold. Together we worked to gather the flock again, and he helped me lead them the rest of the way to pasture.

"You are the daughter of Eliezer, right?" Benaiah said.

"Yes."

"What is your name?"

"Hannah."

"It's a good name—a lovely name!"

I smiled. "And you are Benaiah, son of Serah, right?"

"Yes I am," he said, with some hesitation in his voice. He studied my reaction closely.

"Your mother is very kind," I said. "She's been so good to my mother and me!" I could tell he wasn't expecting that response.

He smiled again, warmly and handsomely. "Thank you. She's the kindest woman I know."

"Thank you for your help! I must be keeping you from your work! I'm sorry."

"I don't mind," he said, looking deep into my eyes.

Until then, I had felt like I was just barely a woman, yet in that moment, I felt older. I was young, but many girls my age were already betrothed and some were fully married. Benaiah was several years older than I. He filled my thoughts from that day on, and a strong, unreasonable ache fired in my soul. My heart started thundering in my chest. He seemed so confident, so strong, and so mysterious.

I had heard the villagers talk of him and how frightening and violent he was, always fighting with other boys. I had over-heard Mother and Father talking about how he had been in trouble with the elders several times. They disapproved of him and called him a "wild one." He seemed so different in person. His smile was bright and friendly. His touch was so gentle.

That night I told Father about his help. He was surprised that Benaiah acted so kindly. He needed help in the fields that year. It was the year after my brother died, and my father was left with only me to care for and no sons to help with his work. After hearing my story, he went to Piram and asked if Benaiah could help in his fields. Piram agreed, but my father had to pay some of his grain or fruit to Piram each month as part of the agreement. After that, Benaiah would spend several days a week working hard with my father in his fields. My father spoke well of him. He was impressed by his hard work, his strength, and his character. Once, when he was in trouble with the elders, Benaiah's punishment was lessened because Father went and defended him. Often he was in trouble because of the other village boys. They would band together against him, hurt him, and belittle him. When something was stolen or broken, they would avoid punishment by pointing blame at Benaiah, even though he didn't do it. The villagers were only too ready to believe them, despite Benaiah's protests. So, Benaiah was often held responsible for their thieving and roughhousing, and his reputation suffered again and again. It didn't help that Benaiah was half-heathen on top of it all.

I felt so sad for him, and I was so upset when Father would tell me about his troubles in the village. In some ways, his suffering made me even more interested in him. He was a strong yet tragic figure, and I wanted to soothe his pain and support him.

My interest in him grew stronger as time went on. How I loved to go to the fields and watch Benaiah working with my father. I often brought them meals or water, and I even helped them if their workload was heavy. Benaiah would come over in the evenings and talk with us. His eyes would always find mine. There was something unspoken and wonderful between us. We grew to be good friends. How we would laugh! We would talk whenever we got the chance.

Still, Father refused to let me marry him. He said it was not a good match. "Benaiah is a fine man," he would say, "but he's not a good match for you, my dove. He's a good friend, for now, but let me find you a man who can give you a better future—a future in which you'll have a good family, a good home, and a good reputation."

I look up from grinding grain, my happy memories vanish, and I stare at the bare room around me. My eyes are slightly damp with emotion. There's a hole in my heart where Benaiah has always been. Berechiah told me about the mercenaries Piram hired to hunt for Benaiah. I fear the worst—my Benaiah is dead. Will I ever know what happened to him? Will he ever come back? How long has it been since I've seen his smiling face and looked into his soft, brown eyes?

A noise outside the house startles me.

"Hello to the house of Eliezer! Is anyone inside?"

Can it be? I set down the pestle and the grain. "Benaiah?" I shout.

"Hannah?"

I rush through the open door, and my eyes fill with the sight of him. He gathers me into his strong arms. Embracing is something we should not do, but I am carried away by the moment. The sad hole inside me fills with warmth and wonderful joy as I feel his arms around me. "You are alive!"

"I am alive, Hannah, but just barely."

"I was just thinking about you! I was just thinking about that day when I met you, and you helped with the sheep."

His smile is like the morning sunlight. He laughs at the memory.

We sit outside under the tree and talk. I am overjoyed to have him again. He tells me the terrible terms of his return, and my heart breaks for him. He will be abused now more than ever before. "At least I have you to talk to again," he says. "I was so alone out there in the hills." His eyes look far away, and I can see the pain in them.

"You will always have me to talk to," I assure him.

He shakes his head. "Not if your father marries you off to some other man."

"You should talk to him again, Benaiah. Maybe he'll soften this time. Maybe he'll say yes."

Benaiah laughs bitterly. "No he will not—especially not now. Rumor has it that I have done terrible things on the trade route and I am now a criminal. Piram's harsher treatment of me will only confirm the reports. They'll say that I'm being punished less than I deserve, and that Piram is showing mercy by letting me live."

I look down at the ground. What he says makes sense, but I don't want to hear it.

"Maybe we should just leave together," he says. His words hang between us like a cloud of hope.

My heart slows, and I stare into his eyes. We share a moment of silence as love fills my heart like sweet wine. Then I look down abruptly, forcing myself to break the moment. "You know I'll never do that," I say softly with kindness in my voice. "Yahweh does not smile on such things."

A brief flash of anger overcomes his face. "Yahweh is a stormy god. I don't even know if he's my god. Maybe Dagon is more my god than Yahweh. What has Yahweh ever done for me? His people hate me."

"You are one of his people!" I say earnestly, desperate for him to understand.

"Ha! I feel very much a part of his people! I am an outcast, Hannah. Don't you see that? I am not one of his people, even if I am half-Israelite. I am worse than a dog in my own house.

I've worshipped him for years as my mother taught me to, but what good has it ever done me? What good has it done *her* for that matter? Piram belittles and abuses her." As the words shoot out of him, he stands up and throws his arms in the air. He looks down at me and takes a deep breath, relaxing himself and his voice before he goes on. "Just don't get me started on Yahweh. I still worship him, but more out of habit than out of true respect."

His words shock and upset me, but before I can respond, I hear my mother calling from the house. Her voice is cracking and strained. "Hannah! Hannah!"

I stand up and turn to him. "I must go to my mother now. I'm glad you're home. We'll have to talk more another time."

He nods, still pulsing with anger at the God who created him. Sadly, I turn from him and go. When I glance back, he is walking away stiff with anger, staring hard at the faraway hills. He is a strong yet troubled man. How I yearn to help him see the truth.

10

SERVANT OF SAUL

The wind rakes across my body, and my robes billow out around me like a sail. I peer off into the distance and follow the outstretched arm of the watchman. "There it is! Just off that row of hills. Right there!"

I steady myself against the tower's parapet and strain my eyes to see. Through the haze I can just make out the smoke. "Is that the village Makereth?"

"It's the right direction for it," the watchman shouts over the whipping wind.

"All right, I'll tell the king!" I shout back. I make my way to the ladder and feel my stomach turn as I look down. My hands tingle with sweat as I gingerly step my foot on the first rung of the ladder. I curse—the sound lost in the wind—and begin my descent.

It steadies my nerves to think of anything other than the dizzying height of the king's tower, so I focus my thoughts on Makereth. The village is in trouble. The Philistines are on the move, raiding villages and plundering our people again. It won't be long until they invade us again en masse. I reach the bottom rung and jump off, relieved to be on solid ground again. I go through the servants' entrance and straighten out my wind-blown robes. Hoshan is there to meet me, his face wrinkled with worry.

I give him a curt nod. "It's confirmed," I say.

We both turn and enter the throne room together. We bow before the king, and he gestures for us to stand.

"Your Majesty, we've just confirmed the latest report," I say, gesturing to Hoshan to continue.

"Yes, Your Majesty. A messenger arrived moments ago from Makereth. The Philistines struck the town early this morning. The initial report is that seven militia are dead and fifteen wounded. The town was plundered and burned."

I go on. "I just confirmed it with the watchman on the tower. We can see the smoke from here."

Saul stands up abruptly. "That's the fourth village this week! They're getting closer!"

"Yes, Your Majesty." I can barely hide the concern in my voice.

"How are we doing with the standing army?" he barks.

I shoot a nervous glance at Hoshan and then speak. "I can check again with General Abner. Last I heard, we have raw recruits coming in from the north. I'm not sure how many. Several hundred have just arrived from the south. The Benjamites have mustered another entire unit for us, despite their small size."

He waves a hand in frustration. "That's all fine and good, but it's not enough! We need those northern recruits, and we need them now! We need to train them fast and get them ready for battle. I must have a stronger army. The Philistines will invade us again and probably soon! They are aching for revenge after their defeat at Micmash."

"We must all pray to Yahweh to protect us." I say.

"Yahweh! Why bother? He's abandoned us all. The only hope we have is the army. Don't waste your breath."

His words feel like a slap in the face. I'm shocked at his bitterness toward Yahweh, even though I know he had another falling out with the prophet Samuel a while back.

Before I can stop myself, I blurt out, "But Your Majesty—surely the promises—"

The king's sternest look slices into me, and my soul turns to ice. My unspoken words freeze on my lips as I close them into a tight line.

"How dare you talk to me about Yahweh's promises! The only promise I have from Yahweh is that he will tear my kingdom away from me and give it to another. Is that what you want?"

"No, Your Majesty," I whisper. My whole body feels numb as I bow and ask to be excused from his presence.

"You may go," he says coldly. Hoshan and I back away from the king and head for the servants' entrance. My heart is hammering away inside me.

Hoshan looks over at me, his face as white as death. His whisper is almost too quiet to hear. "We will pray, whether the king wants us to or not. You were right. It's all we can do."

11

The water in the ditch is shockingly cold on my hands. I rub them together and watch the bits of mud disappear into the murk. The rain this morning was good for the fields, softening the hard-packed ground. Sullen grey clouds cover the sun. I feel wrung out like a wet rag. Plowing is hard work. The low spot in the field behind me was especially wet and difficult, almost too wet to plow, but I got through it. Arah left with the oxen a little while ago. I am cleaning up, preparing to go home myself. I am eager to rest after another long day.

Piram arrived just as I was finishing the field. He inspected my work and went off again without saying a word. If it weren't for me, he wouldn't even own this field anymore. When was the last time he actually helped with the work? When was the last time he acknowledged me at all? I honestly wish he would die. It's a terrible thought, I suppose, but I hate him. I hate the way he treats me. I especially hate the way he treats my mother. I stare into the mud with a bitter frown, remembering the day I caught him pulling my mother's hair. I should have killed him

that day. I should have ended his reign of torture once and for
all.

My only satisfaction comes from the fact that he's wary of me
now. He still uses his words to demean my mother and me, but
as far as I know, he hasn't laid a hand on her during these past
few months since I've returned. He knows what I can do when
he riles my rage.

As I flick the water off of my hands, I turn around to
see Sennah crossing the field. My fists clench as I watch him
come closer. He stops when he's a stone's throw away right
in the low spot of our field. He's stripped to the waist, all his
brawny power on display. I know the might of those meaty
arms all too well. Sennah is a brute of a man. He's two years
older than I, tall as an oak tree, and strong as a young ox.
He's always eager for a fight. He's fought and defeated almost
every young man in Pirathon, and he flaunts it. Now his
two younger brothers and several other youths from town are
coming up behind him. *Why can't they just leave me alone?* I am
tired and in no mood for Sennah and his savagery.

"Not tonight, Sennah. Just go home."

He laughs. "Aw! How you whine! Your father wants me to
pay you another visit tonight."

"He's *not* my father!"

He knows exactly what to say to get a rise out of me.

He ignores my interruption. "I'm only too happy to fulfill
his wish! Are you hungry, little pig?" His words are thick with
disdain. "Plenty of mud for you to eat! Come here! Let me feed
you!"

Everyone laughs as he gestures to the ground.

I bristle inside, but fight the urge to lose my composure.
"You *would* be the one to do Piram's bidding. Your mind is the

size of a raisin! What's he paying you this time? A wee little lamb for you to cuddle with at night?"

He snorts in anger. "You're nothing but talk, Benaiah. You've got the mouth of an ass and the strength of a she-lamb to back it up. Don't you remember the last time I was here?"

For the past month, Piram has been using Sennah to get back at me for breaking his ribs. He's hired Sennah to pick fights with me when I'm tired from a long day's work. This is the third time! I turn my gaze northward to find Piram up on the hill watching the whole scene. I'm not surprised at all. There he stands, not far off, with a bird's-eye view and eager to watch a fight. Hateful pig! As if it's not enough to work me like a slave and humiliate me at home and in the village. He relishes watching me in pain!

The last thing I need is a fight tonight. I turn away and look off toward the town, wishing Berechiah was here. I could use a little help, but I'm sure he's long since gone home. Of course they've come when I'm alone.

I turn back to face Sennah and flinch as something flies toward me. A wet clump of mud explodes on my face, splattering filth in one of my eyes. I spit the grit out of my mouth and rub the grime from my eye. Sennah's eleven-year-old brother is doubled over with laughter. Sennah laughs loudly along with him, as if he is just as immature.

Thoughtless fury explodes in my brain, and I lunge at Sennah. He anticipates me and sidesteps. Using my eager momentum against me, he catches me by my hair and shoves me down into the mud face-first. The cold, wet slime wraps around my face and fills my mouth. I roll over as quickly as I can in the sticky muck, spitting and spluttering, trying to grab his leg and pull him down. He kicks me in the stomach—hard. Pain radiates through my gut.

He gives me a little space so I can get up from the muck, all the while taunting me. "Come here, little dog! Is that all you've got?"

I slowly lift myself up and shake some mud out of my hair as I glare at him. His eyes are flames, and he smiles, enjoying himself.

"Hit him hard, Sennah!" his brother shouts. "Put him in the mud for good—where he belongs!" The crowd hisses their hate at me.

"You're no Hebrew! Go back to your real father, wherever he is!"

"Filthy, heathen dog!"

"How does Piram put up with a half-breed like you?"

Their taunts only fuel my rage. It is the same kind of abuse every time—the same angry words designed to antagonize and belittle me.

He comes at me again, lightning-quick, and I'm caught slightly off guard. Despite my frantic attempt to ward him off, his beefy arm wraps around my neck, bending me over backward. As I struggle to break free, he spits in my face and slams me headfirst back into the mud. My brain explodes with pain. His crowd of supporters are laughing and cheering him on.

He walks around me as I slowly rise to my knees. "Piram promised me a whole skin of wine if I bruise *both* your eyes this time! I can taste it already! Piram's wine is the best. Ever had any?"

I shake the fogginess out of my brain and stumble back to my feet. He's already coming at me again, lunging forward with his breakneck speed. This time he slips in the mud and struggles to recover. I seize the advantage as he skids near me, grab a nice handful of his wet hair, and pull as hard as I can. His body swings over, and he rolls into the mud. I'm on top of him in an instant, my knees falling hard on his chest and sliding off to either side. I hear the wind go out of him as he grunts. He starts to roll, trying to get out from under me. I rain blows on his face as fast as I can.

Suddenly, he uses brute force to shove me off of him, and I slide back, off-balance. He gets up, and we face each other. He roars with rage as he charges me again. Back and forth it goes—slipping and sliding, shoving and wrestling. Sennah's jarring blows leave their marks on my face. His fingers feel like claws on my skin. His muscles pulse powerfully against me as we roll around, yet something fuels me on today—a rage I've only felt one other time. It burns through my core, and for the first time, I actually believe I can win.

The sun comes out below the cloud line and hovers over the horizon, shedding brilliant light on us as we fight on. My warm blood trickles from my battered lip and feeds the vengeance ablaze in my heart. Rage boils inside, and I relish its delicious heat. It pulses through me in waves. It fuels me with hot, clean energy. Today is different. Maybe it's something in his eyes that looks slightly defeated. Maybe it's the reserve of power I still feel inside after such a long struggle.

The cold, soft mud squishes between my toes as I brace my feet. The mud makes a sucking sound as Sennah comes up from his knees. He stumbles toward me with a slow, clumsy lunge, his wet hair flapping around his face. Incredibly, he is weakening. It thrills me to see him slightly off-balance and struggling for control. All his pride is finally knocked out of him. I lower my shoulder to meet his and shove hard. Our bodies slam together, dirty skin on dirty, slippery skin, and our feet churn in the cold slime.

After a few desperate moments leaning into each other, Sennah loses his balance. His feet slip out from under him, and his body jerks back wildly. His head hits the muck with a satisfying thump. I surge forward a step as he falls back, but I stay on my feet. I wait, senses on high alert, eyes fixed on his motionless face, keyed up for whatever might happen next. Moments pass. I feel my breath drawing in and out as my heart pounds. I stare hard at the muddy lump on the ground. This time he does not get up. I straighten stiffly and back away—wet, filthy, and triumphant.

I am incredulous. Pure exhilaration fills my bones with warmth. I did it! I finally beat him! I try to wipe the sweat and grime from my face with my dirty hand, making me feel even dirtier, but I don't care. For once I feel proud. For once I feel strong. For once I am no one's dog.

Sennah's brother is gaping at me. The crowd is sullen and stunned into silence. This is not the outcome they expected.

I walk a short distance away, wary and unsure if anyone else is going to try to pick a fight while I'm weak and exhausted. I turn as Sennah stirs from the mud again and sits up with a groan. His head hangs. His disheveled dark hair drapes over his sallow, filthy face. His beard is full of mud. He looks up and catches my gaze, his eyes bright with hate and shock. For the first time in my life, Sennah looks pathetic.

I have always been intimidated. How many times in my life has he pounded me to the ground and humiliated me in the village square or a country field? Today I do not feel the hot shame leaking from my face. Today I am not surrounded by the sound of vicious, taunting laughter as Sennah and his companions spit on me and walk away. I am not lying here, half-conscious, delirious with my pain and loneliness. No. Today is the day I have earned some respect in the village. I am done being their dog and the target of their contempt.

Sennah stands up shakily and spits blood. He sways on his feet like he's drunk. I step back in a better stance, just in case this isn't over. Sennah's eyes lock with mine, and this time I stare back hard. I refuse to flinch. His black eyes are livid, alive with bitter fury and resentment. He wants me dead—I can feel it burning out of him—but sheer physical exhaustion holds him back. Every part of him, except for his eyes, looks drained and empty. The fight is almost over, but surprisingly, I feel ready for more. My chest heaves with exertion, but my mood is giddy and reckless.

"How'd that mud taste, Sennah? Are you full of it yet, or would you like a little more?" I spit his insult back in his face.

New shock and hatred blaze from his eyes. He mumbles something unintelligible in reply and turns to his cadre of companions. A few try to help him out of the mud. He shakes them off and almost loses his footing again in the process. His whole group is somber and stunned. They stand around awkwardly, not sure how to react to this unexpected turn of events.

I glare at them, seeing nothing but angry, hostile eyes. I don't feel any respect from them yet, but someday that will change. Somehow I'll force them to respect me. They'll have no choice!

12

BENAIAH

A few shafts of brilliant light gleam across the ground. The glowing sun continues descending beneath the clouds, gilding their edges with gold. As the shadows lengthen, I set out along the path to the village, alone as always with my thoughts. The excitement and energy of winning the fight with Sennah has faded, and I'm beginning to feel the strain. A slow ache spreads all over my body—sore joints, throbbing bruises, and a few cuts that ooze blood. My skin is stiff with dried mud and blood. I bend down again at the ditch and wash my hands and arms in the cold water. I'll have to use the water jar at home and try to clean up better later. Gingerly, I touch my face. It is tender and numb where Sennah rammed his head into my lips. A trickle of blood still meanders its way through my beard next to my mouth. I wipe it off with the back of my hand as I get up and begin to walk.

When I am halfway to the village, dizziness overwhelms me. I lean on my walking stick and look for a place to rest. Finding a large stone on the side of the path, I sit down to gather my strength. I don't have far to go, but I have all night to get there. I am not welcome for the evening meal anyway. I watch the orange glow burn at the edge of the sky as the sun melts like wax, merging into the hills. I am spellbound by the raw beauty. I breathe in a deep, slow, delicious breath. The air is crisp and cool. A gentle peace seeps through my tired bones. The breeze softly lifts the hair on my arm. I look down at my hands—nails cracked and dirt finding every tiny crevice, despite my washing. It has been another sweaty, dusty, miserable afternoon in the fields topped off with a grueling fight with Sennah.

Every day I look forward to the evening. I usually stay out in the hills or the fields long after all the other villagers have gone home. I've learned to treasure the last moments of light, the peace of silence, and the savage, lonely places where I dream my faraway dreams. No dreaming tonight. I'm too tired for it. My eyes grow unbelievably heavy, and my head slumps to my chin as I drift toward the edge of consciousness and sleep.

A strange shout jerks me wide awake. *Was I sleeping?* I lift my head and blink in the darkness, every sense fiery and alert. Loud footsteps fall fast on the path behind me. I turn and see a dim figure—a man staggering toward me. His loud, hoarse breathing makes him sound closer than he is. He's been running for some time. I am still groggy and stiff with pain, but I manage to get up and crouch behind the rock I was sitting on. Both hands grip my walking stick as I peer over the top. *Who is this? Why is he running?*

The dim figure collapses in the path, and his feet and hands tear at the ground in his effort to get up again. Behind him, pounding footsteps echo loudly, and another shout follows. Two other men emerge from the growing darkness. They reach the fallen man. There's a grunt of satisfaction and triumph as they kick him in the ribs again and again. One bends down to tear at his robe. *Robbers!* I rise from the ground as soundless as possible like a hunter stalking my prey, ignoring new pains that shoot through my stiff joints. Surprising strength pulses through me at the urgency of the situation, and I forget my wounds for the moment. I crouch down and quietly move forward in the deepening dark. They are so loud and focused on their violence that they do not hear my steps as I approach. They would not expect me on the path this late anyway.

The smaller robber rifles through the man's robes, his back to me. The larger one continues kicking him from the other side. He faces me, and my movement catches his eye a second too late. I let my momentum carry me, and I lower my shoulder and shove hard into the small robber. Pain bursts through me, but I clench my teeth and bear it. The man flies headlong over his victim and into the kicking legs of the other robber. They both tumble to the ground. I have no time to lose. Stepping over the fallen man, I swing my walking stick with all the might I can muster into the face of the larger robber as he struggles to get up. *Thwack!* He howls in pain and tries to grab at my staff. I swing it back, avoiding his grasping hands, and spear him in the ribs with the end of it. He falls back again for the moment. The smaller robber reaches for my legs to trip me, but I quickly slam my staff down hard onto his head. He crumples to the ground in an unconscious heap.

The larger man has rolled over several times to get some distance. Now he's up and coming fast, a streak of blood across his face and a knife in his hand. Caught off guard, I sidestep wildly and feel the rush of air as the knife slices just past my body. I stumble. A sick feeling grips my stomach as I lose my balance.

My staff clatters to the ground, and I fall hard on the rough, rocky ground near the path. The larger man is on me right away. He grabs a handful of my robe and pulls me toward his thrusting knife. Desperately, I grab his wrist and try to force his knife back, twisting my body to avoid the blade. He grunts and shoves me hard. I fall all the way to the ground again and roll onto my back. He raises his arm to throw his knife. Frantically, I wriggle my body backward to get some space. The knife whirrs through the air, and I feel the blade nip the skin under my left arm as it pins the loose cloth of my tunic to the ground. I grab the knife's hilt with my right hand and tug. The thick cloth rips a bit as my body moves, but still I am not free.

Now that he has a moment to breathe, the larger robber unsheathes his short sword and lunges forward for the kill. I frantically grab at the dust, searching for anything to fend him off. My hand closes around a small jagged rock, and I throw it. It's an awkward throw without much power behind it, but the rock strikes the man's cheek and tears it open. He stops and screams in pain, and his free hand reaches up to touch the wound. The slight pause gives me a chance. I twist around and strain to pull the knife out from the ground and free myself. It is lodged in tight and difficult to pull out at such an angle. Seconds of struggle feel like eternities. After two hard and fast tugs, I manage to pull it out of the ground, and I roll over just in time. The edge of the man's sword slices into the ground right where my head had been.

I come up with his knife in my hand and bury the blade in the robber's abdomen. He roars his pain right into my ear. We stand facing each other, body to body, robe to robe. His head slumps over my shoulder, and the hairs of his beard brush the side of my neck. The stench of his sweat fills my nose. Hot blood soaks his robe and runs down my arm. I yank the knife out and plunge it in again, twisting the blade. More blood flows crimson onto the dark sand. His body sags to the ground, contorting in tortured pain. I step back, panting. Unnatural sounds assault my ear as he sucks air like an animal in labor, and his body writhes in the dust.

I watch him die with sickness in my stomach. I lower the knife and feel his blood streaming back down my arm. I hear it drip off his knife and onto the ground. Soon his struggling slows and stops. The moon's light reflects in his sightless eyes. I don't even know him, and I've killed him. There is no time to dwell on it now. Panic sears through me as I remember the other robber. I spin around. *Where is the other man? Is he still unconscious, or is he up again?* I strain my eyes in the dark and find him lying motionless with a dark pool growing around his body and soaking into the dry dust beneath him. The man who was running from them sits off to the side, wiping the blade of his knife. I back away, a bit wary, unsure if he is a friend or foe. I've saved his life, but just what kind of life have I saved?

He seems to read my mind. His voice is loud and deep. "Don't be afraid of me. You saved my life. I won't hurt you." He puts the knife aside and raises his arms in a gesture of peace and goodwill.

I can barely make out his face through the darkness, and I'm surprised when I see a faint smile.

My limbs shake involuntarily, my heart thuds violently, and my head feels like it has been hammered with a mill stone. Now that the urgency is gone, all the energy drains out of me. *What have I just done?* I never dreamed I would kill a man again. For the second time, my hands have ripped the breath out of a man's body. A cold, odd feeling twists in the pit of my gut. I look down at his body—a lifeless, empty shell of skin bleeding in the dirt. The knife in my hand still drips his bright red blood. I back away some more. The knife slips from my fingers into the dirt, and I rub my bloody hand on my cloak.

The man I saved stands up stiffly, favoring his left side. He gathers up several of his supplies that are scattered about and stuffs them back into his bag. He looks up. "Thank you," he says, simply. His voice is husky and deep. "Yahweh sent you just in time."

"I guess so," I stammer, trying to get my breath. "Who are you? Why did they attack you?"

"My name is Adnah, son of Berksha, tribe of Manassah. I am an officer and an emissary from King Saul."

I am shocked. An emissary from the king? Here?

He goes on. "My two assistants and I have been going from town to town in this area gathering strong, eligible young men for Saul's standing army. We search for the strongest and most promising men, and we bring them to Saul. We left Shechem today after assembling a party of men and were on our way here to Pirathon to gather more for the group when we were waylaid by this band of outlaws." He gestures toward the two lifeless lumps near the path.

I let the information sink in as I begin to help him pick up the mess. "Where are your companions? What happened?"

"Killed—almost instantly." He shakes his head slowly and sighs. "It was a total surprise." He kicks his foot at the smaller robber. "This cowardly dog here was hiding behind some rocks not long after we left Shechem. He suddenly began shooting arrows at us. My partner took one in the eye and died right there." He pauses for a somber moment.

The horrific image fills my mind.

"His name was Loman. He was a good soldier," he says.

I lower my head in sympathy as he continues his story.

"As we broke for cover, the one you killed came charging out of a stand of trees we were heading for. My other partner ran right into his sword before he could even draw his own. A third man stepped out and blocked my path. There was no time for thought or hesitation. I was outnumbered, and my partners were dead. I surprised him by running at him full speed, and I rammed my staff under his chin. His head snapped back, and his neck probably broke. I kept going and didn't look back."

He pauses for a moment, looking back down the trail, perhaps thinking of his fallen friends.

"We were not far from Pirathon. Evening was closing in around us. I didn't know how many men were in the ambush. I was hoping they would stay and rob the other two for a while. I run well, and I hoped to make town before they could catch up."

"They didn't stay and rob the others?"

"No—they chased me immediately. I barely outran them this far."

"Are you wealthy? Were they trying to rob you?"

"We had very little for them to rob. We've been traveling fast and light. Our mission is our message. Who knows?" He shrugs his shoulders as a troubled look clouds his face. "They seemed to know we were coming. Hired killers, maybe? Israel has many enemies. Discontented tribesmen?" He sighs. "Not everyone loves Saul. Not everyone wants a strong Israel and an organized standing army. My mission is a dangerous one."

The darkness seems to surround us. The brilliant panorama of stars lights the night sky above us—a breathtaking beauty above that distracts us from the grisly scene in front of us.

"We need to get into the town. Night is no time to be sitting outside the gates. The wild dogs and jackals will catch the scent of blood. They'll be here soon," Adnah says.

"Are you hurt badly? Can you walk?" I ask.

He laughs without mirth and turns to study me in the starlight. "Thanks to you, no, I'm not hurt. I took a few good kicks in my side. You look much worse than I do—believe me! You fought well today. With some training you would make a good soldier. Have you fought before, with the militia or for your village?"

I am flattered. "No. I've never fought in that sense. I have fought local boys since I was young. Just wrestling—no weapons or anything like that."

"You should come with me and join Saul's army. He's training soldiers at Gibeah. Come and fight for Israel. If you would like, I can talk to your father for you."

My pulse quickens again. Some deep yearning wakes in my soul, hungry and eager. I stare hard at the ground. Maybe that is the answer—*become a soldier*. I'd be free of this town and its judgments. I'd make a name for myself on the battlefield and come back a hero. Who would disrespect me then?

Adnah continues, "I'll be gathering men tomorrow and perhaps the next few days, and then we all meet up with the main group of recruits at a place south of Shechem. From there we head back to Gibeah and join the main force."

Together we slowly pick our way up the path toward Pirathon. My household will all be asleep by now. No one expects me home. My body is desperate for food and rest. I need to wash up. My wounds throb—they will need to be dressed and bandaged. My mind is not on the task. Big decisions loom before me.

We reach the village gate, and the watchman recognizes me. He is used to my late arrivals so he lets me pass through. Adnah shows him some credentials from the king. He also briefly explains why he has arrived so late.

The watchman steps back and lets him through. "It's an honor to have you visit our village!" he says.

We pause just inside the town gate.

"This is my last stop," Adnah says. "After this, we rejoin the army with the new recruits. Tomorrow I will hold a contest here in Pirathon and watch for the bravest and strongest young men. Those who do very well will be conscripted into the army—they will have no choice, unless their fathers appeal the decision." Adnah turns and looks right in my eyes. "Tonight, though, you proved yourself in a much more important contest. You have done me a great service, and I want you to join the army. However, I will leave it up to you. I will not force you. Meet me tomorrow evening at the contest and tell me your decision. If you want to join the standing army, you will need to be packed and ready to leave in a few days."

I promise to meet him the next evening with my decision. He tells me he has relatives in Pirathon and will stay with them tonight, so we part ways.

My footsteps crunch loudly in the hushed air as I come down the street to my family's house. I stop outside, take off my outer cloak and tunic, and dip my hands into the stone water jar near the door. It is hard to wash my wounds in the dark, but the cool water feels good on my burning skin. Gingerly, I touch the knife wound on my arm. It's not too serious—just a nick in my flesh and some dried blood surrounding it. I have been hurt much worse. Still, I wince as I touch it and try to bathe it as best I can. I splash water on my face and rub it clean of the dirt, sweat, and blood. It isn't a perfect job, but it will have to do for tonight.

I come through the door as quietly as I can. Our door is a wood slab attached to a pole. We hollowed out the stone above and below the pole to allow the pole to turn, and now we grease it from time to time, but it can still be loud. I try my best to move it slowly, but it still grates a little. Hopefully no one will be woken up by the sound.

A few goats and sheep are penned up just inside to the left, and we keep our pair of oxen in the room to the right. Fortunately, their heavy breathing is undisturbed as I creep past them through the courtyard and into the rear chambers. As always, my mother has left me a few scraps of supper wrapped in a cloth near my sleeping mat in the rear storage room. Tonight my meal consists of cold stew and some hard bread with dipping oil. Very grateful, I eat in silence. I eat like an animal, famished after this long day.

A low fire still burns in the courtyard, giving off a little bit of heat. I sit on my mat and stare at it through the doorway, watching the low embers burn out and listening to the gentle pop and hiss of the flames. I am physically exhausted but unable to sleep. My body feels like a piece of leather, stretched and shrunk. I am glad my family is not awake. I don't need the questions or opinions. I don't need the judgments. I don't need them to poke fun at me for how disheveled I look or prod me for information about my day.

I hear a faint rustle from the other room. A whisper of movement and a dark shape fills the doorway.

"Benaiah? Thank the God of Heaven!" My mother comes in and sits at the edge of my mat. Her face is lined with worry.

I am glad for the darkness that hides my wounds. I finish chewing. "Thank you for the food, Mother."

She nods, silently and painfully. "I am so glad you are okay, my son. I miss our talks together."

What can I say to her? I can't lie. I say it as softly as I can. "I may be leaving, Mother. I plan to join Saul's army and fight for Israel. Please don't beg me to stay."

13

BENAIAH

I feel her staring at me in the semidarkness. A painful silence builds between us, choking my resolve and making me question my heart's desire to leave. A muffled sob escapes her lips, and I realize she's fighting back strong emotion. I gather her frail form into my arms and feel her silent tears wet my neck as she leans into my embrace. Silently I endure the pain as she brushes against my fresh wounds. How broken and fragile she is, even though she rarely shows it. She is always the strong one at home, putting up the bold front and carrying the family along with a quiet determination to be positive in every circumstance. She does whatever is necessary to survive her relationship with Piram, yet she still holds her head high in the village. She seems so indomitable, yet I know the real pain she feels deep in her soul, the memories that gnaw at her, and the fears that whisper coldly in her warm heart. While everyone else sees her strong side—her shell—I see her wounds and her heartache. All these years she has seen me not just as her son but also her best friend and confidant. Growing up I often felt burdened. I was her deepest source of love and friendship. And now, at my age, it is unusual for a son to be so attached to his mother!

Softly, I tell her about Adnah and his offer for me to join Saul's army.

"What would I do without my Benaiah?" she whispers.

I stare into the darkness and refuse to answer. I love my mother, but I am tired of being her strength. My heart is crying loudly for freedom, adventure, and a new start somewhere else. However, deep in my soul I know that I will do whatever she needs. If she asks me to stay, I will stay.

As if in answer, she turns to face me. I cannot read her expression in the dark.

Her voice comes soft and low. "You do whatever you need to do, Benaiah. If you must go, then go with my love and blessing. I'll not stop you. May Yahweh watch your steps and bless your journey."

Her robes rustle as she stands, momentarily blocking the dim glow coming in from the fire, and suddenly she is gone, back to Piram's side in the sleeping chambers.

A cold, unsettled feeling invades me, and I shiver slightly. Wrapping my outer robe tighter around my shoulders, I step out into the courtyard to sit closer to the fire. I glance around through the open doorways. In the dim light and shifting shadows I can barely make out the other bodies in the house—dark lumps rising and falling in gentle rhythm as they sleep.

I was so sure I would join the army, but now questions and worries gnaw at the corners of my decision. My body is hurt and exhausted, but I know I will not sleep. Thoughts pound in my brain like incessant drops of rain. I am wracked with decision, and the weighty pull of the future paralyzes me yet invigorates me at the same time. *What should I do?* I was so sure I would go to war, but what of my mother? Would she be safe with me gone? Would the army really be a better life for me? Other men from this town will join the army too. Such men could easily make my life miserable in the army just as they do here in Pirathon. However, the army is a large group, so perhaps I could avoid them. Besides, if I make a name for myself as a warrior, they would have to stop their tongues. I've already proved that I can fight, and with some training I know I can become a first-class warrior. Who would dare to belittle me then?

Joining the army would also be a chance to get revenge on the Philistines. I hate the Philistines. I ache to feel my blade bite through their armor and spill their blood on the ground.

I have their hated blood in my body. That's why my village hates me. Would they forgive the blood in my veins if I kill enough of the Philistines? Will it convince them that I am a true Israelite like they are? Did they forget that half of my blood is Israelite, coming from the great line of Abdon? Several times in my life we gathered inside the walls of Pirathon, breathlessly waiting an invasion, fearing rumors of a Philistine raid. I'll never forget how the villagers kept their eyes on me, nervous and distrustful. Many of them had argued that I should stay outside the walls. What did they think I would do? Fight for the enemy? I was just a child, born and raised in their village. Did they really think that my Philistine blood would overtake me and that I would betray them all? How desperately alone I felt those days. How I hated the mere mention of the Philistines.

Anger courses through me at the memory. I blow softly on the fire and watch the coals glow bright and then slowly dim. Wild, unruly thoughts erupt in my brain. Many memories tear through me one after the next leaving me feeling bitter and alone. Anger rolls through my heart like the waves of the great sea thrashing against the rocks. How small I have felt in this village!

This is my chance—my moment to prove them all wrong. I will go and be a warrior. I will go and become great. I will have the attention of the whole nation on me and my exploits. I will win their respect. Then I will return to this miserable town, and people will notice. People will look up to me and honor me. Hannah's parents will be proud to give her hand to me in marriage. Instead of having only a few friends in the entire village, everyone will want to be my friend. Everyone will want to get to know me. I will be a powerful, influential leader instead of a despised dog. My mother will finally be honored, too! No more will she be the poor pitied wife of Piram. She will be proud and happy—the mother of the great Benaiah! I will bring her back great wealth and riches that I plunder from our enemies. I will go and be a soldier for her, and for once I will make her life better!

Yet, part of me is also scared to death. Will I be man enough? When the Philistines flood down on all sides, their eyes fierce and eager, their muscles pulsing with power, and their iron weapons sharp and ready, will I have the courage to stand and fight? Could my heart betray me? Could I turn like a gazelle and run? What if I were to die? I can't bear the thought of my mother with tears welling up in her eyes and her tender touch on my lifeless flesh. Or worse yet—my body mauled and mangled, left to rot on some dusty field as the horrible blood-hungry beasts eat my flesh to the bone. My mother would be left to weep and wonder.

And what about Hannah? What would happen to our hopes? Our relationship is young and tender and raw. She feels something for me. I can see it sparkling in her eyes when we talk. She is the one good thing I have going for me here in this village. And if I go to war, will all my hopes of marrying her vanish like smoke in the dark, or will she still wait for me to come home and become her husband? Her parents are so reluctant about the arrangement as it is that they would happily use my leaving as an excuse to marry her off to another man—a man with a higher social standing and a more promising future. If Hannah was not so insistent and strong-willed, they would have already married her off to someone else.

But what might happen if I am gone for long years? Will her feelings change? Will she find someone new?

Even if I survive and come home, will I be the same man after the war? Will I be able to laugh anymore? My uncle, Shem, served in the militia long ago. He came back from war altered in the mind. He would scream the most hair tickling screams late at night. Whenever he came over when I was young, I would often wake up wide-eyed and breathless listening to his harsh breathing and thrashing. War did that to him. He had been a prisoner of war for a time—a slave. He had endured their heartless torture. His own son had died in the battle near his side. He rarely talked about the things he'd seen. He came back as the shell of the man he once was. Could that happen to me if I answer this summons? Could it change me forever? My mind races like a runaway chariot. Thoughts roll around like lightning and thunder in a continuous storm. After a long while, weariness begins to drag at my body. My head starts to droop. I force myself to get up from the fire and go back into the storage room. I lie down on my sleeping mat and fall into a restless sleep.

14

I fight back tears as I turn from my son. How I ache to sit with him and talk all night, but he needs his sleep. I miss him so! I barely see him now, ever since Piram banished him from the evening meals.

I'm still trying to recover from his words. Benaiah *leaving? A soldier?* Part of me wants to go back and beg him to stay. Instead, I force myself to continue walking across the courtyard and into the main sleeping chambers.

Piram is snoring again. I lie down with my back to my husband and ample distance between us as I face the doorway. A movement out in the courtyard startles me. I look intensely into the darkness and then relax as I realize I'm seeing Benaiah's dim form coming into the courtyard. His face is tinged with the light of our dying fire. He looks like he is frowning as he stares at the embers. I strain my eyes to see him better. Is that a bruise on his face? I know that Piram takes delight in antagonizing my Benaiah. I've heard that he even hires rough youths from the town to hurt him. I keep praying that God will give him peace.

Is his becoming a soldier an answer to my prayers? But what peace can come to a man of war? What if he's killed in battle?

Ice runs through my blood at the thought.

Piram shifts in his sleep. I hold my breath until I hear the steady rhythm of his breathing again. I stare out at my son and try to guess what he is thinking, aching for the closeness we used to share. I want to go out and talk with him again, but it doesn't feel right. He's been pulling back from me lately. He seems to want a distance between us now. I feel like our close connection is slipping away…like I'm slowly losing him. I try to crowd the thought out of my mind and convince myself otherwise, but my heart still feels it—the distance grows, and my loneliness intensifies.

The long night stretches on, and my eyelids grow heavy with sleep. I blink. The image of my son sitting at our fire grows hazy and disappears. Memories and dreams swirl together in my mind.

Bright light burns all around. I hear laughter. Youths are playing in the street. I'm a young woman again, and Benaiah is a boy—maybe seven years old or so. We're walking across town together to see the men press the olives in the town square. He's so excited! I feel his fingers straining and tugging against my own. How he wants to run! I laugh and pull him back toward me.

He looks up at me, eyes shining. "Come on, Mother! We're going to miss it!"

"They'll be doing it all day, Benaiah. Slow down and enjoy the walk with me."

"But Mother, I'd rather run! Will you run with me?"

I glance about, wondering if anyone is watching. There's only a few people around. I smile down at him. "Why not?" I let go of his hand, gather my robes, and try to catch up to him as he's already a stone's throw away.

He keeps running faster, and my legs refuse to run. In fact, my legs are slowing down. I try to will them to keep up. Worry wraps its cold fingers around my lungs. I strain forward, but I only slow down. Benaiah is so far ahead now!

I shout to him, "Benaiah, slow down! Come back! Let's walk together again!"

He glances back, smiles, and then keeps running.

Did he hear me? I shout again, "Benaiah, stop running! Come back to me!"

I can barely make out his form. He's merging with the small crowd that has gathered around the olive press. Every breath is a struggle. How can I be so winded? Why can't I run any faster?

Finally I reach the crowd. "Benaiah!" I shout. There's no answer. People look at me strangely as I jostle my way through, looking for my son. "Benaiah!" I shout again. Where could he have gone? Desperately, I plead with several of the women standing there. "Have you seen Benaiah? He was just here a moment ago." They stare at me with puzzled looks and shake their heads. I keep on searching as the long desperate moments pass.

How can this be happening? Where is my son? What will I do if I can't find him? What would I do without him?

Suddenly, a strange man grabs me by my shoulders. "He's gone, Serah! He's been gone a long time now! Go home."

From a foggy place in the back of my mind, a sharp, hissing whisper interrupts my stream of thought. "Stop it! Serah! Stop it!"

My eyes fly open. It is still dark, and I am on my sleeping mat. I freeze in fear. Piram is holding me by my shoulders, shaking me slightly.

"Serah! Stop thrashing about! You'll wake up the whole house with your wildness! You're having a dream!" His eyes are hard, pinning me in place.

I manage a quick nod to show that I understand. "I'm so sorry," I whisper.

He relaxes his grip on my shoulders and slowly backs off of me. My heart is pounding in my ears, not just from the dream that is still so real in my mind, but also from the shock of Piram's hard grip and piercing look. I close my eyes in relief as he settles back into his sleeping position.

"Your dreams betray you, Serah," he whispers gruffly. "You must learn to let go of that bastard son of yours and focus more on the rest of us."

I stare up where the ceiling is and see only nothingness. "How do you know what I'm dreaming?" I whisper back.

"There's only one name that you call out in your sleep, and it certainly isn't mine," he hisses back.

I turn and look out into the courtyard. The fire has almost completely died out. A tiny glow from the coals still fringes the room with light, but my Benaiah is nowhere to be seen.

15

BENAIAH

I wake in the early morning darkness and get ready to go out to the fields. Soreness grips my joints. My body is stiff, and my brain is foggy with lack of sleep. Still, deep down, I feel at peace. I know what I want. I know if I do not go and become a soldier, I'll regret it forever. I don't want to live with that regret.

I step out into the courtyard. Mother is already up and fixing the morning meal. As soon as she sees me covered in cuts and bruises, concern clouds her face. She runs into the back storeroom and comes out with olive oil and healing herbs to dress my wounds. I tell her a little of what happened—just enough to keep her from asking more. She's unusually quiet as she serves our morning meal. I know the thought of my leaving is bothering her. I feel her watching me several times as she works. We exchange a knowing look, and the sadness in her eyes cuts at my heart. After quickly finishing the meal, I gather up my bag and staff and head out the door. I must leave before she tries to change my mind.

My walk out to the fields is joyful. A whole new life is dawning with this day! Even the pain of my wounds can't dampen my excitement. My mind is far from the work that needs to be done today. Part of me wants to walk the other way, back to town, and watch my stepfather's face get red with anger as I announce my decision to him. I am finished being his slave! I want to go to the messenger from Saul right now and tell him I will join the army, but he won't be at the city gate until later in the evening. I will simply have to wait. The eagerness is brimming out of me. It is hard to control my excitement and face another long day of work.

As I walk the path, I pass other villagers who talk excitedly about the man from Saul's army and the contest this evening. From the snatches of conversation that I overhear, I realize there's been an announcement in the town square early this morning. The agent has already been at work talking among the families and letting them know his mission here.

Mahlo joins me on the path as he does almost every morning. Besides Berechiah, he is my only friend. He is the eldest of five sons, and his family is wealthy and very well-respected in the community. Mahlo's father's father is an elder, and his father also helps conduct the business of the village. They have large flocks of sheep and goats and a vast plot of farmland. Sometimes, Mahlo's position in the community affects our relationship. He will distance himself from me if his reputation is ever in jeopardy. I don't like that, but I understand. I respect him and value him as a friend. Perhaps I even envy him.

Even now as I see him coming my way, I am still struck by how well-kept and strong he is. His eyes glow warm and soft, yet there is a confidence and smoothness that flows from him like honey. He is often the calming presence that I need in my life.

Will he become a soldier too? It would surprise me if he did. He is quite important in the village, and his father is eager to have him around to help manage the servants and the fieldwork.

"Benaiah, have you heard the news?"

"Yes, I have! Are you competing in the contest tonight?"

"I'll be there, and I will compete, but Father is against me joining the army. What about you?" He stops in the road, studying my face. "Benaiah, what happened to you? Did Piram send Sennah to beat you again?"

"Yes. I fought Sennah again, but this time I left him in the dust!" The words feel good on my tongue, and I smile at Mahlo.

"Good for you! Wish I could have been there to help! Maybe your father will think twice before he hires him again."

"Maybe Sennah will think twice before he takes such an offer!" I laugh, still filled with the joy of my victory and excited about my future for the first time in my life.

I go on to tell him the other events that happened yesterday and about my decision to go to war.

He looks at me, a strange expression clouding his face. "Benaiah, are you sure this is what you want?"

"I need to get out of this village, Mahlo. You know that. There's no prospect for me here. There's only a life of slavery!"

"I know, but two of my brothers joined Saul's army. It's not as easy nor as exciting as it sounds. Part of me wants to join the army too. It sounds adventurous, but I know better." He pauses and reads my face. "My brother Jolan lost his hand fighting the Philistines. He's not the same man he used to be. I have not seen him in years, but I hear a rumor that he lives as a beggar somewhere down south and is embarrassed to come home to my father. Are you prepared for the toll war might take on you?"

I stop walking for a moment, a little frustrated that Mahlo is trying to discourage me. "I know anything can happen. I may die or get wounded, or I might become a great warrior. No one knows the future. All I know is that I can't stay here anymore. It feels like I'm trapped in a cave, and I can't breathe here. I need to be free of this village!"

"What about Hannah? I thought you wanted her for your wife."

"I still do, Mahlo. I'll come back for her as soon as I make a name for myself."

"What if that never happens? What if she won't wait for you? You're going to give her up just like that? There's no one quite like her, you know."

I sigh, frustrated. "Like I said, I don't know the future. I can't marry Hannah now, anyway. Her parents have fought me every time I try to make the arrangements. Piram won't help me at all. If I go to war and come back a hero, they'll be happy to give her to me in marriage."

"She's a pretty girl, Benaiah, and she's already past the age that most girls get married. I don't think she'll be available anymore by the time you come home."

"I don't know if she will or not, but I'm willing to take that gamble. I'll come back as soon as I can, anyway." There's an edge to my voice now. He's damping my resolve and ruining my good mood.

Mahlo just shakes his head. "All right, Benaiah. Do what you need to do. I won't stop you."

We walk in silence for a few moments.

When we reach his father's fields, he smiles kindly at me. "Take care of yourself, Benaiah. May the God of Abraham smile on you, whatever your journey holds. I know you will make an excellent soldier."

My annoyance evaporates at his warmth and sincerity. I smile back at him. "Thanks, Mahlo. I'll see you at the contest then."

"See you then, Benaiah."

I turn and keep walking to Piram's fields.

My conversation with Mahlo troubles me. What if Hannah *is* married when I return? My heart aches at the thought. I can't stay here in this life, though. I can't keep going on this way. Hannah's father will never give his consent unless I suddenly become wealthy and respected, and that will be impossible if I stay here. My only solution is to become a soldier and try my hand at war for a while. Everything inside of me pulls me in that direction.

"Benaiah! Benaiah!"

The call jerks me from my thoughts. I stop walking and turn around. Berechiah is jogging to catch up with me. He is a head taller than I am and very strong. We would often wrestle around in the fields as boys, and he would easily win every match. I'm glad to see him now. He usually knows how to make me laugh when I can't imagine laughing. He treats me like a younger brother and has always accepted me for who I am. Usually Mahlo, Berechiah, and I all walk to the fields together.

"You are late!" I shout at him as he closes the gap between us. "You shouldn't eat so much for your morning meal—it makes you slow." I smirk.

"Slow? Me?" He shouts back, a mischievous grin on his face. He stops jogging and slows down, dramatically holding his stomach.

"At that rate we'll get there by harvest time!" I laugh.

Giving me no response, he opens his arms in a wide embrace and suddenly sprints at me. Before I know what is happening, he plows right into me, bowling me over to the ground. He's knocked the wind completely out of me, and my sore muscles and bruises have found new reasons to throb with pain. I gasp for air as he rolls off the path and laughs.

"You unclean pig!" I laugh, despite my shock. Berechiah never makes sense. He still acts like a little boy sometimes. "You're out of your mind!"

"Somebody has to shake you up. You looked like you were walking in a funeral procession."

"I was deep in thought."

"I'll bet you were! You're always too serious. Let me guess—daydreaming about your Hannah again?"

"What if I was?" I say, feeling the heat rise to my face. "You goat! Good grief—you broke open all my wounds!"

"Wounds?"

I explain to him what happened last night with Sennah and the agent from King Saul. I tell him about my decision to join the standing army. As I talk, his childish grin disappears, and his eyes take on a deep seriousness.

"If you go to war, Benaiah, I am going with you."

His words are like sunshine for my soul.

We continue down the path, talking about the chores for the day. Soon it is time for Berechiah to turn off the path and go to his family's fields.

"I'll see you tonight at the contest!" he says to me.

"I'll see you there!" I call back.

It won't be long before I arrive at Piram's fields. I don't want to get there too soon. I don't want to see Piram until I absolutely have to. I walk slowly, thinking of Berechiah and his offer to become a soldier with me.

If I hadn't had his friendship growing up, I don't think I would have survived my childhood. He kept me sane.

A few short steps later I arrive at Piram's field. The crops don't look very good this year, compared to last year, and the weeds are beginning to take over the field. Piram and Arah are already out in the field checking crops, and they look up as I approach.

"You're late, son of the dogs!" Piram roars, the vein in his neck bulging with the effort.

Arah grins in expectation.

By the look on Piram's face, today is going to be a long, hard day for me. The only thing that gives me comfort is knowing that soon I will be gone from here and free of all this.

16

HANNAH

I hurry to finish cleaning up after the evening meal, eager for some adventure. Word spread quickly that the king's agent is holding a contest tonight. How I long to see it! I splash water on my face from the washing bowl and feel the cool streams flow down my skin. I use my outer robe to dry off and put the shawl around my hair. Mother is lying down, sick again and confined to her chambers. I glance in on her to make sure she is asleep before I head for the door. Father would not approve of my going, but he will never know. He has gone off to help his friend Jobiah repair a broken cistern tonight. He doesn't agree with the standing army and wants nothing to do with the contest tonight. Jobiah is the same way.

I am joyful as I step lightly out into the street. A few low rays of sunlight split the sky and touch the village houses. Their long shadows cover the street. I smile, my mind on Benaiah. Hopefully I will see him tonight at the contest. He would not miss an opportunity like this. He constantly wants to prove his strength to the other villagers. He will probably be stripped to the waist like he often is in the field when he helps my father. The heat rises to my face just thinking about it.

As I near the town gate, I blend in with the crowd that has already gathered. I weave my way through until I find a place off to the side where I can stand on a low wall and watch over the heads of the crowd.

Where is Benaiah? The crowd around me is alive with anticipation. We have not had excitement like this in the village for a long time. Almost the whole village has turned out to watch. All of the elders and most of the men of the village are here, and many of the women have come as well. I glance off to my left and notice Piram standing with his friend Jobal waiting for the contest to begin. The sight of Piram makes me shudder. The stories Benaiah has told me about his drunkenness and violent temper turn my blood cold. I try to avoid him as much as I can.

Saul's agent steps forward, his arms raised to quiet the crowd. There is an excited gleam in his eyes. His shoulder-length hair is streaked with grey. I am surprised by how rugged and strong he looks for being an older man. Just by the way he holds himself, I can tell he is a man that commands respect.

His deep, husky voice fills the air with sound, and the crowd goes silent immediately. "People of Pirathon: You know well that the Philistines are an ever-present threat to us all. Each tribe has experienced their abuse! They strike us and keep us down. They overcharge us for their services as blacksmiths. They raid and pillage our towns whenever they want. But King Saul, blessed be his name, has gathered an army and bound the tribes together against this common threat. I stand here today on authority from our king to gather strong, capable, courageous men to join him in the standing army and defend our precious people and our God-given land from those murderous Philistines. Who will stand with Saul?"

Several people in the crowd cheer. "We will! Long live our king!"

He holds up his hand to quiet them. "There are people out there who oppose the king, whispering and muttering behind his back. Have no fear. King Saul is strong. Do you not remember the plight of Jabesh-Gilead many years ago and what a victory he won there? You have heard how the king's son Jonathan and the army won a great victory not long ago at Micmash."

Several heads nod at the mention of these great victories. A feeling of pride and hope rises in my heart.

"But do you think they are done harassing us? Even now we hear reports that they are amassing an invasion force to defeat us again. Do you want their outposts scattered among us? Do you want your wives and children to live in fear? Saul is growing his army to defend our people and to destroy the hated Philistine oppressors once and for all!"

A villager standing near me whispers to his friend, "I don't know how we'll ever defeat the Philistines. They have iron weapons—what can we do against that?"

His friend responds, "Exactly. Besides, I've heard rumors from my cousin who lives in Gibeah. Some are saying that King Saul is afflicted by evil spirits. He has fits of rage, and a dark mood possesses him. Some say God has abandoned him."

Another man nearby grunts disgustedly. "Don't believe such lies. Saul is strong! He's building his army now and—"

Saul's agent interrupts. "All men twenty years of age and older are invited to take part in this contest. If you are younger than that, you will not be allowed to compete or join Saul's army. You will remain here as a militia force, should it become necessary for the elders to defend this village against a Philistine raid. If you are chosen for the army and your father has good reason to keep you home, your father must come to me and appeal my decision face to face. If you are not chosen, you also will remain here to defend your village."

The agent continues to tell the latest news from the capital city. I lose interest and scan the crowd that has gathered. I know them all, some faces more than others. Several older men and elders stand near the agent nodding public approval or scowling, depending on their political views. Some are angry that King Saul is demanding men and taxes from Pirathon. They still remember the independence that existed before Saul's reign. Others are glad to have a king and are eager for a more united nation. My eyes keep wandering, searching the crowd for the one face I love more than all the others.

Finally, I spot Benaiah standing against the town wall talking with Berechiah. I love watching him. He's talking animatedly, his eyes lit with bright passion. He intrigues me—a man so abused and neglected yet so quietly strong, with a dignity that no one has ever been able to take from him. I long to know him better.

My heart races even now just looking at him from afar. He turns and looks up. Our eyes meet. I know it may not be proper for a woman to stare so boldly at a man, but I can't look away. My heart slows as deep yearning stirs in my soul. His eyes shine with a mysterious light as he smiles and gazes into my eyes. I return the smile. How I want Benaiah for my husband! What a life we could begin together! Yes, I know I'd have to move in to Piram's household, and Benaiah has told me about the abuse, the pain, and the dysfunction that goes on there, but I feel we could face the future together. If living in Pirathon is too difficult, we could move away and start over somewhere else—perhaps in a bigger city—and create a new life for ourselves.

Our moment of eye contact is not long. It ends abruptly as the competition begins and Benaiah turns to watch. Saul's agent strides forward with a bundle of three spears. He thrusts them one by one into the ground several cubits apart, each one landing with a thud.

"All eligible men must step forward now. We begin with a spear throwing competition."

Suddenly, I feel a sick knot in my stomach. I change my mind. I do not want Benaiah to be part of the contest at all. What if he is chosen and Saul's agent takes him away to fight with the army? Benaiah is too proud to refuse! Also, it would be a great opportunity for him to escape from Piram.

Benaiah is still over by the wall, casually leaning against it. Berechiah stands next to him, pointing and commenting, as they both watch several of the young men line up in front of the spears.

Would Piram allow Benaiah to leave, though? Doesn't he need Benaiah's labor to keep his fields going? That was the whole reason he allowed him to return. Even if Benaiah is chosen, Piram will appeal the decision, and Benaiah will stay here. Yes, that's how it will be. Relief floods over me at the thought.

I am even more relieved and a bit surprised when Benaiah does not step forward from the wall. Berechiah now lines up alongside most of the other young men from Pirathon. Isn't Benaiah supposed to? Does every eligible man have to fight in the contest? I am confused about the rules but glad that he is not coming forward.

A sad thought crosses my mind. What will Benaiah do if Berechiah leaves for war? He will be crushed!

I cheer with the crowd as the spear throwing begins. Sharman son of Arach is the first to take the spear. He lets it fly with all his might. His throw is a bit awkward, and the spear doesn't go very far. His shoulders sag in disappointment as several of the other young men laugh.

Still puzzled that Benaiah is not lining up for the contest, I look again in his direction. Saul's agent has stepped over by him and is talking intently with him. The mood in my heart dips. What are they talking about? Benaiah is not in the competition. He will not be going to war, right?

I will have to ask him tomorrow if I get the chance. Piram and my father have an agreement—Benaiah comes over to help my father in his fields several times a week, and in exchange, my father gives Piram skins of wine or needed supplies from our large garden. Father has this arrangement with several other families, since he has no sons of his own to help him in the fields. Almost every day I go to the fields to bring water to the men or even help with some of the work. It's my favorite time of day, especially when Benaiah is out in our fields.

The crowd leans forward eagerly to watch the first spear throws, and I'm drawn in by the excitement. There are at least thirty young men who have lined up for the competition, and each of them get two chances to throw the spear. One by one the spears sail through the air and slice into the ground. After the first three are thrown, Saul's agent paces out and marks the longest throw with a stone. After all of the competitors have finished, Saul's agent announces the results. Mahlo threw it the farthest, followed by Sennah, and Berechiah came in a close third. Still, Benaiah leans against the wall, watching. Was he disqualified because he is not a full-blooded Israelite?

"Next is a test of strength!" the agent shouts. Large stones ranging from midsize to very large were brought in and placed along the village wall. I can't help but laugh a little to myself as they grunt and groan trying to get those stones off the ground. Hothiah actually lifts the biggest stone, but he's the only one strong enough to do it.

Before long, my favorite event—the footrace—has begun. Bare feet pound the ground as they race around the entire wall of Pirathon seven times. I enjoy watching them disappear from view around the left corner of the wall and then waiting for them to reappear again around the other side. We stand around for several minutes, talking and wondering who will be in first place when the runners reappear. Each time they round the bend, and we break out into another loud cheer. From time to time I steal a look at Benaiah. He's laughing and cheering along with the rest of us.

"Go, Berechiah. Go!" he's shouting.

I wonder how he feels. It must be hard for him not to compete. It must be hard for him to imagine Berechiah going off to war and living without him! How I long to make my way over to Benaiah and talk with him, but there's no opportunity. Besides, he's in the midst of the young men, and it is not my place to approach them.

In the end, Maabar wins the race by a full stone's throw, and we are breathless from shouting. Berechiah was several runners behind him and looks a little disappointed at the results.

"Now for the wrestling!" Saul's agent shouts. The young men get a short break and a drink as they line up opposite each other. The agent pairs them up by size. The first to push his opponent past a certain line wins.

What a power struggle! The men strip to the waist. I can see all their muscles, strained and tense. Their bodies shift and twist as they grapple with each other and try to shove their opponents over the line. Several times they collapse on the ground in a small cloud of dust. Sennah wins again and again against all the rest, despite the fact that he seems a little slower and more sore than usual today. Saul's agent is always close at hand, watching and observing everything and offering words of encouragement to the men.

In the end, Berechiah and Mahlo both do quite well in the competition. Saul's agent calls their names as well as the names of Abdon, Koran, Joshua, Hothiah, Maabar, Methumi, and Sennah, along with several others, and he also honors their fathers. He announces that these are the men he chooses to join the standing army at Gibeah. Fourteen men are turned away—some seem to be relieved, some ashamed, and some disappointed that they were not good enough to make the army. Several fathers of the chosen men step forward to meet with the agent privately to appeal his decision.

This agent of Saul must be wise. He seems to be fostering good relationships between the king and his villages. He has the king's authority to draft any man he wants into service, but he seems to know that if he pushes too hard, the king may have more internal troubles than he can handle. I watch as Mahlo's father pays Saul's agent so that Mahlo can stay home.

I steal another look at Benaiah, and I blush when I see him looking straight at me! I meet his gaze again. There's a strange look in his eyes tonight—a tinge of sadness, perhaps. He must be disappointed that he couldn't impress me with his strength in the competition tonight. I smile widely at him. He gives me a slight smile and nod. It fills my heart. I don't care if he competes or not, as long as he is safely here with me and continues to work toward a betrothal.

Happy and excited, I turn away and head for home. What a fun night! I enjoyed the competition, and I want so badly to hear Benaiah's thoughts about it.

Tomorrow. I will hear all about what he is thinking tomorrow.

17

BENAIAH

Berechiah and I walk homeward after the competition. "You did well out there tonight!" I tell him.

He laughs. "I told you I'd make it into the army. Did you see how slow and awkward Sennah was tonight? I was so close to pushing him over the line until he twisted sideways at the last minute and I lost my balance. You must have really hurt him badly the other day!"

It was my turn to laugh. "Maybe now he'll think twice before trying to fight me again."

"Did you hear—is his father going to go against the agent's choice? Is he going to join the army with us?"

"I don't know. I wish he would stay here. He's the last person I want to see traveling with us to Gibeah."

"I can't believe we are leaving for Gibeah in a couple days. How exciting!" Berechiah says.

"I know. I wonder what Gibeah is like. I've never been there." I look off in that direction, wishing I was going tonight.

"I want to see Saul's fortress. They say it's impressive! It's the strongest fortress in Israel. Can you believe we'll get to see King Saul in person? He's a legend!"

"His son Jonathan is a legend too. Maybe we'll get to fight alongside him. He's just a little older than we are."

We reach the place where we need to part ways, so we pause on the path. Berechiah's eyes are shining with excitement, and it makes my heart full with joy.

"I can't wait to train. Do you think they'll have real weapons for us to use?" Berechiah asks.

"Adnah said most of the soldiers are required to provide their own weapons. There isn't much of an armory there. They have a few weapons captured from the Philistines after Micmash and some that were plundered from the Moabites and Ammorites over the years, but we should still bring whatever we can from home. I'm going to bring my knife and the bow and arrows I use for hunting."

Berechiah paces back and forth, thinking aloud. "I've got a freshly sharpened ax and a few small knives. They'll have to do for now. Maybe we can get some more off the Philistines after we kill a few of them." He stops for a moment, and a serious look shadows his face. "Can you imagine killing someone? I wonder what that will be like. I know it's against Yahweh's commandment...but war is different. I wonder if I'll still feel guilty about it."

I turn my head so Berechiah can't see the look on my face. My thoughts turn back to the blood on my hands and the eerie, animal-like sounds of dying.

Berechiah starts to pace again but stops almost immediately as the realization hits him. "That's right..."

"I don't regret it, of course. It had to be done." I look down, and my voice changes to a near-whisper. "It's not the first time I've killed, either."

Berechiah's eyes widen as he stares at me. "What?"

I look off into the distance. "It was when I was banished from home, off in the hills by myself."

"Benaiah, you never told me this! What happened?"

"I had to defend myself. They were hunting me down."

"Wait. You killed those mercenaries Piram sent after you? That's what happened to them?"

"Yes. I haven't told anyone besides you. I had to do it."

"Then why does it matter if you tell people about it? You should be proud! They were trained killers! I don't know how you survived."

"I don't know either, really. It was like some blind instinct took over my body—like it wasn't even me anymore. I felt it when I killed the man who was chasing Adnah, and I felt it a little when I fought Sennah..." I let my words trail off.

"You'll have to tell me more about it on the trip to Gibeah."

I shake off the bad feeling that has settled over me and focus again on my friend's worried face. "Yeah. I'll tell you more then. I know you have to go home now."

"Are you okay, Benaiah?"

"I'm fine," I say, mustering a smile. "Go, get your bag packed. I'll see you tomorrow."

He returns my smile. "I'll see you tomorrow. Take care of yourself tonight, okay? No more arguments with Piram. Keep your joining the army a secret, all right?"

"I know. I will."

I turn and continue down the path toward home. I'm glad Piram was at the competition and saw that I didn't compete. He will never suspect that I am leaving with the other recruits. Piram thinks I am going to Eliezer's field tomorrow anyway, so he won't expect to see me most of the day. I can spend the time getting ready at home and talking with my mother. I'll leave very early the next day, before Piram has even shaken the sleep out of his eyes. I chuckle to myself in the dark. If only I could see his face when he realizes that I'm gone! Mother will have to act surprised so that she doesn't get into trouble. Berechiah's father and mother have promised me that they'll do their best to protect Mother while I'm gone. This gives me great relief. The only thing that nags at my good mood is the thought of saying goodbye to my mother and Hannah. I am not looking forward to that at all.

18

HANNAH

I wake, as always, in the black of early morning. Household chores consume my time. With mother sick so often, most of the household work falls upon me. I draw water from the well first, when the air is still cool. Today it takes several trips to bring enough water home. Later, I plan to take some to the thirsty men in the field. I cannot wait to see Benaiah again! I know he's working with my father today.

The morning chores wear on, and my mother keeps calling me into her room and adding to my list of work. I have to milk the goats, and since there's no one to help me hold them still, I have to tie each one up and then use my body to pin them against a wall as I squeeze the milk into a wide stone bowl. If only I had a sister to help! Then, I lead the small flock out to pasture for a while. After that, I weed the garden and bring more water from the well to soak the tender plants. I then grind grain and spend time organizing what I need for preparing today's meals.

Finally, the time comes. I wish my mother goodbye and tell her I am taking some water to the men. I lift the skin of water on my shoulder and set out for the fields. As I draw near, I can see the men working hard in the heat. They will be happy to have some fresh water today! My father stands at the edge, pointing and giving some instruction to several young men who have come to help. I look all around, and my heart sinks. Benaiah is not here! Why is he not here today? I'm sick with disappointment.

My father frowns when he sees my face. "What is it, dove?" he asks.

"Nothing, Father."

He presses the issue, perhaps because I'm usually in a good mood and little brings me down. "You seem sad or disappointed. What troubles you?"

"It's nothing, Father. I was just hoping Benaiah would be here today."

Father rolls his eyes. "Child, you need to forget about him. There are other fine young men in the village. He's a wild man with a bad reputation and not worth your time."

I'm indignant. "Why do you have him work in your fields if you can't stand him?"

"He *is* a hard worker and strong. I appreciate his help. He has good qualities that I respect, but he's not a good match for you or our household. Surely you can see that!"

"He *is* a good match, Father. Please give him a chance. Have you even heard his side of the story?"

"I have, and I understand he's had a rough life in Pirathon. He's just not worthy of you, my dove. He gets in fights, and several people have told me he drinks too much wine. His own family barely tolerates him. He has a terrible reputation in this village, especially with the elders, and he does not have a strong faith in Yahweh. Do I need to go on?"

I squeeze my eyes shut, exhausted and disgusted. "No, Father, I know how you feel. I wish you knew the truth about him. He's incredibly kind and compassionate! No one in this village appreciates him or sees him for who he truly is—"

"That's enough Hannah." His voice is gentle, but his eyes are hard. "We are not going to go through all this again—especially not here! You know how I feel."

Reckless anger carries me along. "But Father, you're being unfair to him! You need to give him a chance. Everyone keeps mistreating him and—"

"Hannah! I said that's *enough!*"

I see the threat in his glare, and it stops me cold. My father rarely gets angry. I fight down my frustration and bite my tongue. My shoulders sag in defeat.

When he sees me relent, he changes the subject, his voice stiff with restrained emotion. "Thank you for bringing us the water. How's your mother doing today?"

"She's not well, Father—a little weaker than normal."

He sighs and looks off over the fields toward home. "I'll come back early today. Do you need any help with your chores?"

I look up at him in fake surprise. "You're really going to help this time?"

He smiles back at me—all the tension gone in an instant. I love the wrinkles that form around his eyes when he is on the verge of laughing. He always offers to do the women's work. "Oh yes," he'll say, "I'll help weave that cloth!" or, "Here, let me cook the dinner tonight." Then, later, when I remind him of his offer, he just smiles at me with that mischievous grin of his and says something like, "Oh...not today, my dove! I need to practice first! Can you show me how to do it tomorrow?" Of course, he never actually gets around to doing anything.

When I am done giving them a drink I trudge homeward again, back to my daily chores. My mood has turned sour, and all my excitement about seeing Benaiah has evaporated. Why wasn't Benaiah in the fields today? Father never did give me a reason.

My disappointment lingers the rest of the day. Mother is asleep when I arrive back home. She hasn't been able to do any of the chores. I let out a sigh and start gathering supplies for the evening meal. Then I throw some wood into the oven. While it heats, I spend some time checking the skins of yogurt that are hanging in the back room and looking through the jars to see what we are low on. I discover that we need to grind even more flour, and because this is such a tedious task, I put it off for now. I work for a while at the loom, weaving cloth for Father's new robe. Then my time is consumed with preparing the evening meal. I am doing it all by myself again. I wish Mother would get well enough to help.

As I work at the hot oven, my mind wanders to Benaiah. Will Father ever see him the way I do? Will the villagers ever accept him? It's true he's a bit rough, and he has done a lot of fighting, but his bad reputation is usually not his fault.

The elders have their eyes on him. There have been times when he was punished publicly at the town gate. Heat rises to my face at the memories. One time, two local boys accused him of stealing a ewe lamb from their flock. Their father confirmed their story. They claimed that Benaiah took the lamb in the morning, and instead of working the fields that day, he went off into the wilderness where he roasted and ate the lamb. I was so upset. I knew Benaiah better. He would never do anything like that! But their testimony swayed the elders. Benaiah was forced to take two of Piram's lambs and give them to his accusers. Piram was livid. They tied Benaiah to a pole at the town gate for the rest of the day to shame him. Many people passed by and spit in his direction. They made fun of him and insulted him. I can still see the hurt look in Benaiah's eyes. He stood there so tall and indomitable despite the way he was being treated. Several days later, at the well, I overheard some of the local girls talking about the whole thing. They were the sisters of the boys who accused Benaiah. Their brothers had lost the lamb in the wilderness and didn't want to get in trouble with their father, so they concocted the whole story. Who better to blame than Benaiah, the troublemaker. And there are many such stories! Just thinking about it now makes me angry and irritable.

I finish making the meal and take some warm broth in for Mother to drink. She won't be joining us tonight, which is not unusual these days. Father comes home, and we sit down to eat. I am unusually quiet and somber, still disappointed about my day. Father chatters on, telling stories about his day. I nod and smile, but my thoughts are far away as I wonder about Benaiah and our future.

Later, when we are relaxing after the evening meal, a familiar voice suddenly echoes outside our house. "Greetings, house of Eliezer!"

Benaiah is at the door! My pulse quickens, and my hand flies to my hair, quickly adjusting it and rearranging the shawl atop my head. It is hard to keep myself looking good when I am constantly working. Why is he here? This is not like him! I am excited in so many ways. Perhaps he will try again to arrange something with my father! I work hard to suppress my excitement and appear calm and strong.

My father scowls slightly as he goes to answer the door.

"May I speak with your daughter, Eliezer?" Benaiah says with a humble, hopeful sound to his voice.

He's come just to talk to *me*! This is rare, yet absolutely wonderful!

I can tell Father is far from happy. Reluctantly, he nods his head and beckons for me to come to the door.

His eyes shoot me a warning look, and he regards Benaiah with a stern expression. "Go ahead, to the fig tree, and say what you need to."

My heart is pounding so loud I am afraid Benaiah might hear it as I duck out the door under Father's watchful eyes. We walk the short distance and sit beneath one of my father's fig trees. From here Father can sit outside the house and watch us, and this is exactly what he does.

As I walk beside Benaiah, I am drawn to his strength and confidence. Even now, he walks with no hesitations or wasted movements. I can tell he is slightly nervous, but it makes me all the more excited and curious. We make small talk at first. Daily, mundane things are exciting points of conversation when I am talking with Benaiah.

He pauses, and I see his mind mulling over what he wants to say next. He seems to be trying to form words that will communicate his thoughts to me in just the right way. There is a firm resolve written all over his handsome face. I stare into the soft light in his eyes.

He clears his throat and speaks. "Hannah, you know how tough it's been lately. I am basically a slave in my own house, and the elders keep a watchful eye on me all the time. Sooner or later they'll have me beaten or sold into slavery in some foreign land. If not that, Piram will eventually have me killed when he doesn't need my help anymore. I just can't go on like this. My spirit is broken here." He takes in a deep breath and lets it out. He looks at me, his eyes heavy. "I want to marry you, but Piram refuses to help me arrange anything, and your father constantly brushes me off when I try talking to him about it. I have to get a better reputation. I have to do something to gain everyone's respect, or this is how it will always be. I've talked privately with Saul's agent Adnah about joining the king's standing army at Gibeah. He's offered to take me along, and I have decided to go. I leave tomorrow. I've come to say goodbye to you."

I look at him in disbelief and shock. He's leaving. He's going to war. This is the last thing I expected! My heart freezes, like I've been plunged into a cold river. He is a soldier in the king's standing army.

He looks deeply into my eyes, trying to read my expression. I am angry and hurt, yet still drawn to him in a powerful way. Little does he know that my heart is completely his. He is now crushing it with his decision. I am sure he can see the pain in my eyes as the tension quickly builds between us, and this seems to make him uncomfortable. What can I do? I certainly won't beg him to stay. I am too proud for that. Besides, he is set in his ways, and I know there is no way to change his mind now. I love him and hate him for his stubbornness.

"I will come back, and when I do, this village will see me differently. I will come back a hero and a warrior. Your father will not refuse our marriage then!"

A thought enters my mind that makes me sick. "Maybe Father will arrange a marriage for me with someone else while you're gone. Have you thought of that?"

By the look on his face, my words have wounded his heart. It's true, though. Months, even years, may go by without seeing Benaiah. Who knows what could happen? I love him, but right now, resentment boils in my blood. He is leaving me, and the hole that grows inside me is like the yawning mouth of a deep cave.

The prospect of my life without Benaiah feels crushing, and I can't even wrap my head around it. I stand up and walk hurriedly toward my father. Benaiah walks a few steps behind, trying to catch up to my angry march.

"Hannah, listen! This is something I need to do. Surely you can understand. I'll come back!"

"I understand, Benaiah. Just go do what you need to do."

Part of me does understand. I see what he's trying to do. I know how miserable he is here in Pirathon—especially lately—but my emotions are in a whirlwind. My beautiful dreams are still under that fig tree, shattered into shards. When we are a stone's throw from the door to my house, I stop and turn to face him again. I try so hard to appear calm and indifferent, holding my feelings inside, but when I close my eyes, a tear squeezes itself loose and rolls down my cheek. Soon, streams of disappointment wash down my face, and small sobs escape from my throat.

He reaches out to me to dry my tears, a compassionate glow in his gentle eyes. I rip my eyes away from his intoxicating look and stare at his feet. He holds my shoulders and opens his mouth as if he wants to say comforting words. He is the cause of my pain, though. There's no comforting me at this point.

I shake loose from his hands. "Go, Benaiah. Go fight your war, if that's what you have to do. Just don't count on me waiting for you." I don't care if this hurts him. I need time and distance to ready myself for his absence.

I turn away and keep walking, new tears forming in the corners of my eyes—tears that I will not let Benaiah see. I pass my father quickly. He stands up, obviously confused and curious. I don't want to talk, so I just keep going into the house. I feel my future darkening like a severe thunderstorm spreading over the hill country, bathing the brilliant hills in blackness. He's leaving so soon! Tomorrow already! I steady myself against the wall inside the house.

I can hear my father stopping Benaiah from coming inside, sending him on his way. How will I do this? How can I even wake up tomorrow and the following days and do my household chores over and over again without any prospect of being Benaiah's wife? I must harden my heart, wrap it in stone, and continue on. All those fantasies—those worthless fantasies—must be thrown out of my mind and heart, at least for now. Perhaps when Benaiah returns from war—if he returns at all—I can hope again. But how long can I wait for him? Will my father let me wait for him? What if he dies? *What if I never see him again?* This thought shoots through me like a lightning bolt. My head snaps up, and I turn and burst out the door. Benaiah is already well on his way.

I run several steps toward him and stop. "Benaiah!" I call out.

He turns back and sees me outside my house, next to my father, watching him go.

The wind whips my hair and flows through my robes as I stand tall watching him in the distance. I know he'll soon walk out of sight, my heart leaving with him. I try to send all my love for him through my eyes, hoping that he can see how much I care for him. I drink in the last moments of seeing him and treasure them in my memory. "God be with you, Benaiah! Come home soon! I'll be waiting for you!" I call.

Father grunts in disapproval. "Get back in the house, Hannah!"

Benaiah lifts his hand in a wave, affection shining in his eyes. A mysterious smile suddenly comes over his face. "I will come back for you, Hannah. I promise I will. I love you!"

He turns and continues on his way.

I watch until he is out of sight, and then I sit down in a trance. My father is urging me inside as if I'm some stubborn goat. I can hardly hear him in my present state. I can only think of Benaiah.

19

BENAIAH

I spend the rest of my night lying on my mat trying to sleep, and I can't get her out of my head. Over and over, my mind replays our meeting together. She was so happy to see me. It's been rare for us to get a moment together. Her father guards her closely, and since her mother is often too sick to work, Hannah is busy with all the household chores.

I smile as I remember how her mouth moved as she chatted away about her work for the day, her mother's mood, her father's problems with one of his sheep, and so on. I was only half listening, acknowledging her words with a nod or sound. I wanted to drink her in like wine. I didn't want to forget a thing. If only I could freeze her face in my mind and take it with me. I enjoy everything about her: the curl of her lips when she smiles, the faintest brush of her soft hand against mine, the way her eyes shimmer like candlelight when she laughs, the graceful way she walks, and the liveliness of the single strand of hair that escapes from her shawl and plays in the wind.

A coldness grips the pit of my stomach when I think of leaving her here. She and my mother are the only people I will miss. Will I live to see them again? I shake my head. I can't think like that!

My mind wanders back to the moment I told her I was leaving. I see again her shocked expression. A cold silence settled over her like frost. She hesitated, not sure of what to say at such a moment. Two powerful rivers were flowing in opposite directions within her—duty and obligation pulled a strong current, but the pent-up flood of emotion wouldn't hold back. Anger rolled out first, her gorgeous eyes flashing with light and heat, and her small mouth drawn tight. Words and arguments spilled out of her.

She has a fire in her that thrills me to the center of my soul. Even when she is angry, her eyes fill me with their brightness and passion. I felt absolutely terrible to upset her, yet her anger washed me clean. It drenched me in the feeling of fresh life. It confirmed how much she cares about me. Most people in Pirathon will be glad to see me go, but not her. I love her so much, yet I must leave her here. I must go and fight. There's no other way to have her as my wife. I must leave her so that I can become the man her father will respect and accept.

Even though I want her as my wife, and I want a settled life with children, fields, and flocks…I just don't want that quite yet. First I want to live free and feel the danger electrify my soul. I want to go and see the sights that I have not yet seen. I want to try my muscle, sharpen my mind, and exhaust a few other possibilities in my life. I want a life with Hannah eventually, but right now, faraway dreams seduce me.

It broke my heart when she began to cry. I felt sick, even a little guilty. It was a brief rain that temporarily snuffed my fiery desire to leave. When I turned away, though, my mind filled with unsettling freedom—a feeling that still courses through me. I am so excited for my future, for adventure, for a change of scenery, and for a fresh start and new opportunities. If only I could take Hannah with me! Then my life would be perfect. If only I could marry her first and bring her with me to Gibeah.

I close my eyes and see her again, just as she was when I last saw her today. It's a memory I know I will never forget—an image that will drive me and mesmerize me every day that I am gone. When I turned and looked back at her, her beauty shocked every other thought out of my mind. There she stood outside her house on that cloudy, windy day, with a slight chill in the air that signaled a coming storm. Her garments were flowing in the wind behind her, and strands of her dark hair struggled with a ragged blast of wind. Tears streaked down her face, yet her eyes were clear and bright. A strange mixture of pain and love glowed in their depths and reached out for me across the cold distance. She looked almost like a queen—regal, fierce, and indomitable. Yet at the same time, she was so passionate, vulnerable, and desperate.

I must return for her. I must succeed as a soldier so I can come back and win her as my wife!

20

SERAH

The black sky hangs above me in the earliest hours of morning. Piram sleeps soundly back in the house. It is an hour before we normally wake. I lean against the doorway, my fingers wrapped around the door frame, and my cheek pressed up against the rough wood. I watch the dim form of my Benaiah melt into the blackness, and…he's gone.

Yesterday we worked together packing his things, including some supplies that I prepared for his journey. Now, he's already leaving and I have no idea how long it will be until I see him again. This is the day I have dreaded the most. I can still feel his embrace, his warm arms that were wrapped around me a moment before as we said goodbye. His words of tender love still sit soft in my ear as I watch him walk away.

How strong! He looks manly as he goes off on his new adventure. His heart is set on war, and my heart writhes in pain. I can't hold back the tears that well up in my eyes. It is a relief to be alone in this moment. Crying is not something I allow myself to do, especially not around Piram or the rest of the family. I hate being vulnerable and weak, and Piram does not approve of such emotional displays. I try so hard to arrange my life so that I do not need anything from anyone—ever! Yet this is breaking through all my resolve. My soul is leaving with my son. Without him I am sure that loneliness will break my heart. He doesn't know how badly I want to hold him back. I want him to stay. I know if I had begged him, he might have listened. Our bond is strong—stronger than most mothers have with their sons at his age. I could have doused the fire in his eyes and snuffed out his burning enthusiasm and excitement. I could have stirred the conflict of desire and duty that often rages in his mind. Then he might have stayed. But really, I would never do that to him. I understand how he aches for this change. I know he needs to go. I won't stand in his way, clinging to his robe like a child.

Watching him go, my old wounds tear open fresh. The familiar pain floods my mind. He is the son of my woe, yet I love him more than anyone. Unbidden, the memories tear through my mind like jagged flashes of lightning. Terrible, unsettling weakness blows through me like a cold, violent wind. I step back inside the house and sink to my knees on the dirt. Tears streak down my face, falling and skittering down to the dusty floor where they shatter into tiny balls of mud. I feel my body trembling.

The images come again, so fresh, raw, and real, as if they happened yesterday: I am a young girl again, standing in front of Father's house at the family oven. The oven glows so hot. The flat bread steams, its fragrance wafting into the air with a delicious freshness that warms me inside. My mouth waters. I am so eager for the evening meal with my family gathered around. It is a special occasion. The crop has been very good, and Father has just been honored by the elders for a successful trade venture that greatly helped our village. It is time for a family celebration. Several of our relatives from Shechem are coming to stay with us for a few days. We will feast tonight on fresh goat meat roasted over the coals and seasoned with herbs. Our meal will also include wine, sauces, fresh bread and sweet butter, goat cheese, fig cakes, and other fruits and vegetables.

My job now is to bake the bread and do some other preparations for the meal. Mother is gone in search of some other food for the meal at several of our friends' and relatives' houses and will return shortly. Father and my brothers are out in the fields tending some of our crops. I am just about to take the bread from the oven when a trumpet blasts an ear-shattering signal at the edge of town. It quickly dies off, the sound unnaturally cut short. Sudden wild screams split the air, followed by sounds of violent commotion and crashing metal. My fear is instant. I freeze in place, the little hairs of my arms singing so close to the oven's heat, and the hair on the back of my neck standing on edge.

I quickly recover my senses, and my fear gives way to frantic activity. I quickly finish getting the bread, and I rush into the house, fingers burning. I hastily set the bread on a low table, instinctively covering it with a cloth. What is going on? An attack? Where is my family? Are they safe?

I turn quickly, swinging the wooden door shut. The pole creaks loudly in the hollowed stones below and above. I shut it and bar it. My heart thumping, I flee to a storeroom in back that is filled with stone jars. I huddle in the corner between two large jars, wrapping my robes around me tight, making myself as small as possible. I squeeze my eyes shut and begin praying wildly. "O Yahweh, protect me. O Yahweh, preserve my family. Keep us from whatever is out there threatening our village."

More gut-wrenching screams explode shockingly close—wild screams that run through me like icy fingers freezing my soul. Shouts and mayhem echo out in the street nearby followed by loud crashes and the ear-splitting roars of men making war. I hear feet grinding in the dust and stones of the street, metal clanging against metal, leather and cloth ripping in the scuffle, and the sickening thump of bodies falling.

Fear floods every inch of me. I huddle deeper and deeper in the corner, praying it will be over soon and praying that whoever is attacking will leave. My words come out in a trembling mumble. "O give us peace. O keep my family safe!"

And then I hear a violent thud at the door—our door! My heart jumps into my throat. The warmth in my skin turns cold like frost. I search wildly for a weapon—for *anything*—but all the objects I might use are out in the common room. I dare not go out there now. Just as I start praying that the door will hold, there is an awful crash as it caves through, followed by a gruff manly grunt of pain. In the next room I hear heavy breathing, loud crashes, and furniture splintering as men pillage the house. For some reason, my thoughts turn to the warm bread. Will they spare it? Will I get to taste it? Will I ever taste anything again?

I know it is only a matter of time before they search the rest of the house. I turn toward the wall in sheer terror and begin to claw frantically at the hard-packed earth. My fingernail tears on a stone, and pain slices through me. I force myself not to scream. I keep digging. Glancing over my shoulder, I see no one—yet. I can still hear them rummaging through the house, upsetting everything in a search for something valuable to take.

I turn back to the wall and dig even harder and faster. I don't even know if I can dig a hole through the rocks and mud, but I do know that if this doesn't work, I am doomed.

Suddenly, rough calloused fingers close like talons around my ankles, yanking my body backward. I hear my own scream of shock like it is coming from some throat other than my own. My heart reels as I struggle, desperately throwing dirt and flailing my arms. A huge hand strikes the side of my face like a hammer, and lights explode through my brain. I vaguely hear him shout to someone else in a language I do not understand. Pain pulses in my head as my struggling grows more delirious.

Soon I can see nothing—my robes are pulled up over my face. Strong arms pin me to the dust. My fight is frantic yet helpless. I hear the violent ripping of cloth and feel a rush of cold air surround my body. I scream uncontrollably in absolute terror. The arms pin me back even harder, and an unbelievable weight presses against my body, crushing me into the dust. I try to kick out with my feet as my robes continue to blind me. My whole body shakes through waves of hot pain and pure, loathing disgust. The unnatural pain lasts only a moment, but it might as well have been a thousand years of helpless agony and shame. When he finishes, he strikes me again and again in the head with his heavy, rock-hard hand. I hear my nose break with a sickening crunch, and warm blood gushes on my face beneath my robes. Arrogant laughter echoes in my throbbing ears. Then they shift places, allowing his companion to take a turn. My mind floats away into darkness, and I feel my body being carried down a black river— cold and lifeless to the depths of the grave.

I'm trembling as I remember that evening that is now so fresh in my mind. I forced the memory into a far, dark corner of my mind, yet it tears through me now with such violence I can't hold it back. It still feels so real.

After the attack I woke up in pain that arched my back. My nostrils filled with the thick smell of smoke. The raiders had burned Father's house. Father had arrived just in time to carry my limp body from the burning wreckage. My long, black hair was matted with blood and dirt. Dried sweat and soot clung to my skin. Dried tears stiffened my eyes. A sickness had settled deep in the pit of my stomach. And the shame! I was drenched in self-disgust. I was thoroughly unclean. I was sure no one would ever love me again. My life was destroyed. I was a shadow. I wanted to die. At that moment, I was wishing they would have just killed me. That would have been a mercy.

An unforgettable red, helpless rage blazed on Father's face. Ever after he was a changed man. Mother wept and wept for days—endless days. But the strange thing was that I could not shed a tear. Emptiness filled me. Numbness settled within my heart. This kind of thing happened all the time, but I never thought it would happen to me—though the fear of it had always been there.

It had been a fast raid. A band of Philistines had struck Pirathon in a whirlwind of violence, and then were gone just as quickly. They had not had time to take much. Their goals were simply to terrorize us, bully us, and prove their dominance. They had succeeded with me.

The men of Pirathon had roused a small defense to fend off the attack. Several local men and boys had died at the edge of town. The warning had come too late. After the raid, a group of townsmen had rallied together to avenge themselves on the raiding party, but nothing came of it. Many of the men were accustomed to fighting, but few were well-trained warriors. They were farmers and herdsmen. They kept trees and grew vines. Even though they were strong and able-bodied, and many of them had fought in the militia, they weren't professional soldiers. The raiding party had been moving fast and was well-armed and well-trained. Over the next few days, the people rebuilt several ruined houses in the village and doubled the watch.

A Philistine raid had devastated the village and pillaged my heart, my body, and my soul.

A few weeks later, I discovered I was with child. Fear flooded me anew. In no way was I prepared for this. I couldn't imagine bearing a child that was hardly my own—a child that was forced upon me by violent heathens.

It all seemed so complicated. Not only was I carrying a child with heathen blood, but I also had no husband. I was, however, betrothed to Piram. Several months before the Philistine raid, Piram's wealthy and influential father had approached my father, who then consented to the arrangement. But I feared that this news would change everything. I already feared Piram as it was. He was a stern, cold man—not warm and tender as my own father had always been. He intrigued me, though, because he was handsome and strong, and, at that time, he had the respect of the community.

After finding out I was with child, I questioned everything: What would Piram's reaction be? Would the betrothal fall through? Why had this happened? Was God punishing me? But my questions had no answers. They echoed through my soul, resounding in the newly dead places of my heart. I felt all alone.

As a family we decided to hide the pregnancy until after my marriage to Piram. It was only a few months away at the time, and my belly would not be large enough for him to know. I trembled at the thought of deceiving such a powerful man and his family—the family I would be living with! However, my father insisted on secrecy. He did not want the marriage arrangement to fall through. In his eyes, Piram was my only chance at marriage under the circumstances. The secret weighed heavy on my mind. It gnawed at the insides of my soul. My father told me that all would be well, and that when the baby came no one would know the child was not Piram's. He assured me that when Piram found out, he would make it right. How wrong he was.

My daily chores became a crushing burden. Each day I was more exhausted than the next. Several days in a row I would stay in the house, sick and miserable. My belly grew a bit larger with child. It was so strange to feel movement from inside. The first time I felt it, I was frightened. Later, I was comforted by the little movements. Even so, for a long time I felt almost no connection to the little life growing within. I didn't want it! I didn't want a baby.

When the wedding celebration was only a week away, Piram found out the truth. He had been suspicious for some time. He asked me point blank if I was with child. His eyes were hot and penetrating, slicing through me like darts of flame. I could not lie. I knew my eyes gave my secret away, so I turned my face.

Suddenly, he grabbed me by the shoulders and twisted me around, shaking me slightly. He screamed in my face, "Why do you lie to me? What have you done?"

It was the first time he touched me in anger. I went cold with fear, and all words fled from my tongue. I could only plead for mercy with my eyes as I fought back a flood of tears.

"Who is the father? I'll kill him with my bare hands!" He stormed away furiously.

I was sure he would tell his parents, humiliate me in front of the village, and divorce me. My father found me sobbing in a heap and ran to intercept him.

Father met with his family and told them the whole story about what had happened. He apologized for keeping it a secret. "What would you have done?" he asked them. He then sat with them for some time discussing the situation and soothing their wounded pride.

Father was good at persuasion. He had a way with words, and people listened to him. However, Father also agreed to lower the bride price significantly to influence their decision. Piram's family agreed, reluctantly, to carry on with the wedding. They decided it was still a good match socially, despite the recent developments.

Piram was always upset after that. His whole attitude toward me changed.

When we were first betrothed, his parents had wanted this marriage far more than he did. His father had made the arrangement with my father knowing that having a connection to my family would be beneficial. I had feared that Piram had wanted to take me as his wife more for that reason than out of love for me. However, though he has never been a warm or sentimental man, he had been kind to me at first. From time to time I would even see—maybe only in my imagination—a small spark flicker in his eyes when he looked my way. In those moments I had always wondered if perhaps his love for me was growing.

All that changed when I became pregnant with a heathen baby. After he discovered the truth, Piram started looking at me with a frightening light in his eye. The rest of that week he rarely even talked to me, and when he did, it was all business.

He was short with me. It was obvious that I was a burden to him. I heard rumors that he argued with his parents to break the arrangement. He didn't want me anymore. I feared no one would want me anymore. My future was spinning out of control. My parents thought that once I was married, my life would get better and the shame would go away. They thought that once we were married, Piram and I would grow closer and find the love that Father and Mother had. They assured me that the people in town would forget what had happened and go on with their lives. They were wrong.

The wedding feast came and went, and Piram got so drunk that he spent our first night passed out. He was drunk for many nights after that.

The first time he hurt me was only a week or so after our wedding. I had been bothered by the smell on his breath, so I mentioned it to him once. I also politely asked him not to drink so much wine when we were together. That was the first time I saw that look in his eyes. I was so young and naïve. That fresh pain in my soul hurt far worse than the bruises on my body. After that, I lived in constant fear for my life and for the life of my child. And it has happened so often since then.

The months passed. A dark depression settled on me as I eked out an existence in Piram's father's house. His sisters treated me with disdain. His family used me for my labor, tolerating me at best. They looked the other way when Piram abused me. They gave me the lowest and meanest jobs. I felt so small and ashamed, even though I had done nothing wrong. Everyone in the household treated me coldly. I was lonely and unloved. My mother would visit me, and the loneliness would briefly subside, but then she would leave—how I longed to leave with her!

Finally it was time to give birth. The pains came on me while I was grinding grain. Under normal circumstances, my husband's mother would be one to help me through labor and give me advice, but Piram's mother kept her distance from me and wanted nothing to do with my pregnancy or the birth of my child. She notified the midwife that I was in labor, but while I endured the pains, she and the rest of Piram's family chose not to be present. My own mother came and was a great comfort to me. Without her I don't know how I could have survived it.

Giving birth to Benaiah was the hardest thing I'd ever done. The midwife came with her assistant, a young girl from a neighboring village. She tried to keep me comfortable and knew the right places to rub to ease the pain. She prepared herbs and spices to help me through. Still, it was unbelievable. Screams tore out of my throat. My body was wracked with spasms of intense pain. Waves of agony continuously crashed through me. The final moments were pure torture, and the sounds that erupted from my mouth sounded like they came from a wounded lion. And suddenly, he was there—my little boy! It was unreal how something so incredibly awful could result in such a wonderful blessing! I explored his little ears, nose, and eyes. His little lips trembled as his tiny mouth screamed.

Once I held that helpless, naked little boy skin to skin on my heaving chest, my whole world changed. His tiny fingers curled around mine. Touching his soft baby skin and holding him close to my heart changed how I felt about him. He was so helpless and small. How he needed me! I knew this child was God's gift to me in the midst of such pain and tragedy. Something good had finally come from all the pain and heartache I had endured. This was it. This little boy. This son of my woe.

We named him Benaiah—built by the Lord. Piram had wanted to name him Baal-Marrah, but he relented rather quickly after I insisted on naming him Benaiah. It was obvious that he didn't care. If he had cared, he would have had his way. But no—he was numb toward such things. He was numb toward my little boy and me.

Benaiah was all I had in the world. My parents had married me off into a cold world—a world with a heartless husband and his proud, aloof family. My new husband could barely stand to be near me, and I was often glad when he left me alone. My son became my source of love and my reason to live. I worked hard to fight through my depression and the day-to-day grind of my disappointing life. I fought to survive for Benaiah.

My memories fade away as the faint light of early morning glimmers on the horizon. I slowly get up from the ground and look off into the distance, knowing all too well that Benaiah is too far away for me to see him now. I let a few final tears trickle down my cheeks. A thousand chores are piled up around me, and I am wasting my time languishing in self-pity and fear. I force myself to stand up. Piram will be furious when he finds out Benaiah has left. He relies heavily on Benaiah's help in the fields. The thought stirs a fresh storm of panic in my heart. What will he do now?

21

BENAIAH

The sun blazes down on us as we walk away from Pirathon and away from my tangled past. A chalky dust rises from the road at every step. I look up and soak in the rays of the rising sun, drinking its warmth into my skin. I feel alive in a way I've never felt before—free and excited. The world waits, and I am off to master it! I cast one last look behind me. I whisper, "I will return to you, Pirathon. I will return to you as a conqueror."

I turn back toward the road just as Berechiah jogs up next to me smiling, his eyes shining with excitement. "What a day for a journey! It's going to be strange to have no fieldwork!"

I nod my head and return his smile. "No fieldwork, no Piram, no Sennah—no more Pirathon."

"Sennah didn't come?" Berechiah looks amazed.

"No! Thank the gods! His father refused to let him go. I saw him this morning when we were just about to set out. His father was screaming at Adnah and Sennah, and Sennah was red with anger. His father must have paid Adnah a handsome bribe, because he took Sennah home with him!"

"That's a relief!"

We come up to Adnah and the other recruits. I study Adnah. He is a strong man—a warrior. Some god had been with me when I was able to save his life. Although, I am sure that if he had been alone he would have found some way to fight them off. He is not a handsome man. A scar traces the right side of his neck, and a rough beard wraps around his face. His appearance is wild and raw. You can tell he's an experienced fighter. Every step he takes is deliberate and disciplined. He always conducts himself with the authority and confidence of a man who faced his demons and won. I find myself wanting to be like him. I want people to look at me the way they look at him—with awe and respect.

As we pick our way down the hill and along the path, Adnah passes the time by telling us stories of Saul's early days. His rich, husky voice adds a gentle, welcome rhythm to our walk, and several other young recruits draw near, listening to him with rapt attention.

"By far the best moment has been Micmash. I am sure you heard of it."

I nod, remembering the celebration in the streets of Pirathon when the messenger arrived with the news. I think even the poorest families feasted on meat for the occasion. Piram had gotten extremely drunk and passed out, much to my relief that night.

Adnah continues. "As you know, Prince Jonathan had attacked their outpost at Geba, so they invaded us. The Philistines held nothing back. They managed to move in with their chariots..." His voice trails off for a moment as his mind sees the sight again. "They had thousands of chariots. They completely overran the lower elevations and had an iron-hard grip on the situation. Their troops blanketed our land. It was like a cloud of locusts had descended on Israel. The whole army went into hiding high up in the caves and crags. A few of my fellow soldiers and I hid out in a damp cave. The water dripped from the roof, rodents scurried in the dark gloom, and for days we barely saw any light. Every day, one of us would creep to the entrance and try to get a feel for what was going on. We knew our men were deserting in droves. We thought the end was near. One morning, after what seemed like a week living in the darkness, I was sitting near the entrance keeping watch, and I heard sudden shouts and cries. I looked out and saw Israelites running past, brandishing weapons and raising a war cry. I shouted back to my companions, and we emerged from the cave. Once our eyes were able to adjust to the bright light of day, we saw dead Philistines strewn everywhere. They were on the run, panicked and crazed. We couldn't believe it. We grabbed our weapons and joined in the chase. It was not until later that we learned of Jonathan's daring attack. Yahweh gave us a great victory that day!"

We walk on through the day. Every story Adnah tells makes me eager to go out and get some experience myself. The day flies by as my mind fills with Adnah's words.

Just before night descends on us, we pitch camp near a rare grove of trees. We eat our supper sitting around campfires. Adnah explains to us how to post a guard and sleep in such a way that we can wake up and fight if an enemy attacks us. He tells us never to stare into the fires. If the enemy attacks at night, we don't want to be blind in the dark, leaving us helpless and dead in moments. I soak in all the information I can. Adnah is a fierce, first-class warrior, and if I want to return to Pirathon a hero, I will need to learn fast.

Following the meal, some of the young men sing songs from their local towns. The firelight casts shadows that dance in eerie rituals against the rocks and sand. One man takes out a lyre and plays a haunting melody, his voice wafting out clear and tremulous. Bathed in moonlight, we stare out into the fading light across the hills of Israel. I look at Berechiah, and he smiles at me. We enjoy the moment together in silence.

My body is tired from the journey, but my mind is wide awake with excitement. Images from Adnah's stories replay in my mind all night long. We will arrive at Gibeah sometime tomorrow.

For the most part, the rest of our trip is uneventful. Berechiah and I stay close. The other recruits from Pirathon keep their distance, but they make me wary. I fear they might talk and tell stories, turning the other soldiers against me when they get the chance. For now they seem to be distracted by their excitement and nervousness about joining the army, but that probably won't last forever.

We move at a fast pace, and as the day goes on I grow somewhat tired of the dust that collects in my nostrils, on my feet, and in my clothes. There is also the constant smell of the pack animals and the sweat of men on the move. Finally, just before evening, we reach Gibeah. Other groups of raw recruits are slowly pouring into town from the surrounding areas. Throat tight and palms sweaty, I follow our small group into the main street of town. I am shocked when we draw near to Saul's fortress-like palace. I haven't seen anything like it. Massive stone walls, many cubits thick, thrust up before us. A watch tower rises upward, piercing the sky.

The streets of Gibeah are busy and alive. People bustle about as they wrap up their daily business. Several soldiers run back and forth from the palace. Women carry baskets on their heads, robes swirling behind them. Shouts and laughter echo from a group of travelers enjoying a rest in the shade of a large tree. The savory smell of roasting meat wafts into the air, making my mouth water. Gibeah excites all my senses.

Just on the other side of town we gather with a whirling crowd of men. Not all are new soldiers. Many of the experienced men hang about and razz the new recruits as we walk by.

A tall hawkish man with wild eyes calls out, "Aw! Look at the new little lambs! Ready for a fleecing or a slaughter?" He grins mockingly as he draws his finger along the blade of his sword.

"Saba, you shouldn't taunt them!" Adnah calls back with a twinkle in his eye. "If you're nice to the little lambs, maybe they'll follow you around as their new shepherdess!"

Saba roars with mock rage and brandishes his sword.

Adnah rolls his eyes and laughs.

Another man with dark eyes and a grotesque scar across his cheek emerges from a building as we pass by. He stops and watches us. His eyes pierce us with a look that makes my skin crawl. He says nothing, but keeps his eyes on us, watching our every move. He seems to be appraising us according to some invisible standard. A small sneer slides across his face as he sees Adnah. "Back so soon, son of Gamel?" he calls out, his voice surprisingly smooth and refined.

Adnah turns and recognizes the newcomer. "Yes, I am back, Havel. How did you do in the south?"

"One hundred and twenty-three recruits. And you?"

"Seventy-two, Havel." Adnah rolls his eyes. "I ran into a little trouble on the way to Pirathon. I lost Loman and Simeon in an attack."

"What a pity." His face shows no emotion whatsoever. "Your recruits look awfully green and untried. I hope they don't turn and run at the first sign of the Philistines."

"They won't. We will train them well."

"We'll see when the time comes," Havel says coldly, and he abruptly turns and walks away in the opposite direction.

When we reach the end of the street, Adnah gathers us around. "You'll register here with the army secretary and then join me at the supply tent. Later you will be divided into units and assigned jobs." He points in the direction of the supply tent and walks off to meet up with several other recruiters.

The secretary stands at a low table and tallies the troops. Another commander forms us in lines to register our names and hometowns. Berechiah and I are separated, and he gets through the line much faster than I do. With no one to talk to, I pass the time by looking around at the other recruits. Men of various sizes and ages stand in line before me. Some faces are hard and grim, and others are jovial and eager. I don't recognize any of them. Finally, it is my turn to register, and I stand before the table.

The secretary's voice is nasally and shrill. "Your name, son?"

"Benaiah."

"Father's name?"

I pause uncertainly. Should I give him my stepfather's name? I don't want to be part of his legacy. I owe him no such favor.

The secretary glances up at me, annoyed. The line is long.

"Speak up! What is your father's name?"

Several men around me look up, curious.

"I...I...don't really have a father."

Someone nearby snickers.

The secretary stares at me hard, his beady eyes blazing. His voice rushes out of him in a high pitched crescendo. "You don't have a father?" He pauses dramatically. "Oh yes, let me guess—Yahweh created you out of the dust of the ground, just like Adam? Your mother is the earth, and your father is the sky?"

Everyone has stopped and is staring at us now. I feel an unwelcome heat spreading across my face as the secretary continues.

"I've been doing this for hours today, and there have been a hundred young upstarts like you passing by my table. Do you think you are special?"

I shake my head, speechless.

"Give me your father's name, or I'll send you home. The army doesn't need another weak, arrogant fool."

My face is fully on fire now, and I feel my stomach turn into knots at this unexpected attack. I stammer, "I'm sorry. I just... it's complicated."

Someone nearby laughs outright. "Complicated? He's a bastard! Send him home—he can't fight with us."

My mind is reeling with shame, and a powerful feeling of helplessness overwhelms me. "I do not know my father. I never met him. I don't know his name!" I nearly spit the words in frustration.

A seasoned soldier standing nearby scoffs. "He *is* a bastard! Benaiah the bastard!"

I feel the rage pooling in my bones. I barely stifle the urge to break out of the line and swing and break the man's jaw.

The secretary just shakes his head. "Fine. I'll just register you by your village. What else can I do? What village are you from?"

"Pirathon."

He bends over his tablet and makes the appropriate marks.

"All right, you are registered as Benaiah of Pirathon. Now go over by the supply tents and take your attitude with you. Move along! Next person?"

I storm off in the direction of the supply tent, feeling flustered. I glance up and see the man who called me a bastard leaning against a low wall with a lazy smile on his face. His eyes are mocking me, even challenging me, as he continues to stare. I can hardly believe it. I left home to avoid this, and now here I am, face to face with another Sennah—or worse.

After a few moments of searching, I find Berechiah. He's met up with several of his cousins who are already in the army. He smiles as they chatter excitedly, filling him in on life in the army. I take a deep breath and try to calm down. I don't want to upset them, but I cannot clear my mind. My breath is still coming in short bursts, and my boiling rage is barely contained within me.

Berechiah glances over and reads my mood instantly. His face softens, and he takes me aside. "What is it, Benaiah?"

I tell him what happened at the secretary's table.

"Don't take it so seriously, Benaiah! They'll all forget about it in a moment. We are soldiers now! This is not Pirathon. It's going to be different for you here. I know it!"

A voice echoes over the camp, interrupting our conversation. We both look over at the sound.

"Attention here, recruits!"

All the recruits and the seasoned veterans in the army fall silent in respect.

"Who is that?" I whisper to Berechiah.

He turns with a questioning look to one of his cousins who silently mouths, "Prince Jonathan!"

My eyes widen in realization, and I turn to look again at one of our national heroes. He is a young man, only a few years older than myself, but an incredible confidence and calmness emanates from him. His dark hair and muscular build show off his strength and fine appearance. This is the future king of Israel!

He calls again, "For those of you who do not know me, I am King Saul's son, Jonathan. I've been given the job of introducing you to the army and organizing you into your proper units. First I want you to gather by tribes. We will not necessarily be keeping you with your fellow tribesmen, however. We want men from each tribe working together as one group, fighting together for us as a united nation. At this time, we will divide you among the existing units. When we are finished, each unit will contain approximately one hundred men. You will then eat with your unit and train with them for the first time before the night is through. If there is any bickering or fighting amongst you, you will be dealt with severely by your commander!"

Excitement and nervousness course through my blood. "Here we go!" I say to Berechiah.

"Let's hope we're in a unit together!" he says.

"Yes!" I say.

We assemble by tribe. Prince Jonathan stands on a low stone platform outside the fortress. Behind him I see a tall, fierce, commanding figure. I overhear someone near me whisper, identifying the tall man as General Abner, the commander of the entire army. Several palace guards also stand around Jonathan dressed in their full armor. It is an impressive sight. One by one the various unit commanders step up when the prince calls them, and then the secretary reads the name of one of the recruits on his list. The recruit is then assigned to that commander's unit. Various names are read, and various commanders stand up and receive their recruit.

"Commander Shaminahu," the prince announces.

A large, bulky soldier stands up.

"The lot falls to Daniel son of Morcan son of Allihu."

A tall recruit from the tribe of Benjamin runs up to Commander Shaminahu and bows low. They exchange a formal greeting and clasp hands. The commander gestures toward his unit, which stands assembled nearby, and Daniel walks over to join the ranks.

"Commander Joseph son of El-Machi."

An average-sized man stands up. At first he looks too gentle to be a soldier, like he is a scholar who should be studying the law, but when I look closely, I can see the muscles bulging under his tunic.

"The lot falls to Jonathan son of Arocha—a good name!" Prince Jonathan says with a small smile.

And on it goes like this, name after name being called.

After some time, Commander Ramel comes up in the rotation, and the prince instructs him to stand. Ramel has a leathery, humorless face and a sternness in his eyes. He is not a very large man, but I can tell there is a deep-seated strength in him that naturally commands respect and obedience. Berechiah's name is called to join Ramel's unit. He gives me a faint smile as he walks over to Ramel. He then bows before the commander and presents himself to the unit.

Now I am very nervous. Commander after commander's name is read, and the recruits are chosen to go into their units. I begin to worry and wonder whether my name will be read at all. Every time Commander Ramel stands up to receive a recruit, I hold my breath hoping my name is called. I am disappointed when it is not.

Finally Ramel's turn comes around again, and I am one of the few recruits left standing without a unit. I can count the number of commanders left and the number of recruits that need a unit. If I'm not chosen this time, I will not be in Berechiah's unit. For the first time in many years, I actually offer a small prayer to Yahweh. I do not raise my hands to Heaven, but silently I speak the words, "Yahweh, God of my people, God of my mother, I confess that I do not often go to your shrine at Pirathon. I do not often sacrifice to you, as I ought, but please overlook these failures, and please give me a place in Ramel's unit. If you do, I will worship you exclusively. I will not look about for other gods to give me direction as I have done in the past. I will worship you alone, as my mother does."

I look over as Ramel stands up again, a tired, almost bored look on his leathery features. I hold my breath and focus my eyes on Prince Jonathan's mouth.

"And the lot falls to—"

Jonathan looks down. The suspense is unbearable. I close my eyes and take a deep breath.

"—Benaiah...of Pirathon." He looks over at the secretary who is seated on the platform. "His father's name is not on the list. Are there any other men named Benaiah from Pirathon?"

"No." The secretary says.

Relief floods over me. I walk over and bow to Ramel, presenting myself for service in his unit. He nods slightly, looking me over as if trying to judge my strength and character in a single glance. I walk toward Berechiah and the rest of the unit. From what I can see there are a few other recruits from Pirathon, but I am relieved to see that the man who called me a bastard is not part of this unit. When I reach Berechiah, he is beaming. This could be one of the best days of my life. How eager I am to fight for Israel now!

After the last recruit has been assigned to his unit, we sit around a fire with our unit and are treated to a meal of stew, specially prepared for us by several of King Saul's cooks. Ramel explains during the meal, "When we are out in the field, you will not have this luxury. Most often you will need to find and make your own food. The only exceptions will be if we are able to plunder during one of our campaigns or if the army ever gets its portion from the taxes. There are several flocks of goats and sheep that support the army's needs as well, but usually the meat and dairy from the flocks go to feed those of us who are officers. We will distribute the remainder only to those troops that we feel are worthy or need the extra food. Otherwise you will rely on individual citizens of Israel to sponsor you and provide your needs, or your families can send supplies to supplement your diet."

After the light meal of stew, our first training session begins. The seasoned soldiers are in charge of training us and showing us how to more effectively use the weapons we brought from home. I am surprised that only a small number of men in the army have decent swords, and the few that do have professionally made armor and weapons are the king's elite troops. I ask one of my trainers about the lack of weapons.

He shakes his head. "As you know, the Philistines still dominate the production of iron. The only weapons we have are old ones made from bronze, or makeshift weapons we've made out of farm implements. I dream of the day when we will have a proper armory!"

Ramel's voice bellows, "All recruits! Line up at the far end of the field with your weapon in hand. You will sprint from that great fig tree at the edge of the field until you pass where I am standing."

We all jog out to the other end of the field and turn around, waiting for the signal. Ramel's voice booms out again, and we're off. The veterans in our unit cheer us on and make fun of those who lag behind. I run as fast as I can—head throbbing, blood pumping, breath searing through me—and I am still only in the middle of the group as we pass by Ramel. A sinking feeling settles on me as I see all these recruits who are already faster, more experienced, and stronger than I am. I must do better!

We continue by doing some sparring and mock fighting, as the experienced soldiers shout out advice and methods. Then the archers in our unit practice in front of us and show us how they use the bow and arrow. This is the weapon I brought from home, and I am eager to learn it better. The only experiences I've had with it are the times I've gone hunting. The idea of being able to hit an opponent from far away intrigues me.

At the end of the night, we practice moving in formation. We do a fast march followed by a slow march, and then we practice the all-out charge. Our feet pound the dust with a churning fury. It is exhilarating to run with the troops, moving as one man and hearing the clanking armor, the rustle of cloth, and the rapid patter of swift-moving feet. My nose and throat fill with the dust we kick up together, and I taste its tartness on my tongue. I discover there's nothing like gripping a solid weapon in my hand and adding my voice to a shout that rivals the mightiest waterfall. Ah, what a pure feeling it is! Finally, I am part of something bigger than myself—I am part of an army. I feel a newfound satisfaction filling a dark, lonely place in my soul.

22

SERAH

"Maybe he went to the fields early this morning," I say, trying to sound calm and disinterested. "Why would he go before the morning meal—and without any tools? He's run away or worse! And I think you know where!"

"No, my lord. I haven't seen him this morning. I am just as surprised as you are that he is gone!" I appear confident and poised.

"You're lying!" Spit flies from Piram's mouth. "And when I can prove that you're lying, you'll regret it!" He storms out of the house, muttering in anger.

As soon as he is gone, I take a deep breath and go to help Jadia clean up after the morning meal. As my fingers work, my mind fills with dread. What will happen to me if he finds out?

After Benaiah left this morning, I managed to slip back to the sleeping mat quietly, and I pretended to sleep until it was time to get up for the chores. From the moment Piram realized

Benaiah was not here, he flew into a bitter rage. He sent Arah into town to look for Benaiah at the break of day. All of us avoided eye contact with him as he ate in a fury. When he finished, he got up abruptly, grabbed my arm, and propelled me out into the courtyard to question me. He threatened. He yelled. He insinuated that I knew more than I was telling him. I did my best to stay calm against his onslaught of anger and insults.

I feel a momentary relief now that he is gone, but I know it won't last long. He knows how close I am with Benaiah. He knows Benaiah would never leave without telling me any of his plans. A terrifying thought suddenly grips my mind: He might kill me this time.

I stop working and hold my hand up against the wall to steady myself. For an awful moment I can already feel his hands striking me in anger, and I hear his violent words filling my ears. Jadia stops what she is doing and comes over to me. She touches my back, and I instantly cringe at the contact.

"Are you all right? Can I get you something?"

I turn to face her and manage a weak smile. "No, no. I'll be all right. I just feel a little faint— nothing to worry about."

I force myself to go back to work. I need to keep active and keep these terrible thoughts out of my head. "I'm going to bake some extra bread today and take it over to the house of Eliezer. Miriam is not well, and Hannah could use the extra food. I may stay and see how they are doing for a little while," I tell Jadia.

"Would you like me to do it? You don't seem well."

"No, no. I am fine. I want to do it myself. You have enough to do here as it is."

I go into the storeroom to get out some of the flour that we ground yesterday and some oil, and I begin to make the dough. Going to see Hannah will be just what I need today. She and I are the only people in this village who will miss Benaiah. It will be so good to talk to her and commiserate with her.

Later, when the bread is ready, I gather it up and wrap it in a cloth. The warm, fresh smell fills me with hope. I tell Jadia that I am leaving, and then I step out into the sunlight.

My walk to the household of Eliezer is brief and uneventful. When I reach the home, I call out, "Hello to the house of Eliezer. Is anyone home?"

After a moment, Hannah opens the door. "Oh, Serah! It's you!" Her words are a gasp.

Immediately, tears well up in my eyes. I can tell she's had a rough night of it as well. Her eyes are red with crying and lack of sleep. I just nod my head silently, too emotional to speak. I hold up the bread for her to take.

"Oh Serah, I miss him already!" she says as she takes the bread. "Thank you! You didn't have to go to the trouble!"

"Honestly, I just wanted an excuse to come here and see you for a little while, but I know you need whatever we can give you. How is your mother today?"

"The same as always... She's in bed now. I'd take you to her, but I think she's asleep, and she needs the rest."

"That's fine," I say. "I really want to talk to you, anyway. Do you have the time?"

"Of course I do. I need to talk to you too." She leads me across the room to a low bench along the wall, and we both sit down. "How was he when he left?" Hannah's eyes glisten as she asks the question.

I draw a deep breath. "He seemed eager to leave," I say with some sadness. "Not that I blame him, really. He's had a rough time here."

"I know, Serah, but what if he doesn't make it back?"

"Don't say that, Hannah. He *must* make it back, or I will lose my mind. All we can do is pray for him now."

"Yes, I know," Hannah says as her eyes drop to the floor.

"Benaiah cares for you a great deal. He made me promise to come here and call on you often."

Hannah lifts her eyes and looks straight into mine. She seems touched by Benaiah's concern for her. Her eyes are kind and so mesmerizing. I can see how Benaiah loses himself looking into them. A shadow of concern crosses them.

"How did Piram take the news?" she asks quietly.

"He's furious. He doesn't know where Benaiah is yet, unless one of the men has told him by now." I look out the open door, half expecting to see him coming down the path in a rage. "He can never know that I helped Benaiah leave. He might kill me."

"Do you think he would go that far?" Hannah seems shocked. She's never seen Piram when he gets into one of his fits of drunken anger.

"You haven't lived with him like I have," I say softly.

"I wish he'd never left!" Hannah's words come out fast with an edge to them. "He was only thinking of himself. He's left you in danger. He's left me to fend for myself against my father and his string of suitors. What if my father marries me off to some other man while Benaiah is away?"

I shake my head. "I don't know. Something changed in Benaiah ever since Piram banished him and sent those mercenaries after him. He never talks about those days in the wilderness, not even to me, and he tells me everything."

"He wouldn't tell me about them either," Hannah says thoughtfully. "I think you're right, though. I think he just couldn't take it anymore, and when Saul's agent showed up, he found an opportunity to escape."

"Are you angry at him, Hannah?"

"Yes...a little. I miss him terribly. He said he is doing it for me. He wants to make a name for himself and earn Father's respect. Then he thinks he'll be able to marry me when he returns. I wish instead that he was right here fighting for me and working on getting the arrangements made with my father. Now who knows what the future will bring?"

"Yahweh will work it out, somehow. At least that's what I keep telling myself to get me through the morning."

"I know you're right. It's just hard to see what he's trying to do. Wouldn't it be nice if one of his prophets could just come and announce the future for us?"

I smile at Hannah. "Yes, it would be nice. I think he wants our trust, though. When we can't see the future, he wants our eyes fixed on his promises and our feet walking his paths. I know he'll do what's best for us in the end." I sound more confident than I feel. It's easy to talk about trusting Yahweh, but when pain surprises and trouble threatens—how quickly the doubt floods in!

Hannah nods slowly. She opens her mouth to ask a question but is interrupted by her mother coughing loudly in the other room.

"Hannah...?" Miriam's voice is strained and hollow.

"Just a minute, Mother. Serah is visiting us."

Another loud cough echoes in the other room as Miriam tries to say something else and fails.

"I'd better get going anyway," I say as we both get up. "It was nice to talk to you. Feel free to come over whenever you want, especially if you're feeling lonely."

I see the warm gratitude in Hannah's eyes.

"I will, Serah. Thank you!"

I let myself out as Hannah goes to tend to her mother. I do understand why Benaiah is doing this, but I can't help but think he's missing out on such a great opportunity to be happy. Hannah and Benaiah would make a wonderful couple. They could have moved to Arumah or some other neighboring village, far from the negative reputation that haunts them here in Pirathon. I shake my head as I walk homeward. I just hope that Benaiah hasn't made a big mistake. I know that Eliezer will make the most of this time, trying to turn his daughter's heart to another man or even arranging a marriage against her will. Benaiah has been fortunate that Eliezer hasn't already forced the issue, because it certainly would be within his rights to do so. Now Benaiah could easily lose her.

When I return to the house, I find Jadia working in the garden, and I join her. We silently pull weeds and gather herbs that are ready for drying.

Jadia and I are not close. We work well together, and she treats me as her superior, as is proper, but there is no warmth between us. She spends her time focusing on her work and tending to Arah, when he is home, and she turns a blind eye to Piram and everything he does to me. She seems to be uncomfortable talking about him, too. There was a time that I attempted to get closer to her after a humiliating night with Piram. I opened up to her, seeking some sympathy, but she responded awkwardly by averting her eyes and mumbling short responses, obviously trying to avoid the conversation. I think it is her fear of Piram that prevents her from comforting me. Whatever the reason for her distance from me, it is what keeps us from having a deeper relationship. Being around Jadia makes me feel more alone than ever.

When Piram arrives home from the fields, he storms through the door without even bothering to wash up. I am so startled at his sudden appearance, I drop food in the fire.

"Benaiah joined the *army*! He's *gone*! Are you *happy*? He's off playing soldier, and I'm stuck here playing in the mud *alone*! Who's going to do his work? Answer me that!" He slams his hand against the wall.

I step back from the fire. My mind is racing to find answers or come up with any way to calm him down.

His face is red and twisted with rage. His eyes spear me in place. "You helped him, didn't you? You knew he was leaving, *didn't you?*" His voice thunders.

I swallow hard and try to speak. "I...really...I had no idea."

The back of his hand knocks my words out of my mouth, and fear explodes full force in my chest.

23

BENAIAH

Several days into our training, Ramel calls together all ten of the new recruits in his unit and introduces us to an old soldier named Shoham—one of the army's best men with a spear. He shows us a spear that is bronze tipped and only a few cubits long. I'm fascinated as he demonstrates how the spear can be used for both hand-to-hand combat and for inflicting injury from a distance when it is thrown. Using Berechiah as a model, he shows us how to thrust through various spots of armor and how to use the spear defensively to ward off enemy blows. He then takes us out to a field where he has gathered several spears so we can practice throwing them.

My first few tries are clumsy, and the spear doesn't go very far. I have only tried using a spear once before, when Berechiah and I were out hunting, so my skill is lacking. Shoham takes me aside and shows me how to hold it and when to release it. I watch dumbstruck as he takes his few steps—like a ritual dance—spins his body in rhythm, and releases the shaft at the perfect moment. The spear sails out into the air like a low flying hawk and dives in perfect form. It pummels into the ground with a thump, and the shaft shivers with the impact. Shoham grins at the awed expression on my face.

"You'll get it, Benaiah! One more time now!"

I make one more attempt at it, trying my best to imitate his movements. When I release the spear, it goes a little farther than before but fails to lodge itself into the ground.

"Better! Maybe by the time I lie in my grave, you'll have it down," Shoham says.

I roll my eyes at his sarcasm.

Berechiah's spear has sailed perfectly twice already, and he squints into the distance in the direction of the spear's path. "Maybe you'll have to imagine Sennah is standing out there—then you'll get it to stick in the ground!"

"Maybe *you* should go stand out there!" I say, brandishing my spear at him.

Berechiah laughs and runs out to retrieve his third perfect spear throw. Halfway there, he turns around, throws up his arms, and shouts back, "Now's your chance! Go ahead—try to hit me! After your last throw, I feel pretty safe out here!"

"Don't tempt me!" I shout.

After several more tries, I finally get it to stick in the ground. It isn't a pretty flight, but I'm satisfied for now.

Shoham gives me a few words of praise and then calls us all in for a break.

We gather at the edge of the field. I lift one of the skins of water and take a long swig, and then I pass it to several other recruits who stand near me immersed in conversation. Shoham stands next to me and leans on his favorite spear as he watches all of us. He is shorter than most of the other soldiers. Laugh lines wrinkle his face. An old scar winds around his neck, sticking out like a red snake. The wound must have almost killed him.

"How did you get your scar?" I ask.

The other recruits fall silent. They turn and gather closer to listen.

"A bold question," he says. "Most avoid looking at it as long as possible. Are you sure you want to know?"

I nod my head.

The suspense builds as he looks around at us for a moment before continuing. "I've been fighting with Saul a long time, ever since Jabesh-Gilead at the very beginning. I was a younger man then. Now look at me—an old, broken-down donkey."

I laugh. "You're not quite broken if you can still throw a spear like that! About being a donkey, though, I haven't made up my mind yet."

He feigns shock and anger. "You young people are all alike. All talk!" He speaks the last word with force as he strikes the back of my leg with the flat end of his spear.

"Ow!"

"Serves you right!"

I hop on one leg as several of my companions laugh at my embarrassment. My injured leg burns with pain, like it will never be the same again. I fear I may have taken my sarcasm with Shoham too far. His lighthearted and casual nature has disarmed me. "I was only joking! I'm sorry!"

"You think you can joke with me?" He raises the spear again, threateningly.

I stumble backward, afraid he might actually slap me with it again. He lowers the spear, though, with a twinkle in his eye. I relax a little.

Suddenly, his expression becomes serious. "Be on your guard, boy. If you're not alert, you're dead. I learned that the day I got this scar." Involuntarily, he draws his finger across the ugly band of raised skin.

"Almost died that day." His voice sounds far away, as if his thoughts have transported him years into the past. "I was a young man then—about your age, maybe a little older. A messenger from King Saul arrived at our village. I'll never forget it. The man rode his horse into the center of the street, and we all gathered around him. My grandfather was one of the elders, and he asked the messenger for his report. It was not often that a messenger came, and it was our first message from King Saul, who had just recently been crowned king, so we all leaned forward in eager curiosity to hear him. I think we all knew, intuitively, that this message would have long-lasting implications for our people. Suddenly, the messenger opened a goatskin bag and emptied its contents out onto the middle of the street. We all gasped, horrified."

Shoham pauses, dramatically, like he is lost in thought. We stare at him, waiting, and no one says a word.

He continues. "It was a bloody slab of meat."

Several of us gasp. "What?"

"As you can imagine, we were all shocked. He had our undivided attention. The messenger spoke. 'Now hear the word of your king: Jabesh-Gilead needs you. The Ammonites have surrounded them and have given them an ultimatum. The Ammonites will spare the men of Jabesh-Gilead only at the cost of their right eyes.' We were all outraged. I pictured the devastating humiliation those men would endure if they lost an eye. They would be useless in battle.

"The messenger continued. 'Your king, Saul of the tribe of Benjamin, has cut up his oxen—see here the left flank of his favorite ox. If you do not join Saul and rescue the town of Jabesh-Gilead, Saul has promised to make your oxen like his! Do the right thing. Join together and save Jabesh-Gilead. Saul musters men at Bezek. Join him there.' With that, he dismounted, quickly gathered up the hunk of flesh back into his goatskin bag, and rode off to deliver the news to the next town.

"We stared at each other in stunned silence for a moment. A feeling I had never felt before descended upon me. It was fear mingled with rage and determination. All of us were deeply stirred. Almost all the men in our village turned out at Bezek and joined the militia that Saul had mustered. I'll never forget it—thousands of Israelites gathering for one purpose, all of us angry and determined. I had never seen so many Israelites together in one place. For once I felt like I was part of a wider nation. I was not just a townsman of the tribe of Judah, isolated from the rest of the Israelites spread about in this land. I was part of something much bigger. King Saul was in fine form, all his might on display. He was a head taller than anyone and very strong. He was wise, too. He divided us into three groups for the attack, and with his strategy we caught them completely by surprise."

Shoham pauses for a moment, filled with the memory.

"Yahweh gave us a great victory that day. When it was all over, Ammonite soldiers lay dead everywhere, while we had sustained only a few casualties. We returned home to the village as heroes, but we all knew King Saul was the greatest hero of us all."

I can't help but envy him. How I want to return to Pirathon with that kind of welcome!

Shoham stands up abruptly. "All right, enough lazing about! Get up, and bring your spear."

The day of training exhausts us all. By the end of it, I still haven't quite mastered the spear throw, but at least I've improved. When night falls, we return to the training camp. Stiff and store, I stretch out on my mat and enjoy the stillness. As I wait for sleep to steal me away, I stare at the sky and enjoy the brilliant panorama of stars. My mind drifts back to Shoham's story. I *will* win a battle and come home a hero!

Suddenly, I realize Shoham never did tell us how he got that scar.

24

BENAIAH

My eyes fly open as a trumpet blasts at the edge of camp. I roll out of my sleeping mat and jump to my feet, dagger in hand. I listen as the trumpet blasts again. It is not a normal signal. Several men around me also stir from their sleep and get up. We're all curious and on edge. Is it an invasion? Are we going into battle? Is this some strange training drill, meant to keep us alert?

The past few weeks have been hard. Every day I have trained and exerted myself nearly to exhaustion. Despite another day of hard training, I feel my body pulsing with power and eager for a fight. My mind feels ready to go. Fear still whispers in my soul, but the training has helped to prepare my spirit as well as my body.

One of the soldiers in my unit, Eliab son of Jesse, curses as the trumpet continues to blast away. He's a commanding figure, a head taller than the rest of the unit, muscular and strong. Right now his hair is tangled and wild from sleep, but his eyes are bright and fierce with fury. "Why don't they come up with a better signal—one that we can understand!" he grumbles.

"What do you think it is?" I ask no one in particular.

Eliab curses again. "Who cares? Probably some stupid training drill again!"

His brother Abinidab, who is also in our unit, is more thoughtful. "It could be important. We'll just have to wait and see."

We gather outside the tent in the dark. One of the officers walks up to us bearing a torch.

"A messenger has just arrived," he announces. "We'll be heading out soon. Gear up and get ready for your first taste of battle!"

We look at each other, our eyes on fire with excitement.

Eliab's other brother, Shammah, asks the question we're all wondering. "Sir, can you tell us more?"

He grunts impatiently. "I have to keep spreading the news. All I know is that the Philistines have raided several towns to the north. It's probably just a searching party sent to test defenses, plunder from our land, and spread general terror among the people. We have to respond quickly and decisively to discourage them from turning it into an all-out invasion."

Quickly, we put on our tunics and armor and pick up our weapons. Then we all gather around Ramel as he explains the situation more in depth.

"A villager from Darbath brought a report to the camp tonight and gave us their most recent location. The Philistines think themselves to be well hidden. They are in a dense wood with a small clearing. They've arranged their tents back in the dark of the clearing. They have no fires for cooking, so there is no smell or smoke to give their location away. In the past, they would not have cared about such caution. They would have camped in the open plain and dared anyone to challenge them. Now, with Saul as king and their recent loss at Micmash, they are not so bold. It is a good sign!"

"How many are there?" Berechiah asks.

"The messenger thought there were twenty or so in the raiding party. They appear to be elite warriors, and they are already deep in our territory. Perhaps they have more than just minor raids in mind. Thirty men from our unit have been chosen to challenge them and drive them back into their own land. We leave immediately."

My heart thrills at his words. I will fight my first battle, and I am eager to do well. It's my first chance to prove myself.

We pack only light provisions and move fast into the night. We need to get close and catch them unawares before they wake up this morning. The cool night air washes around us as we run shoulder to shoulder in the dark. Our weapons are secured to prevent any noise. The only noises we make are the slight rustle of cloth, the occasional squeak of leather, and the soft shuffle of our feet on the trail.

We run for a while, and then we walk, and then we run some more, trying to save our energy for the fight, but also trying to get there before the Philistines break camp or realize that we are hunting them down. The stars wink down at me, but the sky is mostly dark. The moon is a ghostly sliver, like a white sword guarding the dark gates of the sky.

In the early morning, our pace slows dramatically. Suddenly, Ramel holds up his hand. We are close! We move stealthily to the edge of the trees and take up positions. In the past few weeks I have excelled at shooting the bow and arrow, so Ramel chooses me now as one of the men to help take out the Philistine guards as silently as possible. I am eager for the chance. Now I can start to make a name for myself!

I look up at the tense faces around me, and a sudden, wild fear tears through my soul. My hand grips my bow so tightly the shaft might break in two. My heart pounds, shaking my whole body. This is it. This is my first test as a warrior. Am I ready? Will I live? Or... My next thought sends a chill up my spine. What is it like to die? I have seen dead men before—cold, empty, rigid. Their staring, lifeless eyes still haunt my dreams. What is it like to feel the warm life empty from your flesh? What does it feel like to be stabbed with a spear or hacked with a sword—to see your own arm lying on the ground or your own blood gushing from an open wound?

Worse yet, where do you go when you die? Does your spirit linger on the earth and watch life from a grey haze? Do you live in some damp underground world? Some hold fast to the old laws of Moses. Like my mother, they cling to the hope of Yahweh and his loyal love. They dream of some hero that will come and save our people. I remember my pledge of loyalty to Yahweh when I was chosen for Ramel's unit. But will Yahweh protect me? Will he guard my soul if I die? I am not so sure. But now is the time to be sure! My heart races in terror for a few minutes as I sling my bow off my back and check the position of my dagger.

I forcefully crowd all the morbid thoughts to the back of my mind. Instead, I paint a picture in my brain. I imagine myself as a famous warrior—alive, strong, victorious, and feared by all! The deafening pounding of my own heart makes it difficult to dream of glory. My mouth goes dry as Ramel signals us forward.

We move off according to plan. I am one of five dark shapes that creep as close as possible to the Philistine encampment. My training and my practice pay off, and we melt into the night like shadows, soundlessly creeping across the ground.

The Philistines have several guards on duty tonight. One stands back behind the camp among the trees. One sits in the long grassy field in front. One ranges about the tents of sleeping soldiers. One is slowly walking out along their perimeter. All are alert and ready. They are experienced raiders doing their job well. How many villages have they already hit before word reached Saul? I think of my mother and the raid that changed her life. Had these filthy heathens ruined other mothers like that? My hate grows thick in the dark night, and it slows my heartbeat to a more determined, steady drumming. I feel my fear begin to clear away as I become even more eager to spill their blood.

The men with me are slowly picking their way through the woods behind the camp. Our immediate mission is to kill their guards. After we kill our targets as silently as possible, we will all gather together behind their camp and begin to pour our arrows into as many sleeping soldiers as we can. While we distract them from behind, the main force will gather and charge from the front en masse across the short open field. When they arrive, we will fall back as the Philistines respond to the action. Because we are outnumbered, we can't afford to waste any of our arrows. We must hit every Philistine we can get.

I take a moment to evaluate the scene. Judging by the Philistines' tents, there are well over fifty in their group. This is not expected! Saul had not anticipated any raiding party of over twenty, and the messenger was wrong as well! There are only thirty men in our entire group, but I hope this surprise attack will be enough to give us the edge. I breathe in the clean, crisp night air as I pick my way quietly through the trees. The damp ground helps to hush our advance. This night will not be silent much longer.

Finally, we are in position and poised for attack. I crouch behind a gnarled old tree and lean on the rough bark with my left hand, holding my bow at the ready.

I peer carefully around the tree to see my target. The Philistine guard stands alert among the trees, looking off somewhere to my right with his back to the camp. He is just a dim, large shape, barely discernible in the looming darkness. I pull an arrow out, notch it in my bow, and wait for the sign.

Ramel is going to throw a tiny rock off to our right as a way of distracting the guards for a split second and giving us our opportunity to come out and fire our arrows. We have to strike swiftly and each kill our target with minimum noise. We do not want to wake the camp until our whole attack party is ready and in position.

I wait, so tense that my breathing seems too loud and every rustle in the trees seems magnified a hundred times.

Suddenly, I hear the slight clatter of a rock off to the right— the signal! The guard in front of me tenses and looks off in that direction. He shifts his body to face the unknown threat.

I spin around the tree, drawing the arrow back in the bow-string as I come around. I have to shoot this guard before he can raise any alarm. My legs spring into motion, my mind on fire with fear and wild eagerness, and suddenly I am falling, my body slamming face-first into the ground.

My ears ring with the loud crash of my fall and the startled cries from the Philistine watchman. I feel the wet ground on my face, and I'm aware of my heart pulsing inside me, racing with panic and shame. I look behind me and see the root of the tree that tripped me.

I crawl, desperately searching for my bow in the underbrush. I find it, grab it, and look up at the chaos. The watchmen are all alive and well, raising the alarm throughout the camp. Shouts ring out. The element of surprise is completely gone.

Frantic questions race through my mind. Where are the others? What am I to do? Should I press the attack? Should I flee to the woods? An arrow whizzes by me in the dark and thuds into a tree. My indecision has vanished. I scramble back into the woods looking for any of my companions. I catch a brief glimpse of Ramel slipping back into the trees like a ghost. I run to follow him.

The Philistine camp swarms like a beehive knocked from a tree. Soldiers run from their tents, armor and weapons clanking and clattering as they prepare themselves to meet our threat. Our soldiers across the plain will soon be in position, and now when they arrive they will meet an enemy that is alert and fully armed for their attack—and it is all my fault! Inwardly, I curse at myself. What kind of soldier am I?

I move quickly in the direction where I had seen Ramel run. Another arrow whistles by my head, a near miss. Two more strike the ground at my feet. I glance back. A Philistine guard is pointing in my direction with a drawn sword. Several other soldiers are following his directions and running into the woods to hunt me down. I duck around some tangled branches and run faster.

My only hope is that they believe we are the only ones attacking them. I meet up with Ramel and the others hiding in the rock formations behind their camp. This is the place we had planned to fall back to after we completed our mission. Now here we are, and we've accomplished nothing. We have not gained any time for the main force to attack from the field. Ramel glares at me, too angry to speak. I'm sure that at this point his primary concern is getting us out of here alive.

I look around at the flushed, sweaty faces of the men I have come to know. Their eyes are hard, sullen, and resentful. I have failed. I have ruined it all. I realize that not all the men are here. A soldier named Hazer, an excellent marksman, is missing. Has he died? I can't bear the thought. Has my mistake killed one of our good men? I open my mouth to apologize, but Ramel forcefully motions for silence. My face is hot with shame.

By now the main force is just heading into position to carry out their surprise attack, which is no surprise anymore. We can see little from our position, but as the attack gets underway, the sounds are enough. Shouts echo across the rocks. We hear the crash of metal, the bark of orders, the screams, and the strange cries in the Philistine language that are obvious shouts of triumph. It is not going well.

We come out from behind the rocks stealthily, trying to engage the enemy from behind. There are only a few of us, and it will be difficult for us to make a huge impact from where we are. We come through a small grove of trees and see Hazer facedown in a growing pool of his own blood with an arrowhead sticking up through his shoulder blades. I feel my stomach turn, but I fight the urge to cry out. Ramel gestures to me and another recruit. We pick up Hazer's heavy, limp body and carry it with us out of the woods.

I have to stay focused. We're not quite out of danger yet. We cross a clearing in the woods and look over at the battlefield. The Philistines have successfully pushed our frontal assault back across the field. They are continuing to push them back even farther into the woods beyond. Arrows and spears still fly through the air, but it's clear that we've lost the fight.

That night we beat a hasty retreat and spend the entire next day picking our way back to Saul's camp. As we continue to move fast, I hear bits and pieces from the other men. I learn that we've lost a staggering eleven men on the field, including Hazer, and several more are injured. The raiding party is still intact and will be even more emboldened to spread terror across Israelite territory.

I feel the eyes of my fellow soldiers blaming and judging me. No one is speaking to me except for Berechiah, but I don't even want to talk to him. I don't want anyone's sympathy. I deserve to be shunned. I was clumsy, and my mistake cost us the fight. Men died because of me, and I am guilty of their blood. I half expect the men to stone me to death tonight or knife me while I sleep. I won't blame them if they do.

We reach Gibeah just before night's darkness blankets the hills. I sullenly take off my gear and prepare for sleep, but when I lie down, sleep does not come. I stare at the black sky, wishing Yahweh would take my life rather than make me face another day in this army.

When dawn breaks, I wake to a rough hand on my shoulder. One of Ramel's servants leads me to the commander's tent. My heart hammers as I enter and face him. Ramel's eyes pierce through me as he calmly yet sternly addresses my failures during the fight.

That morning, as part of my discipline, he assembles the men and makes me stand before the unit and explain my carelessness and what happened as a result. My face burns, and my voice sounds harsh, like a fire crackling in the chill. After I am done, Ramel announces that I am not allowed to train with the men for three days. I must sit in the tent alone with my thoughts.

Twice a day, a servant opens the flap to my tent, sets food inside, and walks away. I endure the silence bitterly. Over and over in my mind I replay the events of the fight. Over and over again I feel the rough bark of that tree, the soft breath in my lungs, the thrill, the anticipation of my first fight, and the sick feeling as I fall so carelessly. How thoughtless! Why would I not check my footing? How could I make such a mistake? Will they ever give me another chance?

When my time of seclusion has ended, Berechiah is the first to meet me outside the tent. "Benaiah, my brother, it could have happened to any of us!"

I laugh bitterly and try to ignore him.

"Benaiah, they'll soon forget. You'll do better next time."

"If there is a next time," I whisper. I glance around and see the other men. They keep their eyes down. They don't look my way. I am like a diseased leper that everyone wants to pretend isn't here.

A dark melancholy seeps into my bones. I am angry—angry at myself and angry at Yahweh. Why did this have to happen? I want to be famous and respected. Instead, I see contempt burning in my fellow soldiers' eyes as they shoot me sidelong glances and whisper about me.

Berechiah goes on and on about Yahweh's will as he tries to comfort me. I am sick of it.

"I feel like your god hates me. Why else would he continually make my life miserable?" I ask.

"He doesn't hate you. Don't focus on your feelings. Focus on the facts. He loves you. He's not just my God—you are one of his chosen people too!"

"Maybe you've forgotten, Berechiah, but I'm *not* one of his people." Bitterness is boiling in my blood. "Everything that happens to me proves it!"

"What happens to us is not as important as his truth. His love is for all nations! Don't you remember his promise to Abraham?"

I laugh. "That promise has nothing to do with *me*."

"It has everything to do with you! The mighty God who created all things loves you. The promise proves it!"

"If your god is so powerful, why are his people always so weak?" I argue with him.

He puts his hand on my shoulder and looks straight in my eyes. "Benaiah! Yahweh is *good*! Just think of all the blessings he gives! Without him we'd have nothing. We'd—"

I push his hand away as I cut him off. "If your god is so good, why would he let me fail and let my failure kill some of *his* soldiers?" I walk away from him, shaking my head. The last thing I want to do is hear anything more about Yahweh. Yahweh makes no sense to me.

For many days I avoid Berechiah when he comes near. Our friendship is fading. I don't want any more talk about Yahweh and his will or his love. It is a ridiculous topic, and I can't stand discussing it. He has always been my most faithful friend, closer than any of my brothers and almost as dear to me as my mother, but this talk of Yahweh is getting out of control. Doesn't he see? Can't he understand? God does not love me. Perhaps it is time to sacrifice to some other god, some forgotten god of my ancestors—a god who can actually help me out and give me something to live for.

25

SERVANT OF SAUL

I hold the tiny lamp as high as I can, and the shadows scatter momentarily and cringe in the corners of the room. I hate going into the storeroom at night, but I cannot sleep until I make sure that the merchants brought us exactly twenty-three jars of oil. The farmers we traded with brought the jars in late this afternoon, and even though Elmar told me the number was correct, I need to see for myself. Elmar sometimes misses things and miscounts things, and the olive oil is too important to risk a mistake.

The jars stand in a rigid line along the back wall. As I come closer, I lower the lamp, and the light pours over their curves. I bend down to inspect them and make sure that these are the jars of oil that came today. A clattering noise at the entrance to the storeroom startles me. Who is in here this late at night? A thief? Is there a thief in the storeroom? Panic pulses in my chest. I cry out almost too loudly, "Who's there?"

I hold the light as high as I can and peer into the shadows. "Who's there?" I repeat, even louder this time. "Show yourself, now!"

Through the shadows I hear Shamra's familiar voice echo from across the room. "It's me. It's Shamra. I…I've been looking for you. You weren't in your room, so I've been wandering around the entire palace trying to find you."

My heart slows, but my curiosity rises. "Well, now you found me. What do you need?"

"The king is calling for you."

"At this hour?"

"Yes. I'm on duty, and the king called me into his chambers. He seems troubled. He wanted me to wake you and bring you to him as soon as possible."

"Did he say what he wanted?" I am puzzled. It is rare for the king to call for me so late. Usually if he needs something in the middle of the night, the servant on duty is more than capable of attending to him.

"He did not. Not long ago, a late night messenger arrived at the palace and sought an audience with the king. The guards let him in, and I woke the king. After the messenger left, the king looked so troubled and agitated that I thought the evil spirit was on him again. Then he told me to find you."

"All right, I'm coming." I hurry toward the entrance, weaving around and through the various baskets and jars stacked around the supply room. As I come around the corner, I find Shamra standing in the doorway. He steps back to let me through.

"Let's go," I say, and we both hike up our robes and run in the direction of the king's chambers.

When we reach the door, I knock—three short raps, then a pause, followed by another three short raps. It is the code we servants use to notify the king that it is one of us.

"Enter!" The king's voice booms from behind the door.

As soon as I enter the door, the king explodes. "Where have you been? What has taken you so long?"

"A thousand apologies, Your Majesty! I was in the storeroom checking on the latest shipment, and Shamra had some trouble finding me."

The king waves his hand impatiently. "Never mind that. Shut the door behind you!"

I motion to Shamra to stay just outside the chambers, and I swing the door shut. I turn and bow to the king.

It's as if King Saul is suddenly lost in his own mind. Instead of addressing me, he is pacing the floor of his chambers, his hands clenching and unclenching at his sides. I wait, impatient to know what I've been summoned for at this late hour.

In the silence, I can't help but notice the king's appearance. His hair hangs undone and flows slightly as he walks, the locks tainted with grey but long and healthy. He is still large and strong, but there's something missing—there's a hollowness about him that is difficult to understand. It isn't like the glory days when he waged war, and our enemies all around feared the name of Saul like they feared their gods. He was our national hero, doing what no one dared to do. He fought and won battle after battle and pushed back almost all of our enemies around us. Because of what Saul has done, we are united as a nation like never before. Yes, our army is still poorly equipped, and the Philistines are still a constant threat, but we have come so far! However, ever since the great prophet

Samuel refused to come and consult with him, things have slowly been falling apart.

The king stops pacing and looks up at me, his attitude somewhat calmer. "We've had another setback."

"How so, Your Majesty?"

"The Philistine raiding parties are getting bolder. Early this morning I received word that our men have again failed to curb another raiding party. We had information beforehand! We went out to surprise them and were utterly defeated!" His calmness is starting to slip away again.

I shake my head in sadness, and fear plays at the edge of my heart, though I am still not sure what this has to do with me.

"According to the report, a new recruit was responsible for ruining the surprise and alerting the Philistines just prior to our attack. Moments ago I received an urgent message from this soldier's hometown of Pirathon. The message came from a very prominent family and warned me that this new recruit is a half-blooded Israelite. His father was a Philistine. They have informed me that he is not to be trusted."

My eyes narrow. "So you think he may be a Philistine spy in our army?"

"I don't know. That's why you are here. I want you to go and inform General Abner of my suspicions as well as the man's unit commander, Ramel. I want you to do so tonight, under the cover of darkness, without anyone else becoming aware of the situation. You have proven yourself trustworthy during your many years of service. This information is for General Abner, Commander Ramel, and you only. I merely want them to keep a wary eye on this young soldier and report any further suspicious activity directly to me. If he is working for the enemy, chances are he is not working alone."

The king walks over to his low writing table and picks up two small scrolls already rolled and sealed. He hands both of them to me. Though they are light to the touch, I feel the weight of this new responsibility when my fingers wrap around them.

"These scrolls are identical. One is for Abner, and the other is for Ramel. They include all the instructions and warnings about this young soldier. Go deliver them tonight. Wake the men if you need to, and watch them as they read this. When they are finished, take the scrolls and burn them. If they have any questions, tell them to come to me in private. I fear this may be a widespread conspiracy, and I want to get to the bottom of it as soon as I can. When you are finished, come straight back to me and tell me how they reacted and what they propose to do about it."

"Yes, Your Majesty. I will go immediately." I bow low and exit the chambers.

My heart is hammering, and my mouth is dry. It is not the first time I've taken an active role in King Saul's official activities, but it is certainly the most important responsibility I've been given so far. I will not fail my king tonight.

26

SERAH

Yellow eyes. Terrible yellow eyes surround the village, bobbing in the semi-dark of early evening. My breath is sucked out of my body, and I am transfixed. Strange creatures begin to take form as they emerge from the dim light. They have the bodies of men, but their heads are like snakes. I motion frantically as these bizarre demonic creatures invade our land. I scream for people to hear me, yet everyone shrugs indifferently as they keep busy with their daily work. They roll their eyes and shake their heads as if I am crazy. Piram stands outside our house joking with his friend Jobal, pointing and laughing at me.

I realize that I am the only one who can see them. I alone hear their violent hissing and clicking as they climb effort-lessly over the walls and into our village. They are swarming onto our streets. One of the terrible creatures comes near me, and I smell his awful stench. My mouth opens to scream, but no sound comes out. I try to draw back, but he grabs my arm and holds a short sword against my chest. I feel the point prick the skin beneath my robe. He fixes me with his piercing gaze. Suddenly, a long, thin red tongue stretches out from his serpent-like mouth. I shiver as I feel it touch my neck—cold, wet, and abrasive. It slides along my skin and wraps around my throat. I tremble in helpless terror. The snake head opens its massive jaws. I cringe at the razor-sharp teeth. Again I try to scream, but the tongue tightens around my throat, cutting off all sound. Pure terror fills me as the creature's tongue drags me neck-first into his mouth to my certain death.

My eyes shoot open, and my chest heaves as my breath comes in several short bursts. Somehow my fingers have gripped full handfuls of my sleeping mat, clenching down. Just a dream… It was just a dream. I breathe out, trying to slow my racing heart. Grateful to be alive, I say a short prayer to Yahweh.

Since I was a girl, I have had many nightmares, but they seem to come more frequently now that Benaiah has gone away. Did I cry out? Did I wake Piram? I look to my left to find the large, dark shape looming next to me moving up and down with his breathing. He shifts slightly in his sleep. The house is as silent as the grave. The terrible images still linger in my head, and my heart is only now beginning to recover. It is still early, but I want to get up. I want to distract myself from the dream and have a few moments to myself before I must begin the many tasks of the day.

As I try to ease myself off of the sleeping mat, I feel a gentle tug as I attempt to move my head. Piram has fallen asleep with his fingers entwined in my hair. Do I dare try to move them and risk waking him up? I ease myself back down at his side. A powerful feeling of annoyance stirs in my chest. Piram always holds me back. He drags me down when I need to get up. Right now

I need to breathe. I need to get free. Yet instead I lie back down as carefully as I can. Wide awake, I stare at the dim patterns on the dark ceiling, still trying to shake the terrible dream from my mind.

I force my mind to think of something else. Naturally my thoughts turn to my son. What is he doing now? Where is he? Is he still alive? My heart aches to learn about my Benaiah. It has been terrible here since he left. I have no one to talk to—no one to turn to when Piram's anger flares. My friends in the village and I do not speak of it. I have always drawn strength from my son, and now I have no one—but I should not think like that. It is selfish. I know Benaiah needed to break free from Piram and find a new life.

But Piram has grown so much worse ever since Benaiah left! His fields have suffered. His trade has plummeted. He is angry all the time. We are barely making enough food to survive. I have had to borrow such daily necessities as grain or garden vegetables from our neighbors and friends. Eliezer and his household have been especially kind to us, but they don't have much themselves. Piram did not realize how much work Benaiah was doing for him. Without Benaiah's careful management of the fieldwork and the household affairs, Piram is lost. It is just like it was when Benaiah was banished and Piram knew he needed him back.

I think back to the day my son left. My arms still remember his warm embrace, perhaps the last embrace I will ever enjoy with my son. I pray not, but who knows? I can still smell him and feel his hair in my hand as I wrapped my arms around him that last time. How my heart yearns to see him again. Just one more look into his eyes would put my soul at peace. My dear boy! Where is he now?

I cringe as I remember Piram's violent rage when he knew I'd helped Benaiah leave. I thought I would die! His face was so red with anger, it looked like he had burned it in a fire. He struck me again and again. For a whole week I did not venture out of the house except if it was extremely necessary. A scar still remains from that day.

I try to twist a little bit into a more comfortable position, but my neck is cramped as I lie in this awkward way, held down by my husband, my hair still tangled in his fingers. The annoyance and anger rises violently inside me again. How dare he hold me down! How dare he treat me like I am his slave—his thing to beat when he gets angry. Does he not see all the work I do for him? Does he not care? Is he just as calloused about my work as he was about Benaiah's? What if I stopped making his meals and tending his garden? What if I stopped cleaning up after him and doing the thousands of chores that keep our family going? Does he ever appreciate me? Does he ever give thanks for the wife God has given him?

Disgusted, I pull my head free from his fingers and get out of bed. Behind me I hear him stir in his sleep.

Go ahead, wake up. I don't care anymore, I think in my head as I slip out of the room and into the main chambers of the house.

Free at last, I walk through the courtyard and outside into the dark. I breathe in the chill night air and look up at the sky full of stars. I stretch my neck and rub it, working out the kinks.

Should I run away like my son? Should I try to find a new life for myself? Does Yahweh allow for it? Would Yahweh still be my God if I did it? Would the village stone me if I left Piram? The questions burn hot holes inside my soul. No answers come from the dark night. Suddenly, though, I am determined to be free.

The need for it overwhelms my soul. There's a newborn fire in my heart that no amount of beating will put out. I need to be free of this man. I need to live outside of his gloomy shadow and his violence. I don't know how, and I don't know when, but I am going to leave him. My heart roars at the thought. Boldness flows through me like a flooding river. I've never felt this way before, and it feels good!

I hear a noise, and I turn around. Piram stands in the doorway of the house. His arms are crossed. His eyes are hard.

"Who are you waiting for out here, you perverse woman? I should have known you were an adulteress! Who is he? I'll tear him up with my bare hands, and you with him!"

27

HANNAH

My fingers work flawlessly and fast as I weave the strands back and forth across the loom. It is one of those tasks I do so often, I could shut my eyes and work just as fast. My mind is racing with angry thoughts. No news from Benaiah. It has been weeks, and there has been no communication. If he wants to marry me so badly, why doesn't he ever send a message to me? Doesn't he realize that I love him? Doesn't he realize that the longer he makes me wait, the more frustrated I feel, and the angrier and lonelier I get?

Travelers from Gibeah arrived a few weeks ago and passed through our village. They brought word from several of the young men in the army, but Benaiah didn't give them a message for me. Jorman, a prominent citizen of Pirathon, had also been to the army camp to see his sons and nephew and to bring them some fresh food from home. He brought home news and reports to all the other family members waiting for word of their sons in the army, but when I asked him about Benaiah, he had no information. Just yesterday, I went to Benaiah's mother and

I WAS THERE WHEN THE GIANT FELL

asked her for any news, and she also had heard nothing. It is all so frustrating.

Mother calls from the other room, interrupting my thoughts. I stop weaving the strands of wool and let out a sigh. Duty calls. There is always something that she needs me to do, yet she does less and less herself. I suppose I should not complain. She cared for me when I was young.

I get up and go into her room. My heart softens at the sight of her, and my annoyance disappears. Mother's face is ashen white, and her eyes are bloodshot and sunken into her face. Her voice comes out like a strained whisper.

"Could you fetch me some extra water from the well and… and heat it on the fire? I'm feeling…a c…coldness in my bones today. Could you make some warm broth for me?"

Despite her pain and her weariness, her eyes are unusually tender. I do know that she loves me deeply.

"Yes, of course, Mother. Is there anything else I can get you? Can I help you feel more comfortable at all?"

"No child, just the broth. Perhaps you should fetch your father. I…I feel faint."

Concern shoots through me. "Are you okay, Mother?"

"I don't know, Hannah. It feels worse today. Perhaps Yahweh is calling me home to my fathers soon."

I'm alarmed. "Don't talk like that, Mother! I'm sure you'll feel better soon. Let me get that broth going!"

I hurry out of the room, wiping a tear that has collected in the corner of my eye. She's always been such a strong woman, and seeing her so weak and frail unsettles me deeply. I run off with the jar and head toward the well. My feet fly down the path, and I am out of breath when I reach the well. I take a moment and steady myself against a tree, drawing in deep gulps of air.

The water jug is heavy and cold against my skin as I carry it toward our home from the well. As I come around the corner near the city gate, my heart skips. Mahlo and his father stand at the city gates talking with my father. Why is Father here? Why is he talking with them? Is it business or trade? Or is it something else? Intense curiosity courses through me. I stop and carefully place the jar on the ground. Quietly, I slide along the wall and creep a little closer until I can hear bits and pieces of the conversation.

"You do us a great honor by coming, Mahlo," my father is saying. "You could not find a better wife among all the sons of Ephraim."

Mahlo's father clears his throat. "My son has been asking me to approach you for some time now. He's eager for a betrothal."

"Of course. I don't see any reason to delay."

I cannot breathe. It is like someone has punched me in the stomach. They can only be talking about me. Fear and disgust fill me. Father knows my wishes. He knows that Benaiah and I are close. Would he go against my wishes? He can. It is in his power to do so. He can choose whomever he wants for me, and I will have to live with it.

I hear the men saying goodbye to each other. I hear the crunch of their steps as they leave. How long have they been here talking about this? My mind reels. What if they already made the arrangements? What if I am already betrothed to Mahlo right now? My heart beats frantically. I feel faint. My back slides against the rough wall, and I sit down in the dust. Hot tears form in the corners of my eyes. Why? Why is this happening? Where is Benaiah? I need him here, now. Not off fighting some losing battle! Not off getting hurt on some battlefield! A few moments pass, and the panic inside me subsides a little. I gather my emotions and steel myself for the confrontation with my father. I need to find out what has happened. What has father done?

My thoughts consume me as I carry the water jug home.

When I come through the doorway of our house, Father is nowhere to be found. Where could he have gone? Did he go back out to the fields? Why the secrecy? Why wouldn't he tell me he was arranging all this?

I stoke the fire and pour some water into the pot. I gather what I need for the broth and begin to cook it on the fire. I look in through the doorway at my mother. She's sleeping peacefully now. I'm glad she has some relief. I go back to the loom and continue working while the broth heats. My mind is buzzing with what I saw at the town gate.

Me betrothed to Mahlo? I consider him. He is tall and handsome, important and strong. He has quite a bit of influence in our village and the surrounding area. His family is wealthy. There are many positives to the match. Also, even though I do not love Mahlo, perhaps I could learn to love him. Perhaps over time we could grow close as married couples often do. My heart reels at this thought, though. I barely know him! Even more, he's a friend of Benaiah's! He must know that Benaiah wants me as his wife! I yearn for Benaiah! We have so much in common, and our relationship has come so far. My heart burns when we talk with each other. Why did he choose to be a soldier now? Why is Father making arrangements? I am so confused and troubled. I wish my mother and I were close. I wish I could talk to her about my feelings. I wish she wasn't so sick.

A violent hissing sound snatches my attention away. The broth! It is boiling over, bubbling into the fire. I run over and pull the pot off of the coals. I will have to let it cool before it goes to Mother. I place it on some cold stones and stir it a little. When I go in to check on her, I find her still asleep. As I approach her, an unsettling feeling gushes through me like a cold river. Something is wrong. Her chest is not rising and falling with her breath. Is she breathing? I put my ear up to her lips. Nothing! My heart is raging in fear. I shake her slightly, and she does not wake.

"Mother!" I whisper violently into her ear. "Mother! Mother!" My voice rises with every attempt until I am shouting her name. She doesn't wake up, and I know she will not. She has gone to be with her fathers.

28

BENAIAH

Hundreds of enemy eyes gleam beneath hundreds of helmets piercing our army with hatred as we draw up our battle lines to meet them. I can already tell it will be the biggest battle I have been a part of yet. Ramel has passed on some of the intelligence he's received from the other commanders and the meetings with Abner. They know an invasion is inevitable, but they do not know if this is the main invasion or just another feinting thrust across our lines to see how we might respond.

I have now been in several skirmishes and countless hours of training. It has become so familiar to me—the strain and energy of war. My life in Pirathon seems a distant whisper, an era passed and gone. As I stare out at the enemy priming for battle before us, I feel the energy of war coming over me, a passion rising from deep inside. The Philistines are just starting to beat their drums and raise their war cry. Soon we shall match them voice for voice.

Berechiah is at my side, as always, though we have not spoken much since our last unpleasant conversation about Yahweh. He encouraged me again and again to trust Yahweh's promises, pointing out that they don't change when life gets hard. I barely know this god, and I can hardly trust that he loves me! I told him that he doesn't understand what it feels like to be part of an army that looks at you like you're worthless and small. I told him that he doesn't understand me and my heathen blood, and that perhaps Dagon, the god of the Philistines, holds some sway over my soul. He responded to me with patience as he again directed me to Yahweh and his covenant with the people of Israel. I barked at him. I hate his patience. I want him to be angry, like I am. At least then we would have something in common again.

He looks at me now as we prepare for battle. There's no anger, just a tinge of sadness in his eyes. "Yahweh be with you today, my friend," he says softly.

I can only manage a nod in reply. My anger is still here, brooding beneath the surface. I fear if I open my mouth, it will come out across my tongue. I'll spit sharp words that I won't be able to take back.

"Never forget your name, Benaiah. You were built by Yahweh. You may have turned from him, but he has not turned from you." He smiles that reckless smile of his. A spark of the old familiar gleam dances in his eyes. "Put your anger to use and kill some Philistines with it! We'll talk when this battle's through."

I feel some of the anger leave me at his cheerful words and indomitable grin. I open my mouth to speak, but I'm interrupted by Ramel's shout as he signals our advance. Berechiah and I turn to face the enemy.

We all raise the war cry and hammer our weapons against our shields, creating a crashing crescendo of noise. We surge forward, hearts riled by that roaring drumbeat of war. I feel the soft earth give slightly beneath my sandals, and the ground shakes with the pound of hundreds of feet. Time seems to slow. My breath comes steady and full, filling my lungs and sending power coursing through my blood. I taste the acrid dust as it plumes around us.

I run forward, hurling myself toward death. In front of me, I see the first wave of destruction as Israelites and Philistines crash into each other, weapons clanking and blood spattering from their collapsing bodies. Thoughtless rage explodes in my brain and pulses through my body like a throbbing heat, yet I harness the energy of that rage and let it carry me toward the fight. As I run, I check the position of the knife in my belt, making sure it is easy to reach. I also have a shield and sword that I picked off the field after the last skirmish, so I'm ready for action.

Soon I'm in the thick of the struggle. Eerie shafts of dust-streaked sunlight pierce through the haze of battle. I struggle to stay focused despite feeling like I am in a herd of stampeding animals. My throat is chalky with dust, and I gag on the stench of freshly torn bodies.

Suddenly, Philistine warriors appear through the haze, hurling themselves at me. My time has come. I swing my arms, relying on my native instinct and my training. My sword slices and turns. Blood sprays. I balance, strike, and avoid. I stab and release. I stick up my shield and feel the pound of an enemy's blow—a blow strong enough to break a bone—yet my shield protects me. I feel the surging movement of men massing forward and backward, like an ocean of humanity writhing in tides of passion, shattering life on the sharp shoals of death.

I notice Berechiah off to my right—a fury of muscles battling with a large Philistine warrior. His spear strikes true, and the man falls in a lump of empty strength. He glances in my direction and a wide grin fills his face. He shouts at me, but the roar of battle carries his words away. Another Philistine is quickly upon him, and he plucks his spear free from the fallen Philistine and lunges to meet his new opponent.

I swing around just in time to see two Philistines charging at me. I duck down, narrowly avoiding a club smashing into my face. I spin sideways, slashing my sword toward the enemy, but it only clatters on the man's armor, doing no damage. The other warrior comes at me with a spear, and I jab upward with my shield, deflecting the blow. The first man swings his club again, but I rush under it and ram my head into his abdomen with as much force as I can muster. He flounders backward, losing the grip on his club. I roll over him and get up fast, sword in hand. As he struggles to recover, my sword finds its mark.

His companion roars at me in a rage and throws his spear to pin me to the ground. I spin away and feel the rush of air as it narrowly misses my body. I charge him as he draws a sword from his belt. My shield slams into his wrist, breaking it with a crack. He screams in pain, and I silence him with the blade of my sword.

I turn and come face to face with a young Philistine, sweat streaming down his face and fresh blood splattered on his arm. He's out of position. I take a split second to look deep into his eyes before sending my blade up under his shield. Surprise fills his eyes, and the light grows dim inside them. In the midst of the chaos a sudden thought strikes me: how fragile life is—a brief mistake and the light is gone! My eye contact with the dying man is ripped away as I am knocked sideways by two men falling in the fight. I stagger for several steps before I recover my balance. As I turn to meet another threat, I feel a jarring blow to the side of my head. I sense my body swinging free, falling into a cold sea of blackness.

29

HANNAH

We lay Mother to rest in our family burial cave as the light of day melts into darkness. Tears fill the corners of my eyes and spill onto my face. We awoke this morning as a complete family, and we end the day with Mother in the ground. Father is taking it hard. His heart is torn apart. I have never seen him cry, but now as I look across at him, several streaks wet his face. I am unable to hold my emotions in any longer. Sobs start in my throat and shudder through my whole body. Eerie and loud, my mourning cry rises to the sky. Several friends and family stand around in silent reverence as my painful sound echoes across the hills. We were able to afford a few hired mourners, and they join me, mourning and wailing as loudly as possible.

My heart feels empty and cold. My mother and I struggled to stay close, but I miss her intensely already. I will miss her touch, her rare yet beautiful laugh, and especially her love—tender, tough and always evident.

Pangs of regret hit me as I think of how annoyed I've been with her lately. She couldn't help being sick. She didn't ask for it. I should have been more patient with her and not been so bitter about the extra work.

Several men close up the mouth of the cave. Slowly, our friends and relatives depart until it is just Father and I standing, staring into the darkness. No one speaks. Quiet sobs still rise from deep inside me. Suddenly, I feel Father's arms wrap around me from behind, and new tears erupt from my eyes.

In the darkness, he chokes out his words in a whisper. "Your mother is in the grave. She is no longer sick and in pain. She's with her ancestors. She's with Yahweh. We must be strong, Hannah. We must be strong." His words sound distant and unsure, as if he is trying to convince himself that Mother is truly gone and that saying this over and over will somehow help him get through the pain.

I turn around and embrace him. My world is changing so fast, and I have no one to rely on now except for my father. After a moment, he draws back and leads the way home.

We walk in silence; the only sound is the soft shuffle of our feet on the path. The pain in my heart is numbing. I keep seeing Mother's face in my mind, and I'm desperate to memorize every feature of it before her image is lost and forgotten. My thoughts are interrupted as Father turns to me.

"I have some news for you, my dove." His voice is strained.

"Yes, Father?"

"I'm not sure if this is the right time to tell you, but you need to know. I've been talking with Mahlo and his father. I am arranging a marriage for you with him."

My heart sinks. This is certainly not the right time to tell me!

He holds up his hand, anticipating my protest. "Mahlo is a good man and important in the village! He is a better man for you than Benaiah could ever be, and he has asked for your hand in marriage. His father is not fully pleased with the match, but he has consented to take you as his son's wife. It is a generous offer of marriage—one I had stopped dreaming could happen. Please honor me and your late mother's wishes, and do not fight me on this decision. The match will soon be arranged."

It feels like I've been struck in the stomach. The pain is so sharp, it cuts off every word I want to say. Everything is changing too fast. What can I do? I do not want to marry Mahlo! Where is Benaiah? Why did he leave to fight this war? Why didn't he stay home and fight for me?

30

BENAIAH

I wake with pain splitting through my head, wishing I could just go back to sleep. The dirt directly beneath my nose is musty and damp. Another nauseating smell also fills my nose. It reminds me of when we butchered several goats for a festival when I was young. I remember the carcasses hanging in the air, the blood dripping down. Groggy and disoriented, I force my stiff joints to move. *Where am I?*

I try to roll over, and new pains shoot through every part of my body. I slowly realize that something bulky and heavy is flung across my legs, preventing me from turning. I twist my head around and try again to roll free. *What is on top of me?* I crane my head a little more and catch a glimpse of the weight on my legs.

A dead body!

Horror runs through me like an icy brook. I move violently, disregarding the pain, and I force myself to crawl forward. The cold, awful weight of the body slides from my legs and flops off behind me as I move. A wave of nausea overcomes me, causing me to gag.

All at once, the memories rush back to me—the surge of men, the glint of swords, the blood, and my hot rage. Then I remember the jarring blow to my head, the blackness that descended around me, and the feeling of utter helplessness as my limbs went limp and I collapsed against the hard ground. How long have I been left here for dead? Where is Ramel and my unit?

It takes all my willpower to stand. Once up, I sway and stagger as I try to move. I look around, shocked to see the field of bodies, their grey, lifeless forms contorted in grotesque lumps. The silence roars in my ears—a deafening sound of life defeated. I recognize a few faces, yet I am numb to the emotions of the moment. No breath. No life. Hands that once gripped swords, plowed land, and held children are now cold, lifeless clay. The stench of sweat and blood assaults my nostrils. Wispy ghosts of fog hang suspended across the field.

The peace of death is a somber, gruesome peace. The soft stillness masks and sanctifies the horror. A bird sings out somewhere in the distance, adding a note of ironic normality. I look around the battlefield, searching for any movement amid the fallen men, feeling like I am the last surviving man on earth. Never have my eyes seen a sight like this! In the distance, I see a stirring at the edge of the field—a sign of life! It seems to be a few men dragging themselves along, and from this distance I cannot tell if they are friend or foe. I am too weak to defend myself right now, so I crouch down and watch them slowly move out of my field of view.

I look around for my sword and knife. I cannot stay unarmed. The cold bodies brush against my arm as I search the ground around me. I go over the area thoroughly and then move several paces away, trying to remember where I fell. Finally, I find my knife buried to the hilt in a man's abdomen. I discover my sword a stone's throw away on the ground beneath a dead Philistine, but the blade is broken. The dead man's sword lies at his feet. It looks like a good blade, so I take it as my own. *At least we got a few of them!*

I have to get out of here. The stench alone is going to kill me, and people will soon be out here to pick through the dead bodies and collect whatever they can from the victims of this battle. I spot a small grove of trees off to my left and slowly begin to make my way in that direction. My legs hurt. My head feels as if it's filled with sand. I ache in muscles I didn't know existed on my body. Somehow I have to get out of the open field and find some of my companions.

I look down at the bodies as I hobble past. I am oddly fascinated by the mangled, contorted forms, their unresponsive eyes haunting the deepest reaches of my spirit. And then I pause. A face catches my eye. A blank stare that looks so alarmingly familiar yet unearthly at the same time. I drop to my knees to get a closer look. Time stops. The earth gives way beneath me like it has turned to air, and I feel my soul falling to the pits of Sheol.

Berechiah.

His face is cold, empty, lifeless. His body is mangled, torn at the stomach, his organs and bones peeking out through folds of skin, dried blood, and tatters of cloth. Hours ago he walked and talked with me. Hours ago his smile lit up this world, and his words sent cheer and life into the hearts of all around him. Now he is just another body in a field of bodies.

I am so numb from shock and grief I can barely breathe. It is as if someone has reached a cold hand into my body and pulled out my heart. This is not real! Yahweh would not let this happen! This is just a dream, and I will wake up from it. When

I do, I will tell Berechiah about it, and he will laugh and tell me to stop worrying so much.

I rub my eyes in the hopes that the sight will go away, yet I am transfixed on his motionless form. I don't know how long I kneel next to him, staring down at him, but slowly the numbness begins to fade away.

I reach my hand out to touch his face, and it is like touching the winter frost. My hand recoils, and reality rushes upon me like a raiding party plundering my body, stealing every shred of hope away. Fresh, terrible emotion overwhelms me with hot pain. Burning tears pool in my eyes.

"No! No! No!" The words spill out in a tense whisper, and I repeat them over and over again, as if denying the reality in front of my eyes will reverse the truth and restore Berechiah to life again.

Unconsciously, I grab handfuls of dirt and squeeze them in my rock-hard grip as I hunch over and slowly rock back and forth. Tears streak down my cheeks and meander through my dusty beard. "Why?" I shout at the top of my lungs. "*Why?*"

31

SERAH

"Her breathing is still labored…"
I turn slightly toward the voice, but it fades away. My thoughts swim again, swirling into a misty nothingness.

"Serah?"

The voice is back. It is a familiar voice—a woman speaking softly. I shift a little, and pain sears through me. A moan fills the air around me, and after a moment I realize it is coming from my own throat.

"Serah? Can you hear me?"

I try to nod my head, but the effort makes me feel faint, and the darkness threatens to take me away again. My effort seems to be enough—she sees my movement.

"Oh, Serah, I am so glad you are alive! We…we were afraid that you were not going to make it."

With great effort I force my eyes to open. Two bleary forms hover above me.

"She's opening her eyes! Serah? Serah? Can you see me?"

A small memory forms somewhere in the back of my mind and grows like a sunrise. The voice… It is my friend, Ruba—my midwife. Am I having a baby? That's not possible!

"I'll get some more oil." Another woman's voice breaks into my puzzled thoughts—Jadia is also here.

I open my eyes again, and one of the hazy forms walks away and out of my vision. *What is happening to me?*

A warm hand touches my arm. I force myself to focus, trying to remember.

"It's over on the south end of the storeroom," Ruba calls to Jadia.

I am starting to see a little better, and I can make out Ruba's form standing over me, looking at me.

"It's so good to see you open your eyes!"

I try to speak, but the sounds that come out of my lips are only unintelligible mumbles.

Ruba's fingers touch the side of my face, gently. "You've been lying here for a full week trying to recover."

The fog in my brain begins to lift. I shift again, and more sharp pain blazes throughout my body.

"Lie still, Serah. You don't need to move," Ruba says while gently brushing a tendril of hair away from my face.

Jadia comes back with a small jar of oil, and Ruba helps as they unwrap several bandages. I flinch as they begin to clean my wounds and wrap them again. Pain erases all thought, and I sink again into a merciful unconsciousness.

When I wake again, it is night. My eyes open in the darkness, and at first I wonder if I have died. A dull pain throbs at my neck, and my back is burning with agony—I must be alive.

I focus on my breathing, taking in long, fresh drinks of air that rush into my lungs until I push them out again. I am still so confused. I know I must be at Ruba's house, but why is Jadia here? Where are my children? What happened to me? Where is Piram?

Suddenly, the memory rushes upon me like an avalanche—*Piram!*

He thought I was waiting for another man! He was livid! He struck me until I fell to the ground, and then he kicked me over and over again. I remember his rage—he lost all sense! I thought I would surely die.

I twist on the mat, trying to see if Jadia or Ruba are nearby. I want to ask them where Piram is and what has happened this past week. I am so eager to know! In my effort to move, I feel a violent tug at my abdomen followed by a moment of intense pain. A strange warmth spreads along my side and then beneath me across my back. I hold myself still, unsure of what to do. My stomach feels sick and weak, and suddenly my vision blurs, and my world goes dark.

I wake again. How long has it been? The early light of morning is just beginning to creep into the house, and the shadows are slowly retreating.

Something is wrong with me!

All my senses are screaming. I need to do something! I muster the little strength I have left to cry out. A pathetic, whimpering sound fills my ears. I try again, a little louder this time. The effort makes me feel faint, but I know I cannot afford to pass out again. I take a few halting breaths before trying again.

Finally, I see movement in the corner of my eye. Ruba rushes to my side. I hear her gasp in disbelief. She touches me in several places, examining.

"Ruba…," I gasp out.

She looks up, startled, and notices my eyes are open.

"Serah!"

"Wh…what is happening?"

"Serah, lie still. Don't move at all!" Her fingers work frantically. I feel her tugging at me, working with the bandages and inspecting the wound. She can't hide her desperation.

"What is it, Ruba?" Worry floods my mind, and I feel incredibly weak.

"Shhh, Serah. Lie still. One of your worst wounds broke open—you've been bleeding for a long time!"

"Ruba…tell me what happened. Where is Piram?" I manage to stammer my words out, despite an overwhelming desire to scream as the pain shoots through every part of me.

"Serah, I'll tell you, but please don't move!" She speaks while she works, fully focused on what her hands are doing. "Piram is gone. He almost killed you, and the elders found out. Eliezer came by your house that morning and found you lying in a pool of blood. They searched for Piram but couldn't find him anywhere. If he comes back, the elders have promised to deal with him severely."

"Piram…gone?" The news shocks me.

"Yes, Serah, but be quiet and lie still." Ruba continues tugging at my side. "You are at my house. Arah and Joel are both fine—they've been trying to keep up with the work. Jadia has been running your household well. She comes every day to check on you and to help me care for you."

"Thank you, Ruba…"

"Shhh—it's okay. Just try not to move."

I lie silently as Ruba continues to work on me. Piram is gone? The realization is both unsettling and wonderful. Could I finally be free of him? What will happen if he comes back?

"There!" Ruba announces triumphantly. "I think I got it back together, but you've lost a lot of blood. You *must* lie still—no moving at all!"

I manage a slight nod.

Ruba looks down at me for a moment, her eyes filled with worry and tenderness. "I'm so glad that you are awake now!" She gently touches my arm before moving off to continue her other work.

I lie here alone, looking up at the wood beams that hold up the roof. I wish Benaiah was here. How is he doing? Is he alive?

After a while, I drift off to sleep.

When I open my eyes again, it seems to be the middle of the night. A scratching noise by the doorway catches my attention. I dare not move to look at it, but curiosity invades my better sense. I lift my head up slightly and look toward the door, but it is much too dark to see anything. I convince myself that it is probably just a small animal outside the door, and I slowly ease my head back down onto the mat and close my eyes.

Piram! It must be Piram! He's back! My eyes shoot wide open. He'll kill me now for sure! Panic races through my entire body. I hold my breath, straining my ears to hear every possible sound. There it is again! Is it someone brushing against the door, trying to find a way into the house?

Sweat breaks out on my forehead, and my heart thuds wildly. This is torture to lie here motionless. I begin mouthing silent prayers to Yahweh to calm my heart for a moment. The noise comes again, interrupting my prayer. I can't take it anymore. I am too afraid to cry out. I have to move! I lift myself up on my elbows and start to scoot off of the mat. I need to get in by Ruba and her husband—maybe they can protect me! With a surge of effort, I manage to roll my body over onto my stomach so that I can begin to crawl, but the pain is unimaginable. I feel something give way beneath me, and again I feel the warmth spreading under my body. A feeling of incredible weakness spreads over my mind and shivers through every part of me. My vision blurs as tears from the pain fill my eyes. My consciousness starts to slip away from me, and I feel like I'm helplessly drifting out into the deep waters of the great sea.

32

BENAIAH

It's been a week, and I've had no proper time to mourn. I can't shake the sight of Berechiah's dead body. He is in my dreams at night, laughing and joking around as he always did, but when I wake, he is gone. The hole in my soul is desperately deep. It is a living, breathing, bitterly empty expanse sucking the joy out of my life. I feel lost and so bitterly alone. Why did I fight with Berechiah? Why was I angry with him? He was my best friend, and now I'll never see him again. I wasted our last moments together!

I passed out trying to drag his body back to camp. Some men from our unit found me when they were out on a scouting patrol. They helped me carry his body back to camp where we buried him. Eliab and several others tried to comfort me, but I brushed them off. There's no comfort for a man like me. I am cursed.

In the days that followed we fought several more skirmishes with the Philistines, and none of them went well. Now we have a brief respite after another small battle. I look around at the men at my side. Their hair hangs ratty and unkempt, and many scars flare across their faces. The butchery of war has left us more savage than ever.

I wanted glory, but this is not glory. There is nothing glorious about seeing men decapitated, shredded, pierced, and stained with blood. This is not how it should be. If we are God's chosen people, why would he allow such things to take place? Why would he constantly let us suffer and allow his faithful servants, like Berechiah, to die?

I want nothing to do with the cruel god of Berechiah and my people. He has never shown mercy to me, and he did not show mercy to Berechiah.

My reflections are cut off as orders bark out through the camp. Ramel forces us to move and reposition for the next skirmish. We pack up as quickly as we can and head off to the south, following a small path through the hills.

The sun beats down mercilessly with a bright, glaring heat. Sweat drips from my brow, and dirt and grime stick to every crevice of my body. How many days has it been now? How many days of hot, grueling travel and bloody warfare? How many days weighed down by the gloomy prospect of defeat after defeat? We fight, we train, we search for spies and defend our borders, and on and on it goes—a constant power struggle with the enemy. Moreover, we have yet to win a single fight! We occasionally have the upper hand against the Philistines, but they always come back to dominate us once again. Our bronze weapons are no match for their iron weapons!

We come upon a small river winding through the hills. Ramel gathers us about, and we pitch camp for the night. I bathe in the river for the first time in weeks, and I come out refreshed and slightly renewed. I take some time to sharpen my new sword—the one I stole from the Philistines the day that Berechiah died. It is razor sharp, and the hilt feels solid in my tightened grip.

Our spies have reported to Saul that there are signs of a large Philistine movement against our people. When I first joined the army, I would have been thrilled at this prospect, but now it all seems dull to me. My life is a series of hard days with no breaks and no friend by my side to lighten the load.

I spend most of my free time with Eliab, Abinidab, and Shammah, the sons of Jesse. They are friendly to me, but they will never take the place of Berechiah. I am closest with the eldest brother, Eliab. He is just as bitter and frustrated in the army as I am, and we often commiserate.

I am weary of the army and tired of the constant strain. Most men have had several kills and are proud warriors, but I am regarded as an uncoordinated fighter who, albeit strong, still has a long way to go before becoming a "real" soldier. Some still talk about my failure against the raiding party, but for the most part, everyone has forgotten that I exist.

Ramel seems to be continually checking in on me. I'll find him looking at me strangely during a training exercise or fighting near me during a skirmish. It puzzles me. Perhaps he is still wary of my skills after my devastating blunder. This is just another frustration that annoys me and makes me feel small.

We rarely see King Saul. I know that he used to be a great leader and amazing in battle, but I have yet to see a glimpse of this side of him. These days he seems to be erratic and inconsistent. Sometimes he is here with us on the front lines, urging us on to fight, but then he will disappear for months, retreating to his palace in Gibeah. I hear rumors that he has severe fits of anger. Feelings of doubt and instability are spreading through the army like a plague.

I run the sharpening stone across the blade of my sword over and over again, feeling the satisfying grind as the blade thins to a razor's edge. As I work, my sad, puzzled thoughts continue to tumble about in my head.

Several days ago, General Abner sat down with me to talk. He asked me several questions about my family, my desire to be in the army, my training, and my goals as a soldier. It was an intense conversation, not just because Abner is the general of the entire army and a forceful, respected soldier, but also because his eyes seemed to bore through me as if he distrusted all of my answers.

Now I feel like I'm in trouble, but I don't understand why. Every day I am being pushed closer to the edge of the army, like I don't really belong here. Where *do* I belong? The only man I want to talk to about all this is dead! I'm beginning to forget why I became a soldier. What am I trying to accomplish? The only things I have to show for this great adventure I have embarked on are some scars and a rough, cold exterior.

The next day Ramel informs us that the Philistine threat has moved on, and another unit is heading to intercept them. Our mission now is to patrol the area. Smoke from our fire curls lazily into the sky. I strap on my armor, feeling the cold leather heavy against my chest. I am heading out with a group to visit several nearby villages, trying to determine Philistine movements and boost the morale of the towns along the border that live in constant threat of invasion. These are towns that the Philistines have raided again and again. Their loyalty and respect toward Saul ebbs and flows with the tides of this war. He needs these border towns to be strong and supportive. He wants to use them as launching pads for attacks into Philistine territory or strong buffers against Philistine aggression.

We arrive at a tiny border village—a nameless gathering of eight family homes with a crude wall around the perimeter. The chief elder meets us at the city gate. He's a large man, brawny, powerful, and dark. Several other villagers come out to meet us. They wear sackcloth, and their hair and beards are wild and untrimmed. They look to be on the verge of insanity.

"Oh, look, the miserable soldiers of our miserable king!" the chief elder barks out.

Several of the other elders try to hold the large man back, unsuccessfully. He breaks free and gets in Ramel's face.

"Just a week late—that's all! You dogs!"

Ramel is gruff and loud. "Take care! You talk against the army, and you are talking against its king! Treasonous talk will not be tolerated here!"

Bitter, helpless rage spews out of the man's mouth. "Where were you? Fancy soldiers of Saul—useless! What good does it do to send our taxes to Saul's government if this is how we are treated? We should be sending tribute to the Philistines like we used to! It's better to appease our enemies with our hard-earned produce than to send it to Saul so he can fatten his army, guzzle his wine, and sit on his haunches, watching the nation go up in smoke!"

Ramel strikes the man across the mouth with the back of his hand, causing him to stagger at the blow. He recovers and starts coming back at Ramel in a brutal rage, but Ramel's razor-sharp sword is out and ready to swing. The man holds himself back and mumbles in anger.

Another elder turns to us. "You must excuse Barmatha. He is still mourning the loss of two sons and a daughter to the last Philistine raid. The loss is fresh. They terrorized us about a week ago."

Ramel stands back and puts away his sword. He extends his hand to Barmatha. "We are fighting the same enemy. Don't turn against the army or your king. I am sorry for your losses."

Reluctantly, Barmatha takes Ramel's hand and then draws back again. He is sullen and silent, letting the other elders explain the situation in town.

We can hardly blame them for their feelings. What if it had been our sons and daughters? Would we react any differently? We had hoped to gather supplies here for our further journey, but the town is empty of provisions, leaving them hungry and upset. We decide to continue through and not stay the night.

They point us in the direction that leads to other villages. Our morale is low after the encounter and the recent losses we've experienced. How will we ever hope to win this war? The Philistines are unrelenting, constantly coming back against us with greater force.

The tension on the border is palpable. As we go from village to village, we hear strong whispers and rumors of a very large Philistine force gathering for another invasion. We hear about giants in the Philistine camp. They claim the Philistines have hired strange mercenaries that are three heads taller than the average man. They have arms like tree branches and weapons that can crush men's sculls with a single blow. We brush off such rumors uneasily—they can't be true. These foolish country folk are so ready to believe anything. The Philistines are spreading lies and scaring our people. Still, it leaves us unsettled and wary.

33

BENAIAH

We are flanking them to the north, slinking through the rocks and scrubby trees. Today I am part of a contingent of thirty soldiers. Our mission is to hunt down and destroy a small unit of chariots and horsemen. Our spies have discovered the group preparing to move against our main force in the valley.

Three hundred Israelite soldiers, including my unit, have been ordered north to stop a series of devastating Philistine raids. That main force is behind us guarding a strategic valley and blocking several hundred Philistine raiders who want to cross the valley to destroy three more helpless Israelite villages and from there continue to attack and pillage our land. These raids are getting closer and closer to my home of Pirathon. The thought makes me angry. Hannah, Mahlo, and my mother could all be killed, or worse, dragged off as slaves and abused by the Philistines! We must stop them.

Our weapons are inferior, though, and we have no chariots. In the valley, where chariots have space to move, they will be deadly weapons against us. Tomorrow there will be a major battle for control of the valley. Our unit commanders believe that they are planning to send foot soldiers first, holding these hidden chariots and horsemen in reserve. After they draw our forces into the valley, they will strike with their chariots when we are most exposed out on the plain. They could easily decimate our ranks if they succeed. We've been told they have about ten chariots and twenty horsemen hiding somewhere before us, just within reach of the valley below. Because our spies have discovered them, we at least have a fighting chance. But if we don't find and destroy these hidden chariots soon, we'll all be dead by tomorrow.

A bitter rage boils inside me today. It blinds me. I cannot wait to strike them down. I ache to slice my knife into their flesh and watch my arrows strike home. They have killed Berechiah! It still seems unfathomable that he is gone. I have tried so hard to drown myself in the missions and suppress thoughts of Berechiah, but in my dreams he is still alive. Last night I dreamt we were out in the fields together, back home, laughing and facing the world and its hardships together. It was such a real dream. I woke expecting to see him and talk to him, only to be laughed at by some calloused soldier who reminded me that he was dead. It was like I lost him all over again in a moment. Each kill I make today will be for him. Today I will pay them back. I want to kill, and I care very little if I die in the process. What do I have to lose? Who cares if I die? The bitter depression that has lingered like a dark gloomy cloud over my soul has now morphed into a churning storm, charged with hot energy and rumbling with rage.

I glance over toward Ramel, and I see Shammah whispering to him and pointing ahead of us. He must see something. Ramel holds up his hand for silence and we stop moving. Looking in the direction that Shammah is pointing, I see slight movement in the distance. We've discovered the place where the charioteers are hiding! There is a small valley between us and them. It must connect to the valley down below where the main force is. We creep to the edge of the forest and look across, making sure to stay well hidden behind the trees and rocks so that their sentinels do not see us and raise the alarm. We will need to cross this valley to attack them, and it will not be easy. Several of their horses are tied up in a stand of trees, shaded by several large rocky outcroppings. It would have been easy to pass them by if we weren't looking for them. They seem completely unaware of our presence so far. There is no alert, no cry, and no tenseness about them. We quickly confer about what to do next. Ramel wants to wait until evening to strike. I do not. I chafe at the idea. I am in such a rage, I want someone to kill right now. I want to unleash all my wrath upon them immediately.

Of course Ramel's wisdom prevails. I have no voice in the decision, and it frustrates me. I am still not highly regarded as a soldier. My failures in battle define my reputation more than anything else. At this point, though, I don't care about anything. I don't care whether or not people ever sing my name in the streets of Pirathon. I don't care about winning or losing the war or about coming home to Mother and Hannah. And I definitely don't care if I die. I actually crave death—an end to my pain and my pointless existence. I am bitter as the frost.

Ramel tells us we will strike as the light fades in the sky. We pass our time, gaining a better position. Slowly and quietly we creep down closer, opposite the valley where they've hidden their chariots. Although we do want to kill the charioteers, our more important goal is to destroy their chariots and kill the skilled horsemen to eliminate their threat. As I fix my eyes on the Philistines ahead, I can't help but remember how I'd alerted the enemy so many months ago when we tried to sneak up behind them. I cannot let it happen again.

It feels like an eternity passes, but time does little to dull the anger that lives in my heart today. I keep on thinking of Berechiah and how I miss him. I think of Yahweh and feel empty and mean. I'm on my own, just like Berechiah was before. No god has ever fought for me. I have no people to call my own. Dagon, the god of my Philistine ancestors, hates me because I fight his people. Yahweh hates me too. It's been obvious my whole life.

Slowly, the sun dips down below the hills, its flames smoldering in the sky. Ramel speaks the word, and we ready ourselves for action. I check my bow and arrows and test the blade of my sword before ramming it into the sheath. My arrows will fly until I'm close enough to make them feel my blade. I stretch and then let my muscles go slack, preparing for the intensity and rough work of killing that I know is soon to come. And though I am slightly on edge, it is not fear so much as tense eagerness. This is not my first time anymore, and there is a reckless confidence riding my soul today. When my death no longer matters, fear has no more force.

We stand poised at the edge of the clearing, waiting for the signal. Ramel motions us forward, and we run, crouched down, hoping they don't see us crossing the clearing until it is too late for them. Tall grass swipes against our legs and sandals as we run. There will be no shouting this time, no alerting the enemy—when they see us, they see us. We just want to strike hard as fast as we can. Halfway across the valley, I hear the first cry of warning in the enemy camp. It's too soon! We are vulnerable, and they can still see in the fading light of evening. Several of them mount horses and come flying around the rock formation. Their spears swing low, glinting points poised to strike. The muscles of their horses ripple as they skillfully careen toward us. Six horses are coming fast, trying to break our advance and gain time for the other horsemen and foot soldiers to come at us. If they succeed, we will all die.

I come to a swift, dead stop, digging my knees into the dirt. With one flowing motion, I draw an arrow from my quiver and unstrap my bow from my back. I notch the arrow and draw back, take aim, and let it fly. My arrow sails straight and true, and even though the horseman is riding fast, the arrow catches him full in the neck. Blood sprays across the field as he pitches back off the horse and crumples into the grass.

There's no time to triumph—the other horsemen will be on us in moments. My head is still full of rage, but my arm moves fast yet calm as I draw another arrow, notch it, and let it fly. Again the arrow flies true, striking the next horseman in the ear, and he too falls helpless into the grass—his warrior scream cut short. His riderless horse veers violently, lost and confused, and fouls up another horse and rider coming up close behind. The Philistine rider loses control and is pitched sideways off his mount, hitting the ground with a sickening thump.

There are three down and three to go, but they are closing the distance fast, and by now several other Philistines are running toward us brandishing spears and swords. Eliab, Shammah, and several other Israelites charge past me toward them. From behind me, several arrows fly at the Philistines, but they all miss their mark. I notch one more arrow and I get it off, just in time, and one more horseman spills backward. The last two horsemen are upon us. Ramel ducks expertly beneath the spear thrust at him and swings hard with his sword at the horse's legs. A shower of blood splatters over him, and horse and rider tumble over into the dust.

The Philistine foot soldiers are now closing in on us. Screams and shouts fill the air as our ranks collide. I am up and running again. I feel the satisfying grip of my sword as I draw it from the sheath and swing it before me. My heart pumps wildly and powerfully in my chest. My bloodthirsty rage pulses through me like fire. A Philistine soldier runs at me, and I feel the pressure on my wrist as my sword swings sideways just below his shield and slices across his abdomen. Swiftly, I turn it around, raise it above my head, and let it fall—a mighty blow that severs his skull. I sidestep another incoming Philistine, spinning and ducking to avoid his spear, and then I slam my body into his with brute force. He caves to the ground with a grunt. I spin again, righting myself and chopping down with my sword. The edge disappears into his flesh, and blood paints him dark red.

I look up and see the last, slower horseman bearing down on us close to Ramel, ready to strike him down. Ramel is out of position and reeling off-balance, unable to defend himself. I let my sword fall to the ground, disregarding the danger in front me. As fast as I can, I swing my bow out, draw the arrow, and let it fly. It hits the horseman in the leg and passes into the horse. The horse rears up in pain, and the rider is wrenched backward, tearing his leg as the arrow stays embedded in the horse. His spear, which was inches from Ramel's head, clatters uselessly to the ground. Ramel looks over at me with a mix of relief and awe in his eyes. I've just saved his life, but there's no time to celebrate. I turn back and see that we have contained their charge very effectively—their foot soldiers are fleeing toward the safety of their hiding place once more, and we are right on their heels. I let a few arrows fly to encourage them along, and then I join the chase.

Moments later, we crash into the trees, following close behind the fleeing Philistines. Horses rear up, whinnying wildly as we startle them. Men scatter in every direction, disoriented and confused. Only one chariot has been able to get moving, and it is just heading out around the outcropping. The other chariots still stand, helpless, with men running around desperately trying to hook up their horses and get them moving.

Several Philistines turn, brandishing weapons in a desperate attempt to save their chariots from destruction. We mow them down mercilessly with our swords and spears. Again, I lift my bow and notch another arrow, holding it in front of me as I run around the commotion with the relentless speed of a leopard. Only one goal is on my mind: I must get that one chariot that is escaping around the rocks. Even one chariot is too many for them to have when they fight the main force on the other side of the valley!

I let an arrow fly as I run. It misses the charioteer and lodges itself in the wood of the chariot near his arm. He looks back, surprised, and shouts at the horses, trying to gain speed. I draw up and try again. Aiming seems impossible with the chariot veering and speeding along, but even so, my arrow catches the driver in the back. He lurches backward, knocking into his companion who is attempting to notch an arrow and shoot me down. The chariot jostles about violently as the startled horse runs without a driver. It takes a sharp turn, and the chariot pitches sideways, its left wheel bouncing off a boulder and shattering. The body of the chariot falls hard on the ground, dragging in the dirt as the frightened horse strains forward trying to get free. It plows a deep gorge of earth and comes to a violent stop as the horse rears back and falls, dragged back by the sudden resistance from behind.

As quickly as it began, it is all over. Several Philistines have managed to escape, retreating to the higher ground, but we managed to kill thirty-seven men and several horses. Now we quickly gather brush and use the embers of their cooking fire to burn the chariots. The blaze is hot and high, and dark smoke billows up, blackening the eerie night sky.

I stand recklessly staring into the blaze, my nose filling with the smell of burning wood, watching the flames dance and twist. I still feel the anger in my soul. I still want to kill or be killed. Unsatisfied, I look up and around at my fellow soldiers. We only lost one man, speared down by a Philistine foot soldier.

Ramel comes up beside me, his face sooty and streaked with blood. His hard black eyes stare right through me, and I stare back at him.

"Benaiah, you *are* a true Israelite. You saved my life!"

"My pleasure, sir."

"You fought well today. How many did you kill?" He's breathless with excitement, which is unlike him.

I shrug, finding myself surprisingly annoyed. "I don't remember. It doesn't matter."

"If it wasn't for you, that first group of horsemen would have destroyed us."

"It was nothing," I mutter. "I only wish I had killed more of them." I spit into the dirt near the fire as I feel the waves of heat wash over me.

Eliab strides over to me smiling broadly, his eyes twinkling in the firelight. "You fought like a madman! You practically won the fight single-handedly!"

Several others nod their heads in agreement. "You were amazing out there!"

Again, I dismiss them with a shrug. The praise should fill me up with pride. It is what I have always wanted. It is strange, though, how the glory that promised such sweetness tastes bitter and empty now. The rage in my soul has only slightly subsided. I still wish I had died in the fight.

34

HANNAH

I watch my tears fall into the dough that I am mixing. I don't even care anymore. I have tried to appear fine. I have tried to keep it together for weeks now. I am tired of covering up how I feel. I am tired of being strong. I am broken and wounded.

I step back from the mixture and wipe my face and eyes with the front of my robe. Father is out in the fields. I am alone. I am always so completely alone. Maybe it will be good to marry Mahlo, just to feel connected with someone again. I have lost Mother, and I realize now how I took her for granted while she was alive. I let the annoyances and petty differences prevent me from enjoying our last years together. I saw her as a burden instead of seizing the opportunities to serve her and be with her. Guilt poisons my memories of her, and I just want to go back in time and do better.

Father's decision that I marry Mahlo has divided us. I always had such a warm relationship with him, but lately I have argued with him more than ever before. He has only become more forceful in his decision that I must marry Mahlo. We are exasperated with each other. He thinks he's doing what's best for me, but everything inside me feels wrong about it. I don't have a choice, though. The decision is made, and the process is already started. As much as I do not want to marry Mahlo, I must do my duty and follow my father's will. God often has a way of working things out, but I'm confused and hurt. I can't see what God is trying to do. Why did he take my mother away? Why did Benaiah leave? Why must I marry Mahlo? The questions struggle through me as all my dreams vanish—my reality is so disappointing. I sigh, frustrated. I wish God would give me at least *something* that I want.

"Hello there, little bird!" Mahlo's voice surprises me as he sneaks up behind me. He must have come around the back of the house.

The surprise melts into annoyance when his words sink in. *I don't like being called "little bird."* I barely manage to control my tongue from saying several things I'd regret.

"Is something wrong?"

"No," I say, managing a gentle tone.

"You look like you've been crying."

I feel vulnerable and uncomfortable opening up to him. He seems more of a stranger to me now than ever before.

"It's just the leeks I was cutting up for the dinner tonight." It's easy to lie to strangers.

"Oh. Good to hear. I...came by to tell you some news, but I don't want to upset you more if you are already troubled."

Instantly curious, I look up and try to read his expression. His face is somber and sad. My eyes communicate the question that my lips don't dare to ask.

He says it bluntly. "Berechiah died fighting the Philistines."

"What?" I gasp in disbelief. Instantly, memories rush through my head in waves: Berechiah's bright, indomitable smile that always lifted my heart, the stories he told that made Benaiah and I laugh so hard we couldn't breathe, and the way Benaiah's eyes always shined when he talked to me about his friend. Suddenly, I see the vivid image of Berechiah and Benaiah walking away together to become soldiers.

"It's true. The messenger arrived yesterday. Several other families got the same sad news."

I step back and sit down on a stone outside our home, feeling sick and numb. The empty feeling in my stomach has become all too familiar, and it fills with fresh pain at the shock of a new loss. I shake my head as tears spring into my eyes and run down my cheeks. "No..."

"I know. It's such a terrible shock. I...I hardly believe it myself." Mahlo stares off into the distance as he speaks.

For the first time, I crave his touch. I want someone to embrace me and hold me together while my life falls apart around me. But he does not embrace me. He just stands in front of me and stares, experiencing his own pain in his own way.

And how I ache for Benaiah! I can only imagine what he is going through. Sadness overwhelms me, and I begin to sob uncontrollably.

Mahlo clears his throat awkwardly and coughs. His words tumble out. "Benaiah might also be dead."

Shock and horror race through me. "What! Why do you say that?"

"He and Berechiah were in the same unit together. They were always side by side. I can only imagine that if Berechiah is dead, Benaiah was close by and probably died trying to save him."

His words make sense, and they sit heavy on my heart. *Benaiah—dead?*

"Also..." He pauses, unsure. "The messenger who brought word of Berechiah's death went to visit Piram's household too. I heard it from Arah. No one was there to get the message, since Serah is still in a very serious condition, and Jadia was with her at the time. Piram, of course, has disappeared. Arah saw the man from a distance, but when he got up to the house, the messenger had already left."

"This can't...it's...it's too much," I manage to whisper through the pain in my heart.

"I know. I can't believe it either." Mahlo is staring off into the distance again, seemingly void of emotion. He's not helping. Why doesn't he just go?

"At least one good thing comes of it all." He pauses again, bringing his focus back to me. "With Benaiah gone, our wedding will be easier."

Anger flares through me at his callousness. He sees this, yet his eyes seem cold.

"I know he loved you, but you have to know it wasn't a good match," he says, taking a step toward me.

"You need to leave." My words are abrupt but soft. They come out of my mouth before I can think better of it. "Benaiah was twice the man you'll ever be. At least he went to war! At least he fought for us! What have *you* ever done?"

Mahlo's hand cracks across my face, and lights explode in my head as I fall off the stone I was sitting on.

"How dare you talk to me like that!" he barks.

I stay on my hands and knees, breathing in the dust that plumed up around me after I hit the ground. I am sick with disbelief and pain. I never would have dreamed that Mahlo would strike me!

He takes a moment to compose himself before saying in a calmer voice, "I'm sorry for striking you, but that is no way to talk to me! I'll leave and let you grieve in peace. I'll call on you tomorrow when you are in better spirits."

I close my eyes and listen to the sounds of his sandals crunching on the path as he leaves. My face is throbbing with pain. *This is the man my father has chosen for me to marry?* I have never seen Mahlo like this. I know he's grieving too, but...he struck me! I should not have talked to him like that. What was I thinking?

35

SERAH

The sounds are all mumbled together in a meaningless noise, but they slowly begin to take shape and form words.

"...a great victory..."

"...safe...for now...."

"...men lost..."

"...soon..."

It feels like a heavy stone is tied to my head, but despite the pain, I try to move.

Suddenly, the noises stop, and the words disappear into a black silence. A soft hand touches my face, and a warm feeling fills me, easing my agony. I take a deep, painful breath and open my eyes. Murky shapes blend and blur above me. I feel the hand again, gently brushing the hair from my eyes.

"Our excitement must have woken her!"

The words are clear now. It's Ruba! I'm still at Ruba's? I'm still alive?

"Serah, please, please don't move!" She whispers the words close to my ear, and I feel her gentle, warm breath. Her blurry form shifts as she turns to several other shapes that float above me. "She lost so much blood last time! I didn't think she would make it!"

I see her form turn back to me and come close.

"Serah, you almost died again! You've been hanging on in a deep sleep for several weeks now. I didn't think you'd ever wake up!"

I manage a soft groan in response.

"We're...we're celebrating, Serah. My husband and the other elders just got word that King Saul's army defeated the Philistine raiders that were threatening this area."

My mouth feels unnaturally dry. It's hard for me to choke out my words. "Have...you...heard..." I try to swallow but instead I cough dry air out of my throat. I pause and let the burning sensation in my throat subside. I need to continue. "...Benaiah..."

Ruba turns again to the others. My eyes are beginning to focus. I can see Ruba a little more clearly. I sense that something is wrong. The silence is telling.

"Tell me...please!" I manage.

Once more I feel Ruba's fingers caress my face. My breathing is irregularly fast from the effort of trying to speak.

"We...we don't really know," she says, almost too carefully. "We haven't heard anything about Benaiah yet."

I close my eyes, feeling a little relief, and I focus on my breathing for a moment.

"Several other families have lost their sons, though. I can tell you more when you are feeling better. When I hear something definite about Benaiah, I'll be sure to tell you. Now please rest, okay?"

I nod my head slightly. A dull ache has spread all over my stiff body.

Suddenly, my eyes open wide. "Ruba!"

"Yes, Serah—what is it?"

"Has...Piram...?"

"No one has seen Piram for weeks. Ever since he hurt you, he's disappeared. Don't worry about him. If he comes back, the elders have promised to punish him severely."

It unsettles me that he might be somewhere nearby. Fear creeps through me at the thought. He's going to blame all of this on me. He's going to be so very angry. I know he will come back. I know he will not rest until he's killed me. I try to breathe through my panic, but I can't stop my mind from racing about. My heart begins pounding—the rhythm strange and frantic. Something feels very wrong inside me.

Using what little consciousness I have left, I pray to Yahweh and lay before him all my fears—for myself and for my son. It eases my mind, and I can sense my heart slowing. I know I can trust God's promises! His love is mine, no matter what—even now! I begin to feel a strange and wonderful peace come over my whole body. My ears catch a faint sound of singing. Ruba must be singing a song about Yahweh. It is beautiful! I open my eyes to see if I can catch a glimpse of her, but the room is empty now. I close my eyes again, my consciousness swirls into darkness, and I feel myself carried away by the best sleep I've ever known.

36

I lead the way to the king's chambers in silence. The messenger follows behind me. He is out of breath and clearly agitated and tense. I try hard to fight down the curiosity that is surging inside me. I want to turn around and ask him what the news is, but I know it is not my place. Instead, I maintain my composure and my silence. Last week we had a messenger arrive from the north. Several units from our standing army had won a decisive battle with the Philistines. Our forces pushed a large Philistine raiding party back into their territory and totally defeated them. They even destroyed several of their chariots! Commander Ramel and Abner also gave a glowing description of the suspected spy, Benaiah from Pirathon. They told of his superb fighting against the Philistines and that he was a key component to our success. The king was very impressed, and no one doubts the young soldier's loyalty anymore. It was a crucial victory and such a welcome relief to get some good news for a change! However, it now looks like bad news has arrived again.

We reach the door, and I knock. The attendant on duty swings the door open.

I turn to the messenger. "Wait here. I will let you in soon."

He nods and looks around impatiently, eager to speak to the king.

I cross the throne room and approach the king who is just coming out of his private chambers.

He sees me and can tell something is wrong. "What's going on?"

"A messenger, my lord. It seems urgent."

"Let him in, then." The king's voice is tired and a bit gruff.

I show the messenger in and shut the door behind him. I lean close to the door to listen, but I cannot hear what is going on inside. I just have to wait.

After what seems like forever, the messenger steps out of the room, and I show him out of the palace. I immediately return to the king's chambers to see if he needs anything, hopeful to get some sense of what the message is about.

As soon as I see him, I can tell he is in a violent mood. He passes back and forth near the foot of his throne, a fierce scowl darkening his face.

I bow before him and ask, "Can I do anything for you, Your Majesty?"

He shakes his head, hardly acknowledging me.

I wait, unsure if I should stay or go.

Suddenly, words start spilling out of him. "Philistines again! They are always on the march, eating at our borders." He curses violently and mutters several words I can't understand, his long hair shaking with the effort.

I watch his frustration and feel great empathy for him. He has had such success against all our other enemies, but that has never been good enough. The Philistines are like fierce, mangy dogs that hang at our heels, always ready to strike, hoping to deal the deathblow and devour us.

King Saul stops pacing and stares hard at the floor, his fingers stroking his beard. "Actually, you can do something for me. Go summon Abner. I need to consult with him and assess our military strength. We're going to have to muster whatever militia we can from every nearby village. The Philistines are preparing an invasion, and we must be ready to meet them. When you've notified Abner, oversee the preparations for my departure. I will be accompanying the men to the battlefield."

I bow low to the ground and back out of the entrance door. I call to one of my other attendants and send him to find General Abner quickly and deliver the king's command. I give orders to several attendants to begin preparations for the king's departure. Then I go into my own room and shut the door. Some deep disturbance rises inside me—a nameless, pent-up flood of emotion boiling to the surface. The world seems chaotic and uncontrolled. Why would God not give us the victory? Why are we so weak and floundering as a nation? Aren't we the people of God? Isn't he the God who created all things? Aren't we special to him? His chosen ones?

I had so hoped that when Saul became king, things would be different. I had been a starry-eyed idealist back then when I first became his attendant. I idolized him, thinking he was invincible. I thought we'd be a strong nation. I thought God would give us victories, and we would make the earth ring with his name. But over the years, I have lost my confidence in my king. I have seen all too clearly how troubled and weak he has become. Yes, with Saul in charge, things are still better for us now than they were before, but we are continually plagued by the same problems.

I raise my hands to the heavens and pray for King Saul, our nation, and our army. I pray for victory and peace. I pray that God will give us triumph. When I finish praying, a calmness fills me. I take a deep breath. A sudden knock on my door makes my heart skip a beat. I quickly wipe several newly formed tears from my eyes. It will do no good to cry like a woman now or show weakness or fear to the other attendants. I must lead them. I must appear stronger than I feel.

Hoshan greets me at the entrance, his face grim and tight. "What is it?" I say, instantly concerned.

"We've just had another message arrive. It's confirmed. The Philistines are on the move. They just overran four villages on the border. It's a huge force--far greater than we first believed. I fear for our army and our king."

I sigh, sad and upset. Why does God answer prayer that way, as if it doesn't do any good? "Thank you, Hoshan. Alert the other attendants. Prepare the king's supplies and his war tent, and make sure his armor and weapons are in good shape. Tell his armor-bearers the news—they will need to help with the preparations."

He nods curtly and leaves.

How uncertain peace is.

My nerves are beginning to fray as internal strife wears away at me. How can we survive? We're surrounded by tension and unrest. Our enemies are resilient, and our king is weak. What if Saul has another fit with the evil spirit while he's out fighting the Philistines? We'd be the laughing-stock of the world! I can't let my mind wander, though. I have to be strong.

I take a deep breath and force myself to think of the here and now. Mentally, I begin to check off the preparations I will need to make. There are several scheduled events for the king that I need to cancel. I will have to oversee the other attendants as they pack Saul's supplies for the trip. I will need to pack my own supplies, because several of us will accompany the king to the battlefield, while others will stay back and continue the day-to-day procedures of the palace. I take another deep breath. As long as I stay busy with the preparations, I will be able to stay calm and focused.

I take a few moments to pack up several of my own things for the journey, all the while wrestling away the worry that tries to invade my mind.

After a short time, Hoshan appears at my door. "Abner is on his way. The king is asking for you again."

Immediately, I drop what I am holding and hurry toward the king's chambers, my heart beating faster with every step. When I enter the chambers, the king is pacing nervously, and several servants are bustling about gathering supplies, food, clothing, and tents. The king looks up as I approach. I bow, and he waves his hand impatiently.

"Have you notified my armor-bearers?" he barks.

"Yes. I sent Hoshan to notify them."

"Good. Get everything ready fast. We leave tonight."

A gasp escapes from my lips and startles me, since I rarely display any kind of emotion in the king's presence.

A note of surprise shows on his face. His eyes narrow as he looks at me. "What's wrong?"

"Nothing, my lord. I am just troubled by this turn of events. I assume it must be bad if we are rushing our departure."

He nods, but still regards me with a curious look. "Yes, we must hurry. If my reports are accurate, this is a very large Philistine force. They are moving fast, and according to several reports, they have a new secret weapon that they are planning to use against us."

His words send my thoughts reeling again. What kind of secret weapon could they possibly have? They already have iron weapons—technology that is much more advanced than anything we have. They also have chariots that they can use against us when the terrain allows it. Even though fresh worries flood my brain, I do not let it show on my face. I cannot risk that in Saul's presence.

Suddenly, Abner sweeps into the room. He's already dressed in his leather armor, and his sword is fastened neatly to his waist. He has a violent, commanding presence about him, intensified now by his stern expression.

"So they march again, Saul?"

"Yes, they are on the move. We must hurry and intercept them at the Valley of Elah before they can push the advantage and invade our territory."

"Of course."

"Alert all the commanders of the army, and send word to the elders in the neighboring villages. Get messengers out to the villages all around and raise as many militia as you can. Get the standing army ready to move tonight. I want every unit in the army heading to intercept the Philistine advance. Also inform Jonathan that he will stay here to protect Gibeah with the palace guard and the local militia."

"Yes, my lord. I will do so at once."

I admire the general. He seems unafraid, with no hesitation and no questions. He is strong and in charge—the way Saul once was. He turns to leave, but the king stops him short.

"Abner—after you pass on the word and muster the men, return here. I'll fill you in on all the details that I have."

"Yes, my lord." He strides out of the room without another word.

The air seems charged with his presence, even after he is gone. It gives me some small hope. Maybe we have a chance after all.

37

BENAIAH

The sunrise gleams across the valley of Elah, burning the hills red with the first blush of morning heat and chasing away the gloomy chill of night. All is settled in stillness, yet soon this silent peace will be sheared apart in violent warfare, determining death or life—victory or defeat.

Every fight has led me here, to this moment. We didn't have long to celebrate our victory in the north. As soon as word reached us that the Philistines were massing an invasion force, we quickly marched southward. Now here we are, ready to meet their threat. It's the biggest battle I've faced so far. A strange nervousness has settled upon my bones. I try to shake it off, but my breath comes and goes in heaving bursts. The recklessness and rage that spurred me on in the last fight has drained out of me.

Maybe it's the beauty of this place in the early morning light that makes me want to live again. Maybe it's Hannah. As we traveled south from the last battle, my thoughts turned to her over and over again, and my reckless rage subsided. We were not far from Pirathon, and I had hoped to have a chance to visit. I long to see her. I miss her smile and her voice. I don't want to die now. I want to marry her and grow old with her—but first, our land needs to be at peace.

To have peace, we must be victorious today. If we lose this battle, we may very well lose our independence and our existence as a nation. Even King Saul is with us today. Every unit in the army is gathered here for war, as well as thousands of militia from the nearby villages. I look about at the white knuckles gripping the handles of swords. I hear the shuffle of feet in the dust. Someone sneezes. Metal clinks on metal, and leather creaks as we move into our positions. An eerie anticipation has fallen on us all. We know they are just up ahead, just over the horizon—a massive invasion force.

"There!" someone says aloud, breaking the stillness.

We stretch our necks, trying to see what he's pointing at.

"Right there at the edge of the hill!" he says breathlessly. "See?"

Dim, blurry shapes move along the skyline as the enemy army comes into view. The metal of their helmets and weapons flash in the early rays of the sun. At first it sounds like a rolling thunder, until I realize it's the pounding of thousands of weapons on shields. I watch them creep over the hill like a swarm of locusts looming dark on the horizon, ready to eat everything good in sight. We watch them form ranks across the valley and then stop. Our armies face each other, waiting for the command to charge. They are close enough now that I can see their individual faces staring at us across the divide.

A chilling thrill fills me at the sight. Fear makes everything intense—the smell of sweat and leather is sharp in my nose, and every inch of my armor feels tight against my skin.

I curse under my breath. Why do I feel this lingering doubt and fear? I've done this before. Although, this is a much bigger battle than I'm used to. I clench my fist around my sword and try to shut out the voice inside me that says I'm too small, too weak, and too cursed to fight this fight.

Ramel's booming voice shatters the stillness as he shouts down the line of soldiers. "We are the army of Israel!" he roars. "Who slaughtered the Philistines at Micmash?"

Hundreds of voices answer, "We did!"

He continues. "We are mighty and invincible! We are fierce, and no one can defeat us! Who will spill Philistine blood with me today?"

Voices cry out, even louder, "We will! Let's destroy them!"

"In no time, these Philistine dogs will be on the run. They will cower and cringe before us. No one can defeat King Saul, the mighty champion of Israel, and his army! Today they will taste the bite of our swords! Today we will push them back into the sea where they belong! Today *nothing* can stop you. You are mighty. You are invincible. You are God's warriors!"

His chanting words settle my jittery spirit. I am ready. I can do this. I hunch my shoulders and ready my legs for running. I clear my heart for war. These are the Philistines that killed Berechiah.

I feel that familiar fire of rage spark again. I stoke it with every memory of pain, every shameful experience, every moment of doubt, and every weakness I've ever felt. Soon, my whole being is overcome by it. Rage for the impossibilities and difficulties of my brief life. Rage for the oppression of my people. Rage for Israel's god who I am supposed to believe in, but who still seems so small and far off. Rage for the weaknesses of my past and all my own insecurities bubbling to the surface of my soul. It all boils out of me in one surge and flood of passionate rage.

I look out at the enemy as if I could kill them with my eyes. My heart leaps, and my muscles grow tense and eager. I am poised and ready to run, waiting desperately for the signal to charge, but I hear nothing. Time hangs in an agonizing pause.

Waves of pent-up frustration wash over me. What are we waiting for? I need to fight! I need to vent my rage on my enemies!

I suddenly become aware of the soldiers around me. They are talking amongst themselves, impatiently questioning the lull in action.

The Philistines still stand in battle formation across the valley, but they aren't moving either. It is eerie. We glare at each other across the divide.

"What are we waiting for?" I hiss at Eliab, who stands next to me.

"I don't know! Maybe we're going to stare them to death!" Eliab says without any humor in his voice.

I strain my neck to see what is happening along the lines. The irritated whispering and questioning grow louder. No one understands what is going on. Suddenly, all sound melts into one loud gasp rippling around me like a wave of audible despair.

Eliab grabs my shoulder and points off to my left. I turn my head, and my heart stops. All the fight drains out of my bones in one cruel instant. The boiling rage evaporates, and fear rushes into me like a cold wind.

"The rumors are true!" Eliab whispers incredulously.

There in the valley, between the lines, is a mountainous beast of a man. I've never seen anyone like him. He is gigantic. The Philistines are shouting and jumping around as if they've already won the war. Not long ago they had suffered a humiliating defeat at the hands of Saul and the forces of Israel. Now they've regrouped. Now they have come back with their secret weapon. Who knew that giants still existed?

"Goliath of Gath! Goliath of Gath!" The Philistines chant their hero's name at the top of their lungs.

Goliath towers above us. I feel like a grasshopper looking up at him, and I am not even near him. How can we possibly fight them if they have men like that? My weapons now look useless and pathetic. I look around at my fellow Israelites, and they are tiny and insignificant. The fear in their eyes and the doubt that hangs in the air around us is crushingly terrifying. I want to sink down into the ground and die.

I can't keep my eyes off of the massive warrior. I am fixated by his awful size and his piercing eyes. His laughter echoes across the valley like human thunder, and we draw back in terror. A few Israelites back away and run from the battle line in cowardly fear. I almost feel like joining them. This is hopeless. Why did I bother training and planning for war? What good am I against a warrior like this?

All of a sudden, he opens his mouth to speak. "Why come out and line up for battle?" His voice booms across the valley. I fear the rocks on the hills might shake loose at the sound.

He laughs, cruel, careless laughter. The sneer in his voice is thick. "Am I not a Philistine, and are you not servants of Saul?" He spits Saul's name as if it has a sour taste. "Come on! Choose a man to come down here. *If* he is able to fight and kill *me*, we'll be your slaves!" He bows dramatically. "But if I kill him, you'll be ours!"

I hear footsteps and turn around just in time to see more of our men fleeing into the hills behind, trickling away from this fearsome sight. There is a deathly chill that fills my throat and ices my hands. I am petrified. How can *anyone* fight this giant?

His helmet is gleaming bronze. His coat of armor looks impenetrable. It is made out of bronze scales and probably weighs as much as I do with my armor on! Even his lower legs are protected by bronze armor. The tip of his spear is iron—that fearsome, secret metal that only the Philistines can make—and it is the size of a small boulder. One blow and it is certain death.

There is an intense pause. His fierce eyes sweep across the ranks of Israel. His glare seems to pick out every single soldier and slice through any confidence he might have left.

His voice shatters the stillness again. "Today I *defy* the ranks of Israel! Send a man over, and let's fight each other!" A bloodthirsty thrill laces his words. Killing is Goliath's business, and he's a professional. His muscles bulge beneath his armor as he stands still for a moment surveying us with a haughty look.

His words sink like cold stones in our hearts. We stare at him in awestruck agony. He resumes taunting us, each insult more vehement than the last. Finally, he settles down to wait and see if we send anyone out to challenge him.

I stand paralyzed, staring out at the mass of Philistines across the valley and the towering giant who stands before their ranks.

"We are finished. We don't have a chance," Eliab says, gaping ahead with empty eyes.

I nod, looking around at the dazed faces full of fear and despair. We were not ready for this. I had been ready to fight. Now I am ready to run. What's the use?

I look toward Adnah off to my right, his sword dangling point-first into the ground. The same stunned expression fills his eyes. My heart sinks even further into despair. If a seasoned soldier like Adnah is afraid, what hope do any of us have?

I take a few steps closer to him and venture a conversation. "Adnah?"

"Not now, Benaiah." His deep voice trembles. His lips move beneath his beard, but no sound comes out. I realize that he's mumbling a prayer.

I turn back and look across the valley. Is any Israelite answering the summons? I can hear the laughter and jeers echoing across the distance. The Philistines are having their fun, enjoying their victory before the battle has even begun.

I long for Berechiah to be here to steady my nerves. Instead, doubts and insecurities flood my brain. How quickly things turn around.

We're at a stalemate. The sun rises, hot in the sky. The day wears on. No one goes forward. Goliath's challenge hangs in the air like a crack of lightning. The air is still charged with energy, and fear burns through us all.

When night falls, we pitch camp dejectedly, talking in low mumbles and whispers as if the Philistines will hear us. I do not envy the sentinels on guard duty tonight, staring out into the inky blackness, ever imagining the shape of a giant emerging from the gloom.

When I finally fall asleep, the Philistine giant fills my dreams. I am alone in thick hanging fog, lost in the strange light of early morning. A booming voice explodes off to my right, so close that it shakes my body from the inside. I see nothing. My eyes desperately strain into the eerie haze. I notch an arrow and hold my bow at the ready, terror ripping through my body. Suddenly, the bow snaps in my hand and falls useless to the ground. The voice explodes again, causing me to stumble backward and claw at the ground beneath me. I struggle to my feet and run for my life. As I run blindly, I dig at my belt trying to find my dagger, until suddenly I slam into a stone wall and slump to the ground. I look up and find myself staring into the gleaming, mocking eyes of the Philistine. I feel like I am the tiny child at Piram's mercy again. I gasp out soundless cries. He smiles and raises his spear, its enormous, lethal point hovering over my heart. I close my eyes and scream.

I wake, my body drenched in sweat. I've rolled off of my sleeping mat and lie in the gravel and dust. I rest here for a while with my chest heaving, my mind still reeling from the images that have just vanished. It all seems so real. Am I dead? Where is Berechiah? Did I really cry out? A few moments pass. I sit up, head pounding. I spend the rest of the night trying in vain to go back to sleep.

Finally the morning light peeks above the hills. The camp stirs to life. We are all somber, alert, and afraid.

Suddenly, we're startled by that awful, thundering voice. "Up, up, children of Israel! Is there a single man among you, or have you all become little girls?" He laughs mercilessly. "Who wants to sleep the sleep of death? Who will come and fight me?"

The Philistine's voice sends another wave of fear through us as his words torture our ears. I can feel the army around me wilt and wither. We stare at each other, eyes alive with panic, as the giant Goliath of Gath continues his taunts. He strides back and forth, spewing endless words of hate and derision.

The days pass, each one drearier than the last. Every day, Goliath's words echo across the divide. Morning and evening, Goliath strides forth and challenges us. Anxiety reigns over our army. Many soldiers have deserted. Some were successful in their escape, and others were caught and executed for their treason. The thought of escape tempts us all. Why stay here? Eventually the Philistines will kill us or make us their slaves.

King Saul has offered great rewards for the man brave enough to challenge Goliath: abundant wealth, the king's daughter in marriage, and tax exemption in Israel. Every day, the king sends messengers around the camp to remind us of his offers. Several men, tempted by the rewards, have come forward to fight Goliath, but as soon as Goliath appears, they instantly lose their courage and refuse to go through with it.

Israel has become a laughing-stock, and I am convinced now more than ever that Yahweh is a weak god. Dagon must be stronger. We are small and terrified because Yahweh is small and terrified. He cannot defend us—or worse, he simply does not care. Putting trust in only one god doesn't seem to do any good, anyway. It has been a long time since I have offered any sacrifices, but perhaps now is a good time to sacrifice to several gods. Maybe one of them could help.

Several soldiers want to go get the ark and bring it into battle with us, convinced that if we have the ark, we will enjoy victory. If ever there is a time to bring Yahweh into battle with us, it is now. Many others strongly disagree. We tried that before, and the Philistines stole the ark and defeated us.

Twenty days pass, each a miserable copy of the last. Every day we wake up, reluctantly draw up for battle, and spend the day waiting for the giant to come forward and threaten us. He does this at least twice a day, yet we are still not used to seeing him. Our fear feels fresh every time. Ramel says that if we don't find a man brave enough to fight this giant, our only hope is that they abandon this strategy and agree to fight a regular battle with all our forces. Perhaps they don't want to risk this, though, since we defeated them at Micmash and overpowered their raiders in the north.

Another week passes, and something finally breaks the mo-
notony. Jorman arrives all the way from Pirathon to check on
his sons and bring supplies. Since his last visit, there have been
many casualties, including his nephew who died in the same
battle that claimed Berechiah's life. Jorman looks older and
wearier than when I saw him last. I stand nearby, eager to hear
any news from home. I need to ask him about Hannah and my
mother, but I'm not sure he'll talk to me. I don't know him that
well, and almost everyone in Pirathon has a bad opinion of me.

I am surprised when Jorman calls my name and asks me to
come over.

He hands me a satchel of parched grain and some dried
fruit. "From Berechiah's father," he says. His eyes are sad and
concerned.

I am moved by the thought of Berechiah's family reaching
out to me. "Thank him for me, Jorman."

He nods.

My supplies have really been running low. The military has
provided some rations for us, but usually by forcing several villages nearby to supply our needs. We have been in this place far
too long. Most of the army also receives help from back home,
but for me, this is rare. I must make do with what the army gives
me and what I'm able to find on my own.

"Jorman? How is my mother? How is Hannah?" I'm suddenly
desperate for news of them. I haven't had much time to worry
about them, but now that all I've been doing is sitting in fear, I
haven't been able to stop thinking about them and wondering
how they are doing.

Jorman pauses, a bit unsure of himself, and his eyes are
heavy with news. "Your mother, Benaiah, she...she has gone to
her fathers."

"What?" I cry in disbelief. I am shattered.

"Piram hurt her badly." Jorman shakes his head. "She hung on for a long time, but her wounds were too much for her."

I am speechless with pain, and Jorman can read it all over my face. He looks down at his feet for a moment.

"I'm sorry, Benaiah—truly I am. No one deserves to lose their mother like that."

"What about Piram? Has he been stoned to death?"

"He's run off. No one has seen him. No one can find him."

My head is spinning, and my bones grow heavy with despair. "I should have been there!" The words explode out of me. "Why did I leave? I could have… I should have…"

Jorman reaches out and grabs my shoulder. He looks me in the eye. "We all should have done more. There were many rumors about Piram—we just never interfered. It was a mistake."

His words barely make it through my ears. I feel so incredibly numb and wounded. My mother! I can't believe she's dead. She trusted Yahweh completely, just like Berechiah did, and Yahweh let *her* die too! What kind of god would let that happen?

I spend the day in a stupor, and when night falls, the weight of the pain collapses all of the resolve I have to hold myself together. I weep as I have never wept before. Thankfully, the other soldiers in the tent leave me alone and let me mourn. Guilt washes over me in merciless waves. *Why? Why did I ever leave? I could have protected her! I failed her when she needed me most.*

38

BENAIAH

It has now been forty days. Forty long days of dreary nothing. The inactivity has been pure torture for me. All I do is think of my mother's death and hate myself for leaving her. I swing back and forth between intense sadness and bitter blasts of rage. If I ever see Piram again, he will wish he was never born. His face haunts my nights. Sometimes he and Goliath are together in my dreams, and I am helpless and afraid. Other times I dream of my revenge on him. I make him hurt the way he made my mother hurt.

More than anything, I want to abandon this empty battle and head back to Pirathon. I need to see Hannah again. I need to mourn properly for my mother. I need to find Piram and plant his body under a pile of rocks. Maybe some of the villagers will even help me avenge my mother's death. The thought surprises me. I was so ready to be free of Pirathon and become a soldier, but now, strangely, I long to see that collection of mud brick homes again, hear the children playing in the street, and watch the sun cast shadows along the village wall.

The day after I heard of my mother's death, I asked Ramel for permission to go, but he wouldn't allow it.

"Usually I'd let you go for something like this, but I can't," he said. "This standoff won't last forever. We'll need you soon enough! You've become an excellent soldier—one of the best fighters in my unit. We've lost so many men as it is, and this battle is vital to the safety of our nation!"

I responded with resentment. "What good am I? All we do is sit around, waiting for the next round of fear! I'd rather die than sit here."

"Benaiah!" His voice was sharper than I expected. "I know you are in pain, and I feel especially indebted to you after you saved my life. But if you even think about abandoning us now, you'll regret it the rest of your life. Believe me!"

His words have hung in my heart ever since. There's much that I regret in my life, and leaving the army would just add to those regrets. I decided to stay, but every day I feel the pull to leave.

The morning drags on, just like all the mornings before. I sit with Eliab and his brothers, Abinidab and Shammah. We glumly sharpen our knives and swords for the hundredth time, no one saying a word. We know it is almost that time again—time to muster whatever courage we have and line up for battle, hoping against all hope that today will be different from every other day and we will charge across the valley to meet the Philistines in open battle. We know this won't be the case, though. We know that Goliath will saunter out before their lines yet again, goading us with insults and trying to get under the skin of just one hot-headed soldier who might rush out to fight before he knows what he's doing. I shake my head and Eliab sighs in frustration as we prepare for the inevitable.

Suddenly, Ramel stands near. "Form your battle lines. Up! Get up! Perhaps today's the day!"

I roll my eyes. Ramel says this every day, and I'm so sick of hearing it. He is desperately trying to muster our courage and erase the boredom, despair, and helplessness that have settled on us, but it never seems to work. Reluctantly, we draw up our battle lines and raise the war cry—a pathetic ritual which none of us have the heart for anymore, yet shouting it out does serve as one of the only releases for our pent-up tension. The shout echoes and reverberates among the rocks and down the valley and then fades in the distance, sounding tinny and small. We hear the Philistines laughing on the other side when it is done.

As we stand ready in our battle positions, Eliab, Shammah, and I are lined up next to each other, poised and on edge. Abdon and Meshumi are next to us on our left, and Abinidab is on the other side of them, near Ramel and Saba. Suddenly, we hear footsteps on the path behind us. I swing my head around and see a young man coming up the path. He looks just a few years too young to be in the army. I watch, half aware, as he goes over by Abinidab and begins talking to him. Abinidab turns and embraces him.

My attention is ripped away by the sound of the Philistines' roar as their massive champion strolls out between the lines. His familiar voice echoes across the valley, and my familiar pang of fear echoes through my chest. His neck is like the solid trunk of a tree, and I can almost see the veins jumping out of it as he brandishes his weapons and violently curses Yahweh. His muscles bulge with every movement. More of our men flee for the hills. I am surprised we have any soldiers left.

I look back and see the young man near Abinidab. It will be the first time he's seen the giant, and I'm curious how he'll react. His face is hard and rigid with rage. He looks intently across the field at Goliath and spits into the dust. Perhaps it is boyish pride or foolish immaturity, but he does not look afraid—he looks furious. I'm curious to find out more about him. There's something in the way he holds himself that intrigues me. I can't quite put my finger on it.

Eliab sees the boy, and a gasp of annoyance escapes him. "Little fool!" he mutters.

"Who is that?" I ask.

"It's my little brother, David. What on earth is he doing here?" He heads down the path, and I follow closely behind.

As we come closer, I hear David's voice rise in anger as he talks with Abdon and Meshumi. "Who does he think he is anyway, this uncircumcised Philistine dog, that he should defy the armies of the only real God?" Concern and indignation radiate out of his face.

We reach David, and Eliab explodes in anger. "What are you doing here?"

David looks up, surprised at the sudden vehemence. I wonder how long it has been since they have seen each other.

"Who's watching Father's sheep out in the desert? You're so conceited! You just wanted to watch a battle! Have you seen enough yet?" He spits on the ground at David's feet. "This is men's work! Go back to your sheep where you belong!"

"What have I done?" David says, his voice shockingly quiet and restrained. I am surprised by how mature he sounds compared to his brother. "Can't I even speak?" he asks with a quizzical look. He then turns away without another word.

Eliab scowls. "That boy is nothing but trouble."

39

SERVANT OF SAUL

His booming voice fills the tent yet again. Even though the monster Goliath is halfway across this cursed valley, he sounds like he's right outside. I still cannot believe that we've been waiting here for forty days—forty endless, dreary days without a single reason for hope. I am utterly annoyed today.

The Israelites let out their war cry a few moments ago, and now they stand in line for battle, trembling at the giant's voice as it whips the fight out of them for the eightieth time. Morning and evening for the past forty days they have heard his challenge, and every day they have quaked in fear and frustration. Not to say that I haven't been feeling the same fear. I wouldn't fight that mammoth man for five years of my salary. It would be utterly suicidal.

King Saul, on the other hand, is the savior of our nation—a head taller than anyone I've ever known, strong as an ox, and quick on his feet. From a distance, I've watched him swing his sword with such brute force and precision that I believe he could chop an arrow in half mid-flight. His spear is a terror to be reckoned with. Yet here he sits doing absolutely nothing as the troops stand in line for battle. He doesn't even bother to get dressed for battle anymore! He sits in complete numbness and confusion, absolutely incapacitated by this turn of events in his battle plans.

A few moments pass, and General Abner steps into the tent. Abner is another amazing warrior who has certainly proved his strength on a thousand battlefields. Why doesn't he just challenge this giant and get it over with? And my dark thoughts roll on. I take a deep breath, knowing that it does no good to worry about this. Let the king do as he will. My job is just to make sure he has his supplies in order and everything is polished and ready in case he ever decides to spring into action.

Yes, during the first few days of this campaign I was scared out of my wits as well. I couldn't believe that men the size of Goliath even existed. He looked like a war god come to earth to destroy us all! At that point I knew we had little hope of winning as long as they had men like that on their side. Today, I am still in awe of his sheer size and the power that emanates out of him. But forty days? This could go on forever! I would almost prefer being their slave over sitting here and waiting for something— *anything*—to happen.

The king's tired voice interrupts my thoughts. "Abner, how is it with the men?"

He sighs, frustrated. "The same. I've been up and down our lines over and over again. Everyone in the army knows the rewards that you've offered. I'm at my wits' end. Fear has paralyzed us all. No one will fight him!"

I turn away and roll my eyes so they don't see. Here are the best two fighters in all of Israel talking like this. It is unreal to me. If only the king's son Jonathan was here! He has the heart of a lion and strength to go with it. He's been the national hero before. We can use him here now!

I sent a messenger to Gibeah a few days ago, without the king's knowledge, asking Jonathan to come and help us. It was a personal message from me describing our situation, so I don't know if he'll come. I hope the king does not get angry when he finds out. I just wonder why Saul couldn't have left someone else in charge back home in Gibeah. If King Saul won't fight Goliath, I know Prince Jonathan will do it.

Saul continues. "They need to give up this strategy so we can fight a normal battle, but they're showing no signs of backing down. Unless we find a suitable challenger, we'll have to hold our lines and wait for them to change tactics."

Abner paces back and forth. "The men are terrified. It's shameful! We can't let it go on. We *must* find someone who can meet this challenge!"

I hear Hoshan's voice just outside the tent asking permission to enter. The guard lets him through.

He ventures a tentative step into the tent. "Your Majesty, I hope I'm not disturbing you."

"What is it?"

"Pardon me, Your Majesty, but one of your armor-bearers is going throughout the camp asking about the Philistine and the reward for fighting him."

"One of my armor-bearers?" A dark, puzzled look clouds the king's face. "Why isn't he training or doing his duty around camp?"

"It is David, the boy from Bethlehem. You have a special arrangement with him, remember?"

"David?" Saul says, obviously still baffled.

"He's the harp player from Bethlehem. You took an interest in him and made him an armor-bearer. He's the one who goes back and forth between your court and his father's house in Bethlehem."

"Oh, yes…that's right. Well, what brings him to the battle-front today? Usually he only comes when I call for him at the palace."

"He was bringing supplies to his brothers who are in the army."

"I see. Well, go get him and bring him here. I would enjoy talking with him, especially if he is interested in what is going on here. I long for a fresh perspective, and a little harp music would be nice too."

Hoshan bows to the king and departs from the tent.

Harp music? I almost swallow my tongue. Why not? Let's play the harp! That sounds like fun! Maybe we could also do a little dance while Goliath chops off our heads!

Several moments later, Hoshan reappears with the boy. He looks a little older than the last time we had him bring his harp to court. He is lithe and strong, but so young. Maybe in a few years he'll be a proper armor-bearer for the king, but I don't think he's fit for the job yet. He certainly isn't dressed appropriately for court today— his robes are the plain robes of a common shepherd, and he's still dirty from the road! I wish Hoshan would have at least had him clean up before seeing the king!

He bows low to the king, and the king nods in return.

"Well, David, you've seen our predicament. What do you think?"

"Why are the men so afraid? No one should lose heart on account of this Philistine; your servant will go and fight him."

Initially, I think he's talking about me, and I almost choke in shock! When I realize he's offering to fight the giant himself, I fight the urge to laugh out loud.

Saul looks him over. "You can't go and fight this Philistine; you're only a boy! He's been a fighting man from his youth—long before you were born."

But the boy replies, "Your servant has been taking care of his father's sheep. When a lion or a bear came and carried off a sheep from the flock, I went after it, attacked it, and rescued the sheep from its mouth. When it turned on me, I grabbed a hold of it by its hair and beat it to death. I've killed both lions and bears. This uncircumcised Philistine will be no different from one of them, because he has defied the armies of the only real God. Yahweh rescued me from the paw of the lion and the paw of the bear. He'll rescue me from this Philistine too."

I can tell that his answer has impressed Saul. He looks at David as if seeing him for the first time. He plies him with questions, and David answers with dignity and confidence. There is something strong about the boy, some indomitable spirit in him that defies identification. He is special, but he is so very young. Saul is deep in thought, staring again at David.

Suddenly, his expression changes—he's made up his mind. "Go, and Yahweh be with you."

Panic erases my every thought. I can't believe it! Is he joking? To entrust the entire future of our army and nation to a young shepherd boy is certainly an act of insanity. Perhaps the evil spirit is in him again! I stare dumbfounded. No harp music can drive this fear from my heart.

I walk out of the tent in a daze. *Maybe I'm dreaming. Maybe this isn't real.* I look around and find myself standing next to a cooking fire. *There's only one way to find out.* I take hold of one of the hot stones at the edge of the fire. Pain sears through my hand, and I cry out. Quickly, I find some water nearby and douse my hand in it. As I look at my red, blistering hand that is festering in pain, I realize that this is definitely not a dream. David will fight Goliath, Goliath will kill him, and all of Israel's armies will become slaves to the Philistines!

Someone coughs uncomfortably, and I look up to see several cooks staring at me like I've gone completely mad. I feel the heat rising on my face.

"Carry on! Carry on! The fire's hot—definitely hot enough." I mumble some more nonsense under my breath and turn back to go to the tent, completely embarrassed.

I enter the tent just in time to hear Saul calling my name.

"Where did you go?" Saul shouts with impatience.

"I'm sorry, Your Majesty. I...I just had to step out to relieve myself." I feel my face on fire with shame. I've never said that to the king before.

"I need my best armor immediately!"

My humiliation disappears, and my heart soars with pride. He's going to fight the Philistine! The arrival of this silly shepherd boy must have stirred something in him again! Oh how God works in mysterious ways! A shepherd boy was all it took to push him in the right direction!

"Yes, Your Majesty, of course! With pleasure!" I hustle back into the supply tent that contains the king's personal armory. I select his best armor—his favorite bronze helmet and the gleaming hilted sword he plundered from the king of the Amalekites a while back. Hoshan comes to help me carry it all back to the king's tent.

I hold the suit of armor up, waiting for the king to step into it. Saul gestures to David and says, "Dress him in my armor!"

"Your Majesty?" I gape at him like a dumb sheep.

"You heard me! Dress him in my armor!"

Disappointment floods my heart. I'm back in the nightmare again!

Reluctantly, Hoshan and I begin to put the armor on the boy. We put the king's tunic on him and then the coat of armor that is obviously too big for him. Next, we place the bronze helmet on his head. It drops down over his eyes, and he staggers under the sudden weight of it. David fastens the king's sword over the tunic and then tries to walk around. He can barely move!

"Your Majesty...I...I'm not sure—" I start to say.

David interrupts me. "Your Majesty, thank you, but I can't go in these—I'm not used to them. If I am to fight him, I need to feel comfortable. I need to use what I've brought."

The king lets out a sigh, but nods his head. Hoshan and I help David take the heavy armor off.

"I can go to the armory tent and find the boy some better fitting armor if you would like, Your Majesty," I offer.

David shakes his head. "No, I have a better idea." He bows to the king. "With your permission, I need to go and make a few preparations. Then I will return."

The king nods and David exits the tent.

I am still reeling inside, and I'm beside myself in fear and anger. I simply cannot believe this. We've found the youngest and least experienced challenger, and to top it off, he's not even in the army! Does anyone else see how stupid this is? And the king is letting this happen! I can hardly contain myself. I need to leave the tent. I ask the king's permission, and I step out into the fresh air.

I do the only thing I can do—I pray. My words tumble out in frustrated desperation. "Yahweh, rescue us from this giant. Give this boy the victory. Work a miracle for your people!"

40

BENAIAH

The sun beats down on us in the afternoon. We have done our best to find or create shady places where we can rest and yet still see into the valley. Several soldiers are always on guard, watching in case the Philistines suddenly change tactics and surge across the gap. The time is drawing near. Nervous, edgy fear is rising in my heart again. I feel like throwing up. I don't want to see Goliath.

I overhear two soldiers from another unit talking excitedly.

"Who could it be?"

"I just can't believe someone is actually going to do it."

"Did you hear when?"

"No—but who is brave enough to face that giant? Shamha? Almon?"

"Maybe Jonathan has arrived from Gibeah!"

"Yes, I bet that's it! Or maybe it's King Saul! Maybe he's been training and getting ready all this time, coming up with a strategy!"

My curiosity overcomes me, and I can't help but interrupt. "Has someone offered to fight Goliath?"

"Yes! At least that's what I heard from Grabiah who heard it from Zabbin who heard it from someone close to the king!"

"We don't know who it is?"

"No, but I can't wait to find out!"

"I hope they have a good plan. We could lose our entire nation in a matter of hours if he fails!" "I know. We could be their slaves by tonight!"

We fall silent at the somber thought. It takes the edge off of our eager excitement.

"Do you think it is King Saul?" I say, somewhat to myself. "What if Goliath kills him? That would devastate our nation!"

"Who needs a king, though, if we're all slaves? If our champion loses, Saul's as good as dead anyway. He'll have to run for his life or die trying to fight them off when they claim their victory."

Our conversation is cut short as we are summoned to our battle lines. It's time again to see the monster and hear his challenge. We take up positions and watch as mighty Goliath strides across the divide with violence seeping from his eyes. Again, he looks bigger than ever.

He shouts his taunts—the same taunts we've heard over and over again for the past forty days. As he curses Yahweh, I sniff in disdain. I'm starting to agree with him about this god! If Yahweh is so strong, as Berechiah and others have claimed, he must be deaf to put up with this for so long. Obviously, he is a pathetic god. I've given up on him. The last forty days have confirmed my feelings. There are much more powerful gods than Yahweh.

A movement off to my left, down on the far side of our lines, catches my eye. I crane my neck to see. A collective gasp of shock goes up from our forces. I struggle to see over the heads of the other soldiers. Finally, I catch a glimpse. Someone is coming out from our lines. Someone is actually going out to meet the giant!

"Who is that?" I let the question hang in the air, not expecting an answer.

He looks small, unimpressive, and so very young.

"He isn't even wearing any armor!" someone gasps out.

I get a better look, and my eyes stretch wide in shock and dismay. Just a boy! All he carries is a mere staff—the kind any shepherd boy might carry. I shake my head, trying to clear it. This must be a bad dream. I hear an angry shout off to my right, and I look to see Eliab roaring in rage.

"What does he think he's doing? When father hears about this, it'll bring his grey head down into the grave! Stupid, headstrong, arrogant, conceited little idiot! Somebody needs to drag him back here right now! I'll tear him from limb to limb!"

It puzzles me at first why Eliab is so worked up until suddenly I realize who it is. The boy in the field is David, Eliab's little brother!

My heart turns sick, like it has filled with rancid oil. *David?* That young boy that was here talking with us this morning? *David?* My mind can't begin to grasp the thought. I shoot a stunned look at several faces around me. They all look as upset and confused as I do. What is going on? Who would allow that boy to go out there now? Who would send a foolish shepherd boy to go and fight a mighty warrior, let alone the mightiest warrior any of us has ever seen? This is absolutely insane!

There's no confident shout from our lines as the boy walks out—just a deathly silence. Doom hangs in the air.

I hear my fellow soldiers whispering in terror and shock.

"A young boy?"

"We're doomed!"

"Who does he think he is?"

"He's not even a soldier!"

"Did King Saul approve this? Does he even know this is happening?"

"Someone *do* something! Go get him and bring him back before Goliath sees him!"

David's brothers are frantic. Eliab is pacing back and forth, grumbling about how he wants to knock some sense into David.

Abinidab tries to charge out to David to protect him, but several men hold him back. "Think of our father, David! Don't do this foolish thing!" he shouts. "What will Father do when you die?" His words do nothing to deter his brother.

Shammah's face is white with fear. He stands in shock, his spear hanging down by his side, its point brushing the dust. He says nothing. He simply stares as David strides confidently out to meet the massive Philistine.

We hold our breath. The Philistine stops sauntering back and forth as he sees movement from our lines. His shield bearer stops as well, setting his massive shield on the ground and peering around it to see why Goliath has stopped.

As Goliath realizes that someone is approaching him, he starts moving across the field toward David, his armor-bearer going on before him. We see him squint and then stop again as he sees his challenger. Suddenly, angry, triumphant laughter booms from deep in his throat. His surprise and disdain are obvious.

Our faces grow hot with embarrassment. We're fools. We're professional soldiers, and we send a shepherd boy out to battle their champion. We send a shepherd boy to prove that our God is stronger than Dagon and their hateful gods. We send a shepherd boy to fight our fight for us. What shame! I shake my head in disbelief. I should be out there instead of him. He has a family—I do not. He has a future—I do not. What has been holding me back? Why am I so afraid? I have nothing to lose. I might as well sacrifice myself on this giant's sword instead of this poor young shepherd boy. I am so shocked that King Saul is letting this happen! What is he thinking?

Goliath's laughter fades. His voice booms, and his words cut right through us. "What is this? A boy? You're attacking me with a *stick*? Do you think I'm a dog?"

He is getting furious. He wants a real fight. He's been primed for a fight for forty days. Disappointment and rage pulse through him. We haven't even seen him angry yet. The sight of it makes us all shudder in fear. Grown men are cringing at the sound of his roar as he curses David with awful, ear-shattering words, invoking the name of his god Dagon with blistering curses against David and Yahweh. David stands there unmoved. He holds his head high and stares straight at Goliath. He doesn't even flinch. I am spellbound by the sight. My eyes fix on him, and my heart slows its frantic beat. His calm helps to make me calm. His bravery stirs some small bravery in me.

"Come here, little lamb!" the Philistine roars at him. "I'll feed your body to the birds and the wild animals!"

We hear David's voice, a much smaller sound than Goliath's, yet strong and clear. "You come against me with sword and spear and javelin, but I come against you in the name of Yahweh— Lord of all and the God of Israel's army. You've insulted him!"

Goliath snorts loudly across the field. "Your god is pathetic. He sends a boy to do a man's work!"

David ignores him and continues clearly and confidently, as if he's discussing an outcome that's already been determined. "This day Yahweh will hand you over to me, and I'll strike you down and cut off your head."

Goliath's eyes go wide with exaggerated mock fear, and he turns to the Philistine ranks. "Stop! You're scaring me to death! What? You're going to cut off my head with a stick? That's going to hurt so much!"

The Philistines roar with laughter. My heart is beating in my throat, and my hands are slick with sweat.

When the laughter dies down, David breaks the silence again with a loud yet calm voice. "Today I will give the carcasses of the Philistine army to the birds and the wild animals, and the whole world will know that there is a mighty God in Israel. Everyone watching here today will see that Yahweh does not need swords or spears to rescue his people. He determines every battle's outcome! He will give all of you into our hands."

Again, laughter echoes down the ranks of Philistine warriors.

Goliath is done playing around. He turns to David and shouts one more time. "Let's see if your god can save you from *this*!"

He brandishes his giant spear, and an enormous hair-raising battle cry erupts from his throat. It sounds like a thousand lions roaring together. We all cringe as he strides forward with the confidence of a warrior who specializes in murder and mayhem, his body advancing with perfectly fluid and efficient movements. He charges quickly for a man so large and so heavily armed. My eyes stretch wide. My breath stops. All I hear is the rhythmic pound of my panicking heart. David is going to die in front of our eyes! We're all going to die in a matter of moments!

I blink, not believing my eyes, as I see David begin to run, not away from, but *toward* the monstrous warrior. He holds his staff at the ready as he runs, but just as he gets into range, he drops it. I gasp in surprise. He continues to run full tilt—*unarmed*?

He reaches into a bag that hangs across his chest, pulls out a large, smooth stone, and notches it into a sling he's been hiding in his hand. As he runs, he whips the sling around above his head—once, twice, three times it spins. Goliath slows, momentarily hesitating, slightly unsure, squinting to see what David is doing.

David releases the stone, powering it forward with all of his momentum, his hand dipping down and following through with the motion. The stone whirrs in the air—it flies straight at Goliath! All of us are entranced. It sails through the air with incredible force and strikes the giant right on his forehead! The sound is like the dull thud of an ax smacking against a tree. The stone disappears in a spray of blood.

The giant man reels, roaring out in surprise and pain. He crashes facedown into the ground. A plume of dust rises up. His massive spear clatters harmlessly in the dirt. The mighty warrior is suddenly a useless heap of muscle.

It's over as fast is it began. I stand frozen in place as my brain tries to grasp the scene.

David doesn't miss a stride. His feet slap the ground as he runs forward. When he gets to the giant's side, he yanks Goliath's sword out of its scabbard. He swings it high above his head and lets it fall. Goliath's massive head rolls free, and his blood is an angry red river gushing over the thirsty dust.

A surprised hush falls over the entire battlefield. We stare, unable to comprehend what has just happened. After a moment, a surprised shout erupts somewhere behind me, and soon more men join in, leaping and yelling in incredulous glee.

We look up from the fallen giant. The entire Philistine battle line stands in total shock, gaping blankly. Suddenly, several of them turn and run. Their line begins to fray, and in no time the whole mass is melting away. All the Philistines are running in full-fledged fear.

Ramel shouts, "Let's go, men! Come on! Now's our chance! Charge their lines!"

We surge forward, several men strapping on their swords at the last minute, unprepared for the sudden turn of events.

A cool wind begins to blow, and the late lingering sun shines down. We charge forward after the fleeing Philistines. I take aim and let a few arrows fly as soon as I am in range. Philistines pitch headfirst into the hard ground. It's almost too easy! They are running as fast as they can, armor clattering, and many of them even drop their weapons to lighten their load as they run. We draw close, some try to turn and raise a spear or sword at us, only to be struck down almost immediately. By evening, Philistine bodies lay grisly and lifeless all along the Shaaraim road to Gath and Ekron.

When darkness falls, we make our way back and plunder food from their abandoned camp. Joy surges through us like never before as we talk about the day's events. We eat like kings, drinking their best wine and feasting on roasted goat meat, cheese, and bread. Victory has never tasted so sweet!

41

BENAIAH

E liab's voice explodes outside the tent, shattering my
sleep.

"You could have been killed! Just because the old prophet Samuel anointed you doesn't make you invincible! You were
testing God. I've never seen such stupid pride!"

David's voice answers, "It wasn't pride that sent me out
there—Yahweh did."

My head still heavy with sleep, I get up and walk outside the
tent into the dim light of early morning. I rub my eyes and see
Eliab and David standing near the fire. They are going to wake
up the whole camp!

Eliab is glaring at the boy. "There you go again. You are not
as special as you think! You are the youngest. Your place is at
home tending sheep, not here on the field of battle."

David shakes his head sadly. "When will you understand,
Eliab? I am not against you. I am not trying to outshine you. I
am simply doing what Yahweh has put in front of me to do! It

has nothing to do with you. Why didn't you fight the giant, if you wanted to so badly? You had forty days to do it!"

I fear that Eliab will strangle the boy. By the look of hatred on his face, he seems ready to strike him. Eliab appears to be the only one who isn't happy about what David has done.

"Eliab," I say, "give the boy a break. What's done is done. He won a great victory for Israel. Why argue anymore?"

Eliab shoots me an ugly look.

I just shake my head. "Why are you so angry?"

Eliab turns toward David and spits. "I'm done with this conversation. I'm glad we won the victory yesterday, but I'm not happy with you!" He stalks off.

David watches him walk off with a sad look on his face. "Can you believe we used to be close?" he says, gesturing in the direction of his brother.

"That surprises me."

"I'm sure you heard him mention how the prophet Samuel anointed me…"

"Yes, I was wondering what that meant."

David turns to look at me. "I'm not fully sure, myself. It isn't something Father wants us talking about and spreading around. He fears King Saul will be angry if he hears. Can you not mention it to anyone?"

"Your secret is safe with me. It's a great honor to be anointed by a prophet, though. Yahweh's favor must rest on you."

"I suppose it does. But no more than his favor rests on any of us."

I frown. Yahweh's favor certainly does not rest on me. "There have been rumors that King Saul is no longer in favor with Yahweh. Some deny it, of course. If the prophet anointed you, I can see how the king might be agitated."

David nods his head. "Eliab is agitated enough for everyone else. He's been angry with me ever since. He's the oldest and thought for sure the prophet would anoint him. He never expected it to be me, and now he resents me." David sits down on a stone near the fire and prods it with a stick.

I draw close to the fire and to David. "I'm Benaiah."

"Benaiah—," he says thoughtfully, "—built by Yahweh. You have a good name!"

I laugh bitterly. "Sometimes I think my name should mean 'destroyed by Yahweh' instead. My life has been anything but built by him." I sit down across from him and watch the sparks fly up between us.

He stops poking at the fire and looks right at me. "I am sure that's not true." His voice is kind and incredibly confident.

I sigh and look down at my feet. "You wouldn't understand."

"Maybe not, but I do know Yahweh. If he can use me, he can use anyone. Look at me! Eliab is right—I'm nothing special. I'm just a shepherd boy, the youngest in my family, and yet Yahweh sent the great prophet Samuel to anoint me. Yahweh sent me to kill Goliath and used me to defeat the Philistines, and he's been with me the whole time. I am so amazed by it all."

I look up at David, filled with pain and questions. Something about this boy has disarmed me, and I suddenly start spilling out my bitter thoughts. "What can Yahweh do for me? I'm not even a full-blooded Israelite! My mother was abused by the Philistines—half my blood comes from our enemies! Can Yahweh really be my god? Why did he kill my best friend? Why did he desert my mother, leaving her in the murderous hands of my stepfather? Why am I treated like an outcast in my own village? He has never shown his love to me. I am cursed!"

I stop myself, suddenly feeling the red rush of embarrassment rising on my face. I'm foolish. I shouldn't be telling him all of this. I have the sudden urge to get up and walk away.

David looks at me. His eyes glow with a kindness and a compassion that I have rarely seen. It transfixes me, and my bitter thoughts subside.

"Yahweh loves you." He says it so simply, as if it's a fact that cannot be questioned.

I just shake my head again.

"He formed you in your mother's womb. He knows everything about you—even your deepest thoughts and flaws—yet his love for you is boundless."

"How can you be so sure? What about all the evil that's happened to me? Yahweh is the god of the Israelites, and I am only part Israelite. How can Yahweh love someone who is not one of his chosen people?"

To my surprise, David smiles. "I have Moabite blood running through my veins."

"What?" The word shoots through my lips. I am shocked.

"My great-grandmother was from Moab. She found love and acceptance with an Israelite man, Boaz. She was poor and humble, and he was rich and influential, yet he loved her and married her, and I am descended from them."

"And still Yahweh favors you?"

"He doesn't favor me any more than he favors you!"

"I thought everyone who wasn't a full-blooded Israelite was probably cursed by him. I've lived my whole life as an outsider."

"No, he doesn't favor me. True, our lives are different—we have different roles to play in God's great plan—but you and I are brothers, chosen by God to be his people. His promise of forgiveness gives us confidence that lasts forever, so we want to honor him with everything we do."

I stare hard into the boy's eyes and see nothing but kindness. I can hardly believe it. Every other time I've mentioned my Philistine blood, people have rejected me or treated me differently. David thinks it is nothing to worry about. I can't believe it!

"What gave you the courage to go and fight Goliath?"

"Yahweh sent me to do it. Any of you could have done it. I am no one special. God does not look at the outward things, like flashy armor and massive swords. He is not impressed by someone's reputation, accomplishments, or wealth. Sure, Goliath was huge, but he was mocking the God who created everything. He was defying God and God's people. He did it for forty days, and no one stopped him."

At the mention of Goliath, my thoughts turn back to him. I see again his immense muscles and weapons. I hear his booming voice. "Everyone was so impressed by his size and strength," I say. "I've fought some fierce battles, but I have to admit, fear overcame me at the sight of him. Everyone assumed it was impossible to fight him." *Yet he fell so quickly in a cloud of dust.*

David nods. "Yes, it looked like it would be impossible. But all along, God saw him as a small, weak, arrogant fool. God gave him forty days to stop his sinful blasphemy, and God used my tongue to tell him the truth and warn him." He leans forward on the stone and looks at me, his gentle eyes catching the reflection of the fire as he continues. "You saw a mighty warrior—brawny, tall, and powerful. God opened my eyes to see him as he actually was—a pathetic fool trying to desecrate God's reputation. God sent me to silence him. He was like a ravenous bear attacking God's flock, and Yahweh anointed me to be the shepherd of his people. He wanted you to see that. He wanted all of Israel to see it." David pauses and looks off toward the hills.

My heart is on fire inside me. I've never met anyone who knows the ways of Yahweh like this young boy does.

His voice seems to come from far away. "The Spirit of God took over me, and I could not help but fight the Philistine. Fear played with my heart as well, but I trusted Yahweh. The battle is always in his hands. It's an honor to be a part of it!"

"You would have liked my friend, Berechiah! He always talked of Yahweh. He worshiped him and often persuaded me to do the same. He is gone now—swallowed by the grave."

"Well then, you shall see him again!"

"What? No one comes back from the grave! He is gone forever, unless I join him in the darkness of the afterlife. I've heard the afterlife is a shadowy place. I hope to find him there, but who knows?"

"Benaiah!"

I look up, and I am again mesmerized by David's shining eyes, so warm, so fired with compassion. My heart slows.

"Those who trust in Yahweh shall live and not die. You will see him again! He lives forever with Yahweh now!"

I almost laugh. "How can you know so much? You are so young! What are you, a prophet?"

He smiles. "No, not a prophet, I have spoken with prophets, though. Yahweh's word is truth. We have all broken Yahweh's rules. We all die because we violate the way he created us to be—perfect like he is. But Yahweh has promised a champion who will come and defeat our sins forever. Trust his love. Trust his promises. Why do you think God asks for all those sacrifices?"

A memory stirs from deep in my mind: my mother's face lighting up as she taught me all the different sacrifices. She taught me many things about Yahweh, but my stepfather always scoffed at his ways and his laws. I turn to David and answer his question. "Supposedly, they take away our guilt and our offenses against Yahweh."

"Right, and God promises that they do, but they also point ahead toward a sacrifice that will take away our sin forever and remove our guilt and make us right with God. Those who trust God's promise will live forever. From what you've said, your friend Berechiah trusted God's promise, and he lives now with God."

Again, I can hardly believe my ears, yet the words he speaks settle in my heart like seeds in freshly tilled soil. They are growing inside me and changing me in ways I cannot put my finger on. My despair is melting away, and confidence is glowing brighter than ever before.

Footsteps fall loud and hard on the path. I glance up. The army messenger is coming into the camp. David and I stand to meet him.

"Benaiah of Pirathon?"

"Yes."

"Commander Ramel sent me to give you a message. Now that the battle's over, he's granted you leave to go home and mourn for your mother. You may leave immediately. You have one month to spend at home, and then you must report back to Gibeah for duty."

My mind struggles to recover and grasp the new information. "Thank you," I finally manage. "I will begin packing."

Turning back to David, I say, "Thank you as well. I have never heard anyone speak of Yahweh the way you do. I long to hear more!"

"I'm sure we'll get the chance. I am one of King Saul's armor-bearers, and after this battle I think I'll be part of the army full-time."

I smile. "I'm sure you will!"

"God's blessings on your journey home!" he says, and he turns to go back to his brothers' tents.

"Thank you! May God bless you as well!"

I turn from David, a little reluctant to leave now that I've found a friend to talk to who knows so much about God. I have so many more questions about Yahweh and his ways, yet Pirathon beckons me. I am eager to be home and mourn for my mother. More than anything, though, I long to see my Hannah. She's all I have left in the world, and I want her as my wife. Hopefully her father will be willing to give her to me in marriage when I return as a soldier. The thought thrills me with a hope I've never dared to feel before.

42

HANNAH

I am surrounded by a flurry of activity, yet I feel abandoned and alone. My chest heaves with panic, and fear's cold grip wraps around my lungs like a snake. It should be a happy day, a day of feasts and joy, but it is far from that. I've lost my will to live. I am resigned to my fate. Mahlo will be my husband. Today is the day of our betrothal. Today we will stand before the elders and pledge our union publicly. It will be official. I am sick with the thought of it.

My Benaiah is dead, and my heart is buried with him on some distant battlefield. My father is thrilled about my betrothal to Mahlo, adding to my uncomfortable depression. My mother is not here to help with my hair and shawl and whisper any rare, soft words of encouragement in my ear. I am alone. Several young women are helping me prepare, but they make me feel more alone. I am not close with them. One of them is sympathetic, and she holds my hand and wipes my tears. Still, I feel so far away, so lost, and so afraid.

I try to argue with my own thoughts. Mahlo is a good man. He is honorable. He has wealth. He is moderately attractive. I still struggle and panic because I feel no connection to him. *Can I trust him? Will he hurt me?* Over and over the questions nag at me.

I know that this is often how it is with marriage—a father chooses a suitable man for his daughter, he sets a bride price, and he settles the arrangement—but for me, it is difficult. I have only dreamed of having Benaiah as my husband. He has dominated my thoughts, and I can see myself with no one else.

Father bustles into the room, his eyes shining and wet with tears. I turn toward the wall so that he will not see the tears in my eyes.

"My dove! You are radiant!" He sucks in his breath in exaggerated wonder as he looks me over. "All is ready. You know I have arranged to have a feast in honor of both of you tonight. It won't be as great as the feast on your actual wedding day, but your betrothal is very special too."

I let his words fall to the floor in silence. I want to scream, "No! I don't want to marry at all now!"

Instead, I sit quietly as he continues on. "Oh how I have waited for this day! Finally, my daughter will start a family! Oh, finally!" He bustles on into the next room.

I let my breath come out in a loud sigh. Why is my heart so heavy? Why can I not get it together and accept this new future for myself? I must learn to, somehow. I must let go of the dreams I have dreamed and do what I need to do to make it through each day. I must forget about Benaiah. I must close the doors on my memories of him and leave them buried. I must find a way to go on.

Soon we are ready and out the door. Father and several young women from town are accompanying me. We walk out to the town gate. The elders are all here, gathered about. I feel like I'm going to a trial. This must be how it feels when a criminal comes before them and gets sentenced to be stoned. I try to shake the thought out of my head. The sky is overcast, and my mood matches the clouds.

Mahlo has already arrived, and he's standing tall and proud, dressed in a fine tunic, with his father at his side. His mother and brothers are also here, standing back a ways and watching it all. My heart goes wild, and I feel faint. This is not even the wedding celebration—what will I do then? What will I do when Mahlo takes me home to his father's house on our wedding night? The thought sends chills up my spine. Today we officially become betrothed. We will make our promise to each other. Our families will exchange gifts and finalize the legal transaction.

I have dreamed of my family and my husband, but my dreams have never looked like this.

All too soon, Mahlo and I are standing before the elders, facing each other. I can barely breathe. Everything seems hazy. Mahlo speaks the words of promise. My turn comes. My lips refuse to move. My heart trembles. Panic erases all my thoughts of duty and obligation. Before I know what I am doing, I am backing up, turning, and running away. My father is shouting as I've never heard him shout. The young women scatter as he tries to reach me and grab me, but I run too fast for him. I don't look back. I don't want to see the confusion behind me. I just want to get away to a place where I can breathe again. They can do the rest without me, if they must. Do they really need me there?

Whether I make the promise or they make it for me, the end is still the same. I will be Mahlo's, and I will be miserable.

I become aware of the burning in my lungs. I slow down and suck deep breaths of air. How far have I run? Where have I gone? What have I done? I will be the talk of Pirathon. Everyone will laugh at me when I walk down the street. I am already quite old for marriage. Most women already have husbands and children at my age, and now I've just run away from the only offer of marriage my father has ever been able to procure.

I turn around and see father running down the path as fast as he can. I have never seen his face so flushed with anger and embarrassment. Shame wells up inside my soul. I have dishonored him and our family. I have disappointed him. I have further ruined our position in the community.

I turn and keep running. Maybe I will never come back. Maybe I will hire myself out as a slave or live with some of our relatives in a neighboring village.

Suddenly, I hear loud voices in front of me. I stop in my tracks. Someone is coming around an outcropping along the path. Where can I turn? Where can I go? My father is catching up behind me. These unseen strangers will soon block my path. What if they grab me? What if they hurt me? My mind is frantic. I try to leave the path and scramble alongside the outcropping.

"Did you hear something?" a voice cries out. "Who's there?"

I try to move a little quieter, but I don't have time to stop.

Another voice comes, a bit quieter than the first, but so close and so unmistakable. "Reminds me of another time we were both on this path, Adnah, only it was dark then."

My heart soars with unspeakable joy at the sound of this voice. Can it be? Is it my Benaiah? Has he come back today of all days? I am breathless again—not just breathless from running, but breathless from the best surprise of my life. The men round the bend, and I look into the eyes of the man I love. My Benaiah is alive! He has returned!

43

SERVANT OF SAUL

It's the morning after the great battle. Joy thunders through me as never before. I can't stop thinking about our victory! The battle is over, but the memories are sweet and fresh. I fold the king's tunics and pack them in the bag as we prepare to journey back to the capital city. My fingers work all on their own as my mind continues rehashing the events that still hardly seem real.

A boy destroyed the giant! The man who had us trembling for forty days fell dead and helpless in a few short moments! Our army swept over the Philistines like a rolling wild fire over a dry grain field. Nothing can chase away the happy smile on my face! Yahweh has answered all our prayers!

Even Prince Jonathan arrived in time to see it. I had finally gone behind the king's back and sent a message to the prince hoping he would come and challenge this Goliath and get it over with. I knew that Saul had been keeping Jonathan away, trying to protect him all this time. But I also knew that Jonathan had the heart of a lion and that if he had any kind of invitation he would come and fight him. He arrived the day that David struck the Philistine champion down. He saw it and cheered louder than us all! When David came back to the camp, Jonathan welcomed him like a brother. They spent the entire evening together talking as if they were old friends.

The king enters the tent, and I notice traces of the old King Saul have come back. He's arrayed in one of his best robes for today's journey, knowing that the people will come out to celebrate our victory as we parade back to the capital city. He holds himself with pride again, and there's a ring of joy and eagerness in his voice.

My thoughts careen into the future. Maybe this battle has changed everything! Now we will defeat the Philistines once and for all. King Saul will lead us as we conquer all the other nations, and they will see that our God is the only God! My heart buzzes with fresh hope and excitement.

Hoshan and I finish packing the tent and the supplies and secure them to several donkeys. General Abner arrives and informs us that the army is ready to go.

The gentle morning sun paints us with light as we begin our victory march. The army moves out with Saul at the front. We walk near him, leading the pack animals. David and Jonathan are right behind, and the rest of the army parades in rows according to rank, beaming with pride and joy. Messengers have carried news of the victory far and wide, and the people are coming out in droves to praise the army and celebrate the victory.

Throughout the day, excited Israelites flock to us from every village that we pass. Everywhere we go, people are celebrating. Many congratulate the soldiers by giving gifts and food. Breathtakingly beautiful women dance in joy at our victory, dressed in their best robes and jewelry. Tambourines shake and chime as they sing beautiful songs of triumph.

They honor Saul and David with their songs: "Saul has killed his thousands and David his tens of thousands!"

I am caught up in the dizzying crescendo of joy as the sound of their sweet voices washes all around me.

We pass through ten villages, and all the women sing the same refrain—it's become a national anthem! Several times I look over at the king as the dancers twirl and the songs of victory echo across the hills, and I am surprised to see that his face is grim and tight. He smiles politely but coldly. Something is wrong with him. Why is he not celebrating? Why does he look upset?

That night, in the tent, I hear him muttering to himself. "Tens of thousands! They credit *him* with *tens* of thousands, while they credit me with only thousands! Don't they know I'm the *king*! What about all my victories? I have fought our enemies over and over and won again and again. How quickly they forget me in favor of some new upstart!"

"Your Majesty," I venture quietly, "I'm sure they mean no disrespect. They are just celebrating David because he fought the Philistine and won the victory—*this* time. They are still acknowledging your greatness."

"Are they? My thousands are nothing compared to his *tens* of thousands!"

I am disturbed by the king's attitude. Why can he not be happy? We just won the greatest battle with the Philistines so far!

"Don't think I'm a fool! Everyone looks at me differently," he grumbles. "They think I should have gone out and fought Goliath. They think I'm old and spent. Little David's the hero now! I'm just cast off like an old used-up wineskin!"

"Your Majesty, please! No one is thinking such terrible things. Everyone loves you. Everyone respects you."

"What do you know? You, too, probably think I should have fought the giant days ago."

Tense caution tingles through me. I pause a moment. My mouth feels dry when I open it again with a lie. "Of course not, Your Majesty."

He grunts in disbelief.

"Yahweh wanted that boy to defeat Goliath. You were not meant to fight him."

"Do *not* talk to me about *Yahweh* and what he *wants!*" The sudden anger explodes out of him.

"A thousand apologies, Your Majesty," I whisper in submission.

We complete the short trip to the capital city the next morning. Every village along the way gives us the same reception, and with every song that praises King Saul and David, the king grows more and more glum and upset.

We arrive at the palace at midday, and I am relieved to be back in familiar surroundings. I greet the servants who were left behind and go about checking over the work they did while I was gone. They have done a passable job of keeping the supplies in order, and I commend them. I check the lists and meet with several of the merchants.

I am in the supply room when Hoshan bursts through the door, panting for air and shouting for my help. I drop the list I am working on and rush to see what is happening.

"What is it, Hoshan?"

"The...the king—he's...he's out of his...mind!"

I run after Hoshan and burst through the servants' door of the throne room. The servants have once again shut the main doors to the throne room trying to contain another outburst. King Saul's face is contorted in an angry snarl, and his eyes are glowing like hot coals. He's chanting strange and unusual things about Yahweh with fierce anger and then screaming at the servants at the top of his lungs.

He shouts like a deranged prophet. "Hate! Yahweh hates me!" He growls a deep, guttural, unearthly sound. "He hates all who have broken his ways!" His eyes dart about like flecks of foam tossing on a violent sea.

No one dares to go near him or tries to control him. He has gone completely crazy.

"Quick, go get David and his harp!" I hiss. "This is the worst I've seen him."

Moments later, David arrives with his harp, and he seems to be completely calm and at peace. His confident presence cools the hot tension in the room. He lifts the instrument and begins to play. He opens his mouth and pours out beautiful, simple words of God's love and peace. Again, I am transfixed by the moment. If this does not calm the king, nothing will!

Suddenly, I hear Hoshan gasp in terror. I look over at the king just in time to see a flash of movement. I hear a sickening thud as one of the king's spears sinks into the far wall, narrowly missing David's head! The shaft twangs and quivers after the impact, and the room fills with an eerie, tense silence. David stares wide-eyed at the king, and the king glowers back at him.

I stand gaping, my mind struggling to comprehend what just happened. Did the king really just try to kill David? Before I can recover, the king reaches down and takes hold of another spear!

"Your Majesty!" I protest involuntarily.

Again, before any of us can move, he thrusts it with all his might at David. David avoids it again with a quick jump to his left, and the spear strikes the wall, glancing off the panels and clattering to the floor.

Servants scatter in every direction. David stands looking at the king in bewilderment.

"Why...why are you trying to kill me, my lord?"

I stare at the king, his eyes glowing with hate as he glares at David for long moment.

"Your Majesty...I just wanted to play you a song on my harp, as I always do. Would that be all right?"

A sigh escapes Saul's lips, and his eyes soften. His hands drop to his side as a great shudder runs through him. Sanity seems to gradually return to him.

"I...forgive me. You're like a son to me, of course. This damned spirit possesses me, and I...I was not thinking. It wasn't me." He shakes his head in frustration, turns, and walks back into his sleeping chambers without another word.

We all look around at each other in wonderment and shock. David is the first to recover.

"We must pray for our king." His eyes travel and rest on each of us for a moment. "Please don't tell anyone about this. King Saul's reputation is at stake."

We nod dumbly, and David quietly leaves the chambers.

After that, I try to avoid the king as much as I can, sending others to do the work that must be done in his presence. I am so disappointed and disillusioned. Rather than celebrate David as the hero that he is, or acknowledge Yahweh and thank him for the victory, the king ruminates in selfish thoughts of inadequacy and jealousy. No one enjoys working near him.

Young David is now at the palace all the time. He is part of the army and given a high rank. Officially and publicly the king praises him and congratulates him, but in private he is extremely bitter and jealous.

I find myself drawn to David. This young man has a heart for Yahweh and courage like I've never seen, and Yahweh is certainly with him in everything he does. As time passes, the thought grows larger and larger inside me: David would be a good king. I hear rumors that he was secretly anointed by the prophet Samuel. I find myself hoping these rumors are true. I hear of his victories and I'm impressed by the way he holds himself in every situation. I try to shake the disloyal thought from my head, but it begins to work itself into my heart and takes hold like a growing root. I want David to be my king instead of Saul!

44

BENAIAH

We are almost to Pirathon. Adnah has come back with me as an official messenger from the army to bring news of the battle in the Valley of Elah. The journey has been uneventful, and I've enjoyed having Adnah along with me. It is strange to walk back with him as an experienced soldier instead of a raw recruit. We trade stories and talk as peers, and it feels good. I marvel at how far I've come since I left the village with him and went off to join the army. Soon we will round a bend in the trail, and I will have a full view of my village. This presents me with mixed emotions—Pirathon is where my Hannah is, yet it is also where so many bad memories were made.

Suddenly, we hear fast footsteps on the other side of a rocky outcropping along the path. Adnah and I stop, all alert, hands poised on our weapons. We are shocked when a woman bursts around the corner of the outcropping.

Can it be? Can it be my Hannah? Her face is flushed and red as the evening sky, and her hair and shawl are tussled and wild.

She's wearing her best robes, but they are scuffed and marred with dirt.

"Hannah!" Incredible happiness fills me immediately.

"Benaiah! I heard your voice! You're really alive?"

She's out of breath, but she runs the short distance between us. Abandoning all restraint, she wraps her arms around me in tight relief. My heart throbs with overwhelming joy as I hold the woman that I love with all my might. Nothing in the world has ever felt so sweet and right.

"Yes!" I laugh. "Of course I am."

I look down into her large round eyes and see them brimming with tears.

"Let's just leave. Let's go away from Pirathon together—right now."

"Run away together? I've just arrived! Why would we run away?"

She looks behind her as if expecting to see someone.

"Why are you running? Why are you so far from the village—and in your best robes?"

"Father has pledged me in marriage to Mahlo. Today is the day of our betrothal before the elders."

A sharp arrow of shock and pain pierces through my heart. "What?"

"Yes. Moments ago we were standing at the gate, ready to make the pledge before the elders. I...I ran away."

All of a sudden, Hannah's father rounds the outcropping, completely out of breath. I have never seen him so flustered and furious. "Hannah!" His voice is a hoarse roar. He sees me, and his anger intensifies.

Our embrace melts away, and we quickly part from each other. Hannah's tears are streaming down her face. She's shaking her head, her long, beautiful strands of hair disheveled and bobbing from side to side.

"Oh, Father! No!"

I am completely in shock. My arms and my heart ache for her, but I also hurt knowing that I've arrived only to lose her forever. The thought fills me with a frightening emptiness.

"Father, please! I can't marry Mahlo! See—Benaiah is home! My heart is his!"

He shakes his head in rage. "Hannah, stop fighting this! You have shamed me as no one ever has. The arrangement is made. You must marry Mahlo. Come back with me at once!" He shoots me a dangerous, challenging look.

I close my eyes. The pain in my heart is sharper and more unbearable than any wound I've ever felt. I want to grab her arm and run away with her immediately.

"Let's go, Hannah. Now!" her father barks.

"Father, I—"

"Hannah! Don't say another word. You have disappointed me in every possible way! Come with me right now!"

I open my eyes in time to see Hannah's head drop in shame and resignation. "Yes, Father." I want to shout. I want to grab her arm and pull her back to me. I lost Berechiah. I lost my mother. Now I'm about to lose Hannah! This loss will be the worst of all because she will still be alive. I'll never stop loving her, yet I'll see her and hear her voice every time I'm in town, knowing we'll never again have the hope of a life together. As for Mahlo, I'm losing him too! Why is he going along with this? How could he betray me? He knows how much I love Hannah. I will never forgive him for this.

Her father grips her hand forcefully and directs her back toward the gate. She follows like a stray lamb pulled along by a shepherd, a lamb that has given up the struggle to be free. I follow closely behind, my heart dying inside.

On the way to the gate I explain the situation to Adnah. He shakes his head and offers me only silence for comfort. He is a great friend on the battlefield, but he is lost when it comes to matters of the heart. I feel truly alone.

When we reach the gate, the elders are clustered about and muttering together in disapproval. Hannah's father is flustered, but tries his best to maintain his composure. Mahlo is upset and embarrassed, but his father is livid, veins pulsing and face flushed. As soon as we reach them, his anger explodes into shouts.

"Your daughter is a disgrace! How dare she run off like that! I've never met a woman so wild and ungrateful!"

Eliezer's voice is a whisper of shame. "I am so very sorry. I don't know why she acted like that. She is here now. She will not run away again. We are ready."

Mahlo's father laughs bitterly. "She will *not* marry my son. I withdraw my offer."

"No! My lord, please don't do that!" Eliezer's voice breaks with emotion.

"We have seen today what kind of a woman she is. I will not have her betrothed to my son. I will not have her as part of my household!"

"Please, it was a moment's foolishness. She's here now. She's come back to her senses!" Hannah's father pleads.

"My mind is made up. No one will want her now! I'll see to it myself when news of her behavior reaches the rest of the village. She has utterly disgraced herself!"

Part of me wants to go over and knock Mahlo's father to the ground, yet part of me is springing alive with new hope.

While the elders talk amongst themselves, one of the chief elders steps forward and speaks to Mahlo's father. His voice is quiet and stern. "Since the betrothal has not yet taken place, we will honor your request to withdraw your offer of marriage." He turns to face Hannah's father. "Eliezer, we are very disappointed in you and the way your daughter has shown such disrespect for these proceedings. We trust that you will teach her to be more respectful in the future if anyone offers her another marriage arrangement."

Eliezer hangs his head at the words. "Yes, of course."

Hannah's eyes fill with tears that are starting to spill down her cheeks. My heart breaks for her and the shame she must be feeling. She and her father are so close, and it's obvious she has wounded him deeply.

The chief elder turns his attention to Adnah. "We apologize for not greeting you properly. We do welcome you to Pirathon once again, Adnah. Do you come on another recruiting mission?"

Adnah bows to the elders. "I do not, my lords. I come to bring you news of a great victory for King Saul and all of Israel in the valley of Elah. The Philistines came full force against us in the valley. They sent forth a monstrous champion, Goliath, to decide the battle's outcome. After a forty-day stalemate and no challenger rising from the ranks of Israel, young David, son of Jesse of Bethlehem, went forward and battled Goliath and felled him with a sling and a stone. After that, we overran their forces and routed them all along the road, slaughtering many of them as they fled in terror from the battle lines. Yahweh has given us a great victory—one of the greatest victories against the Philistines so far!"

As Adnah speaks, the elders' faces light up with joy and relief. They cry out shouts of joy.

"Praise Yahweh!"

"What news!

"We must tell the whole village!"

Adnah clears his throat loudly, and the elders quiet down. "One more thing I must tell you: Your own Benaiah of Pirathon has greatly distinguished himself on the field of battle. Surely you heard of the large raiding party that was threatening your village and the others here in the north. You must know that you owe your safety to the heroic bravery of Benaiah who felled several horsemen with his bow and arrow and fought valiantly so that we could disable their chariots and win the victory in the north!"

A rush of heat rises to my face. I am surprised that Adnah is telling them this. I feel Hannah's eyes on me, so I glance over toward her. Through her tears, she is beaming with pride.

The elders seem to be looking at me as if they've never seen me before. After a moment, the chief elder comes forward and embraces me! I am numb with shock. He stands back and says, "Benaiah, for many years you have been a trouble-maker among us. Many times I myself had to speak stern words to you before the elders and the village, but I am indebted to you for your service in the army and for fighting hard to save your village."

I nod, somewhat embarrassed and unsure how to react. I've never before had the approval of any of these men.

"Adnah is a very respected man, and his endorsement of you is no small thing. We are grateful for what you have done for us all, and I myself will hold a feast tomorrow to honor you for your service! The whole village will be invited!"

I can hardly believe my ears. The other elders are nodding in approval. I have never felt so honored! "Thank you," I say. "I was just doing what I needed to do. I don't deserve such honor."

Instantly, my mind races back to when I left for the army. This is what I wanted all along! Yet, now that I have such honor, I realize how I've changed. I realize now that life is so much more than what others think of me. What I want more than anything now is Hannah's love and to learn more of Yahweh and his love. I want to serve him with my days, whatever those days may hold. The realization strikes me like lightning in that moment, and I hardly think before my mouth opens up again. "Eliezer."

He turns to look at me in surprise, his face still traced with fresh disappointment at the failed betrothal. "What is it, Benaiah?"

"I have asked you this question many times, and I know the answer that you have given me over and over. Today again, in the presence of all the elders of Pirathon, I ask for your daughter's hand in marriage. I promise that I will be worthy of her and work to earn the respect of the village."

Hannah's face comes up at my words, and I see the fire of hope burning in them as she looks eagerly at her father. Her father looks at me, his eyes tinged with sadness and a little resignation.

"I have always known you as a hard worker, Benaiah, but you've had a troubled youth and little respect in the village. However, I am grateful for your service in the king's army and that you fought to save Pirathon...but my daughter is my only child, and my heart has been hers since she was young. I have always wanted what is best for her, and I still do to this day." He pauses, visibly struggling with rarely expressed emotion. He looks deep into my eyes. "If you will promise to take care of her and provide for her, to fill her life with song and joy, and to honor and love her, then I will *consider* giving her to you as your wife."

"I will do all that and more!" My words rush out in eager joy.

I look over at Hannah, and she is crying again—not out of sadness or shame, but out of sheer, exuberant joy.

45

BENAIAH

It is early, but the sun is already quite glaring and hot. Sweat glistens on my skin as I urge the oxen to move. The yoke rattles as they strain forward. The plow blade sinks true into the earth, and fresh, black soil churns upward as I break the ground.

It's been about a year now since I stood before the elders and asked Hannah's father for her hand in marriage. A few days after I came home, he fully agreed to the match. Two weeks later we officially made the arrangement before the elders, and I promised to care for her and to pay Eliezer as much as I could for the bride price. I did not have much, but Eliezer was understanding about it.

Mahlo avoided me for quite a while after I returned, but I went to visit him recently, and we had a long talk. Our friendship will never be the same, but I have managed to forgive him. It surprises me what Yahweh's love has done in my heart.

When I sent word of my betrothal back to the army, commander Ramel responded by generously giving me a full two years' leave from the army. Usually soldiers only get a year off after getting married. I've had plenty of time now to enjoy a short betrothal with Hannah and then our wonderful week-long marriage celebration which still fills my mind with joyful memories. I can't help but smile when I think of her or say her name. Yahweh has blessed me through her in ways I still can't fully appreciate! The way her eyes light up when she sees me thrills me every time. The soft touch of her skin on mine makes me feel like I could fight a thousand Goliaths! We still have much to learn about each other, and sometimes we disagree and get angry with each other throughout our days of hard, grueling work, but I wouldn't trade my life with Hannah for all the adventure in the world.

Time is flying by, and soon enough I will go back and join the men in the army. For now, though, I am enjoying my time of peace. Arah has been good to us. He's let us stay in the household, and I've agreed to help him work the land this year. It is strange to live in the same house when everything is different. I sometimes look up expecting to see Mother come around the corner. Of course, she never does. I still miss her so intensely. It's as if some part of my soul is missing, and I'll never get it back. I mourned for her for a full two weeks when I got home. I wore rough cloth and cut my hair. I visited her grave every day. Hannah was such a comfort to me. If I wouldn't have had her by my side to help me through, I might have slipped back into a cold river of regret and sadness. She kept assuring me with Yahweh's promises, and she always seemed to know just what I needed her to say. I often go and visit Lamich and Ardaliah and pass on some of those condolences to them. They still miss Berechiah fiercely, but it helps when we sit down and share memories together and talk of his strong faith in Yahweh.

I marvel at the changes that have taken place here in Pirathon. I don't feel small anymore. For the most part, the villagers have come to accept me and even respect me. They see me as a strong soldier and a leader. Even Sennah has matured. Now we have developed a friendly rivalry between us. He often jokes with me about the days he used to lay me flat on my back. I remind him of how muddy he was in that field the day I won.

After my reprieve is over, Hannah and I will move closer to the capital city so that I can continue in the army as a soldier. I have been notified that when I return, they will give me a higher rank. Commander Ramel was recently promoted, and I will take his place. I will have a hundred men looking to me for direction! I am a bit nervous to take on such a responsibility, but also honored that they would choose me to do it. I know that Yahweh will help me lead them.

I finish the row and turn the oxen. I steady the plow to begin another row. Arah is doing well for himself. The fields look good this year, and the garden looks like it will do well too. Hannah has enjoyed helping Jadia at home, and they have become quite close. I've had long talks with Hannah and her father about Yahweh and his love, and I've been learning so much more. My heart has newfound peace knowing that I serve the God who created the whole world and that all along he has blessed me in ways I never recognized before. If only Berechiah could see me now! If only I could talk to him! He would be overjoyed at my transformation, and he would teach me so much. I still feel like a toddler in the ways of Yahweh.

I look off to my left and am startled to see a man silhouetted on the hillside. I pull up on the reins, and the oxen stop obediently. I shade my eyes to get a better view, and a vague uneasiness creeps into me. There's something oddly familiar about the large man coming toward me. I secure the oxen so they won't stray, and I start walking across the field to meet the approaching stranger.

His clothes are tattered and worn. His hair is grey, unkempt, and hanging so it almost completely covers his face. I'm on my guard, every sense alert.

"Son of the dogs!" he gruffly announces.

I stop moving. I stop breathing. It's the voice I've heard in a thousand nightmares. Cold fingers of fear reach for my throat. I panic and instantly think of Hannah. I must protect her!

Suddenly, I think of my mother. She died because of *this* man! This man ruined so much of my life! Boiling anger purges my fear. "I ought to kill you right now, Piram!"

"You wouldn't kill your own father, would you, boy?"

His hard voice rips through me. Old wounds inside tear open and bleed—I am raw with fresh rage. I rush toward him, closing the gap between us, my fists clenched for conflict. I stand toe to toe with him and stare into his cold, black eyes.

My words hiss out. "You're *not* my father!"

He stands his ground. "Rumor has it you've made something of yourself in the army." He laughs bitterly and then coughs violently. "I'd have to see it to believe it." He coughs again—a gross, unnatural sound—and then spits into the dirt.

Hot blood pulses through me, and my voice crescendos in trembling rage. "You *killed* my mother! She served you faithfully her whole life, and you destroyed her! What did she ever do to you?" My nails dig into the palms of my hand as my fists clench down even harder. I lift one balled fist and shake it in his face. "If I had a sword right now, I'd cut you down." I look around for my staff, a rock, or anything I can use as a weapon, but then I realize that it would feel better to do it with my own hands.

I look up at Piram, alert and ready to strike him down, and I see something change in his eyes—an invisible wound. Have my words pierced him? I pause and study him as his bravado and confidence vanish. A wave of weariness seems to wash over him. He stumbles a bit, his large form swaying.

"Are you drunk?" I ask.

He shakes his head. "Your mother…I never…I…" His breathing is shallow and strained. He swipes at the hair in front of his eyes. "I…I'm not drunk—not today." His face has gone pale, and his hard expression has melted away into a strange pathetic sadness. "I haven't eaten a meal in five days…haven't slept in a house for months. I've just…followed the trade roads…"

"If you are looking for sympathy, you've come to the wrong place!" I shout at him.

Images of my mother's bruises flash before my eyes. I see again the pained, tortured looks on her face as she endured torment at his hands and the way she looked around nervously when she thought he was near. I hear her crying when she thought no one was listening. The memories roll through my mind, and each one disgusts me. He did that to her! "You deserve nothing but death—a slow, painful, torturous death!"

He sinks to his knees in the freshly tilled earth. He swipes his hair out of his eyes again, and I'm shocked to see tears etching their way through the dirt on his face.

"I never meant to kill her." His words are a pained whisper. "She…she was the best thing in my life, and now she's gone, and I…I did it! I lived in such…anger! Please kill me. That's why I'm here. I don't deserve to live. I…I hate myself. Kill me!"

My mind and heart struggle to take it in. I have never seen him like this in my whole life. He's never once shown any sign of remorse or any twinge of conscience. Never has he apologized.

His broken words have penetrated deep inside my soul. An old, gaping wound somewhere in the depths of my being begins to heal at the sound of his words. My anger starts to fade.

Suddenly, a conversation that I had with Berechiah long ago resurfaces in my thoughts. We were boys, and I remember being so angry with him. He said something infuriating that burned in my thoughts for years to follow.

"We're really no different than Piram, you know," he said. *"We all harbor hatred deep within us. We all act selfishly and get drunk with our own power or shame and lash out. Piram, too, needs Yahweh's mercy. We all do!"*

I didn't speak to him for a full week after he said that. I felt betrayed by him, yet he was right all along!

As I stare down at the broken man who ruined my life, another memory fills my mind. I was sitting with David across the campfire, his tender eyes so alive with the truth he was telling me. I asked him, "What gave you the courage to go and fight Goliath?"

"Yahweh sent me to do it," he said. *"Any of you could have done it. I am no one special. God does not look at outward things, like flashy armor and massive swords. He is not impressed by someone's reputation, accomplishments, or wealth. Sure, Goliath was huge…it looked like it would be impossible. But all along, God saw him as a small, weak, arrogant fool…. You saw a mighty warrior—brawny, tall and powerful. God opened my eyes to see him as he actually was—a pathetic fool…."*

I look down at the pathetic fool in front of me, broken, alone, and without family or hope. All my life I saw him as huge and powerful. All my life I cringed in fear of this man and raged at him in helpless exasperation. He terrorized me and made me feel weak and small. Now my eyes are open. Now I see him as he actually is. Yahweh has brought him to his knees. My giant has fallen, and I can hardly believe it.

"Piram, mercy is Yahweh's greatest gift. It's a gift I never deserved from him, yet he gave it to me. Today I give it to you." My words are slow and quiet, and the anger is no longer in them.

He looks up at me in confusion. "You're not going to kill me?"

"It's what you deserve, but no. Get up! Let's go to the house, and I'll give you some food. You have much to learn about the ways of Yahweh."

He seems utterly incredulous. I reach out to help him up and take hold of his hand—the same hand that beat and killed my mother and the same hand that tortured me as a child. I touch it and am healed.

As we walk the oxen home together, I think of the story of my ancestor, Joseph. His brothers had destroyed his life and sold him into slavery, yet many years later he could say, "You intended to harm me, but God intended it for good to accomplish what is now being done, the saving of many lives."

I look at Piram again and marvel at the ways of Yahweh and his mercy.

EPILOGUE

The feast is over, and the little ones have gathered around me. Little Reuben, his eyes shining like stars, looks up at me in wonder. "Tell us the story! Were you really there? Did you really see Goliath? What was he like?"

I look across the room at my beautiful Hannah. Age has frosted her hair, but her eyes still sparkle like they did when we were young. She looks at me and smiles her easy, honest smile—the one that still makes my heart leap.

I wink and return her smile. "I don't know if your grandmother wants to hear that story again. She's heard it almost a thousand times."

"Do you mind if he tells it again?" Childish enthusiasm spills out of Reuben.

Hannah's eyes shine with amusement. She pauses for a moment, looking down at all the little faces staring eagerly up at her. She lets out an exaggerated sigh. "Well, I suppose I could hear it again, if you must." Her eyes find mine, and we share a hundred memories in a brief glance.

I feel my heart warm at the connection between us, and I smile again. Then I turn to my eager audience and clear my throat as the children lean in with expectation. "You want to hear about Goliath?"

Wide eyes bob up and down.

"Well, he was certainly the largest man I've ever seen in my whole life. He was as tall as that young fig tree growing up on the hill." I point out the open doorway, and the children turn to look at the tree.

"Really?" Four-year-old Serah gasps, and her eyes widen in astonishment. "He must have been a giant!"

"Oh, he was!" Reuben pipes in again. "And King David knocked him down with just a sling and a stone!"

I pause for a moment. "No."

"*No?* But he did, didn't he? Everyone says he did!"

"Who made the stone?" I ask, my eyes shining.

The children grow silent and curious.

"Yahweh made the stone." Little Obed's voice is a whisper as he stares up at me, eyes wide with wonder.

"And who made sure that the stone hit Goliath right where it would knock him down?"

"Yahweh, I guess." Reuben seems to be catching on.

"You guess right."

"So Yahweh really knocked that giant down?"

"Yes, and he used David to do it."

"And you were there? You were really there? You saw it happen?"

I can't help but laugh at their enthusiasm. "Yes, I was there. I was there when the giant fell."

After I answer all of their questions and my dear grandchildren have fallen asleep, I walk out under the winking stars and sit on a stone outside our home to rest and think. So many blessings! Such a life! Such a God!

At my age, I have stored up more memories than I have left to make. Seventy-three years I have walked this earth, most of them fighting for King David as a general in his army. I was honored to be one of thirty of the king's elite fighting men. I could tell countless stories of hundreds of battles, but still none compare to the day I saw Goliath fall, a battle that I watched from a distance. It changed me in ways I will never fully understand. Yahweh has been my God ever since, and I know now that all other gods are empty, powerless, and false.

I look up at the countless stars, the brilliance of God's handiwork. A cool breeze whirls around me, and I breathe in deep, feeling the coolness course through my tired body.

I chuckle, remembering the little faces when I described Goliath. God has blessed Hannah and I in so many amazing ways. He has given us nine children—six boys and three girls— and now a house filled with grandchildren. There is peace in the land these days, and I have every hope that my grandchildren will grow up in the ways of Yahweh, doing great things in his name.

I think back to my younger days when I was dishonored and alone—when the village was against me and I felt that God had put a curse on me. How little I knew! If only I had listened to Mother and Berechiah when they talked of Yahweh and his faithful love. I could have learned to serve God in my pain while understanding that true joy does not fail when life is challenging. I could have understood that peace from God runs deeper than anything else. I tried so hard to gain respect and make a name for myself. What a waste! God found me when I was nothing—when I *hated* him—and he opened my eyes and changed my life. Every experience he gave me was a blessing that made me hungry for his promises, and he filled that hunger with his truth!

Soft hands touch my neck, and a gentle thrill runs through my soul. "My Love!" I say softly. I turn and feast my eyes on my beautiful wife.

"What a wonderful night!" Hannah says, her eyes glowing. She is ageless in her beauty.

"It certainly is! I am enjoying the stars and remembering the old days."

We sit together in comfortable, joyful silence, relishing the last moments of the day together. Hannah rests her head on my shoulder. I close my eyes and give thanks to the God who has given me so much more than I ever could have dreamed—so much more than I have ever deserved.

After a while, she stirs at my side. I feel her warmness leave me as she gets up to go inside, and I ache to have it back.

"Are you coming in? Do you need my help to get up, now that you are old and feeble?" Her voice smiles.

I turn and look into her laughing eyes. Old age, is it?" I laugh. "I'll have to carry you into the house like I did when I was young—*then* you can tell me all about my old age."

"Now that's a tempting offer, but I wouldn't want you to break your back."

I grunt in exaggerated exasperation as she heads inside.

As I get up, I pause to take one last look at the millions of stars that speckle the night sky. God's promise to Abraham flashes into my mind. He promised Abraham descendants as numerous as the stars, and *I* am one of them. I am living proof of God's fulfillment. God also promised him a descendant that would be a blessing to all nations on earth. One day, that ultimate champion will come and battle the most dreadful giants of all—sin and death. Years ago, King David told me about God's promise to him, too: One of his children will be the one. One of his descendants will have his throne forever and be the champion we've yearned for all these years. Maybe soon that promised one will come! Until then, I'll live each day grateful for the God who fights my battles and gives me peace.

I turn and walk toward the house, eager to be warm again and surrounded by those I love. Their faces pass through my mind. I don't know what the future holds for any of them. Will they be important and influential in Israel? Will they do great things and have the love and respect of everyone around them? I hope so, but I am sure they will also experience seasons of loneliness, disrespect, and loss. They may even appear rather small and insignificant throughout their lives. But I know if God can use me—an angry, insignificant outcast—he can also use them, no matter who they become or what they experience. They will always matter to him, because he loves them. My heart rests in that truth.

I take one last look at the sky filled with stars, each one different, each one blazing its tiny light into the darkness, each one carefully set in place by God himself. I marvel at the sight, and the familiar words of worship rush up through me and pour from my lips in an awed whisper. "Give thanks to Yahweh, for he is good. His love endures forever!"

POSTSCRIPT

The young scribe peers over at the master copy. He reads the words aloud. "Among the thirty were Asahel the brother of Joab, Elhanan son of Dodo from Bethlehem, Shammah the Harodite, Elika the Harodite, Helez the Paltite, Benaiah the Pirathonite...Hiddai...Eliahba...Zalmon..." He sighs, exasperated. "Another endless list of names! Don't get me wrong, Master Hagathiah, I am very honored that I am finally qualified to copy the Scriptures. I tremble at this important work! It's just that the lists of names to copy are so long! Why must there be so many names?"

Hagathiah smiles, knowingly. "You are young. This is your first copy of the Scriptures. I have scratched these names on hundreds of scrolls over the years. I've learned to love these lists of names."

The young scribe gestures at the scroll in front of him. "I know nothing of this Elika or this Abiezer or this Benaiah of Pirathon. Their names are in the Scriptures, but nowhere else. Ages of time separate me from them. Why would God have me record each name? Why is it so important that they have a place in his Holy Word until the end of times?" He shoots Hagathiah a pained look of confusion. "You enjoy copying them? How can that be?"

"My son, think of it this way: Each of these names is precious to God. Each one has a life and a story behind it. God knows each life and each story—their sins, their failures, their dreams, their families, and their triumphs. Even if we do not know anything more than a list of their names, their lives are open to God. I think God has put so many long lists of names in his Scriptures so that we remember that each single person is important to him. God loves every single person and has given each one an important life that he weaves into the fabric of his great plan for the world."

The young scribe stares in amazement at the list in front of him. He reads through the list of names again, and this time he imagines a life for each one. His eyes widen in appreciation.

Hagathiah smiles. "You see? Now for the best part—these lists remind us that our names are important to God too! Just like he knows these names and their stories, he knows your name and my name and our stories! He knows all our joys and triumphs as well as our failings, problems, and sins, and he loves us still! He gives us his promises of salvation and eternal life. We too are part of his story—the story that never ends!"

The young scribe turns back to his work with new zeal and carefully continues copying the words of God—the promises that give life and salvation to the world.

BIBLE REFERENCES

This fictional account intersects with and mentions actual biblical events. If you would like to read the biblical accounts, I've included references here. 1 Samuel 8:1 – 18:15 sets the background for most of the novel. There you can gain helpful information about Saul's early days as king, his relationship with the prophet Samuel, his servants, his troubles with the evil spirit, the battle for Jabesh-Gilead, the battle of Micmash, and the famous contest between David and Goliath in chapter 17.

There are several other Scripture sections mentioned briefly in the book. Abdon, Serah's ancestor in the novel, was one of the judges of Israel and was from Pirathon. See Judges 12:13-15. David briefly mentions his grandmother from Moab. Her story is found in the book of Ruth. Benaiah mentions the Philistines' capture of the ark which is recorded in 1 Samuel 4. Towards the end, Benaiah refers to his ancestor Joseph. His story is found in Genesis 37-50. God's promise to Abraham is also mentioned several times. Read Genesis 12:1-3 and Genesis 15:1-6. Benaiah's final words in the novel are Psalm 118:1. This encouraging and beautiful psalm fits themes found in the novel and points us to the Promised One and the world's only Savior, Jesus Christ. The entire Bible is about him. For more information and resources please visit www.whataboutjesus.com.

QUESTIONS FOR DISCUSSION

Benaiah felt like an outcast in his own village. Describe a time that you felt that way in school, society, or even in church. Identify several ways God might use you to help others who feel like outcasts.

Serah and Benaiah struggled with domestic violence. How can a loving God allow such things to go on? Should Serah have handled the situation differently? Why or why not?

Benaiah is bitter, even angry with God at times. When in your life have you been tempted to have a similar attitude toward God? What's the key to countering this temptation?

Yahweh's promises are mentioned several times throughout the book. List as many of God's promises as you can. Which ones are especially helpful to you today? Describe how your life might change if you relied fully on these promises.

For a long time Benaiah was never sure of God's love. How can anyone be sure of it? Find several Bible passages that answer this question.

Throughout the story, God's people appear weak and pathetic. It is a theme found throughout the Scriptures. Find other places in the Bible where God uses people who appear insignificant to accomplish his amazing plans. Why is this so?

List several ways Benaiah has changed by the end of the book. What brought about each of those changes?

ACKNOWLEDGMENTS

First and foremost I thank my Savior Jesus Christ. Without him this project would have been impossible and meaningless. His priceless forgiveness and overwhelming grace astound and motivate me every day. Any good that comes of this is his doing. He deserves all the credit.

Without my wife, Cara, there would be no book. Her love, support, and encouragement along the way have made this book possible. I am awed by her patience, hard work, sacrificial love, and excellent advice during this entire process. (Thank you, Honey!)

Thank you to my editor, Rachel Kamin, for tireless hours of painstaking copy and content editing. She saved me again and again from butchering the English language and its rules of grammar. I appreciate her hard work, dedication, and good advice.

Thank you to Jonathan Mayer of Scapegoat Studios for designing and creating the cover art for the novel.

Thank you to Aaron Biebert for professional photography work and his website help. www.attentionera.com.

Thank you also to all who read through the final versions of the manuscript and helped me with excellent words of advice and

ADAM NITZ

encouragement—especially Pastor Dean Biebert and again, my wife, Cara.

Wherever I have taken wording from a bible translation in the text of this book, these Scriptures were taken from the Holy Bible, New International Version®, NIV®. Copyright © 1973, 1978, 1984, 2011 by Biblica, Inc.™ Used by permission of Zondervan. All rights reserved worldwide. www.zondervan.com The "NIV" and "New International Version" are trademarks registered in the United States Patent and Trademark Office by Biblica, Inc.™

ABOUT THE AUTHOR

Adam Nitz is a graduate of Wisconsin Lutheran Seminary, Mequon, WI and a former pastor. He regularly contributes to the website www.breadforbeggars.com. He has always had a love and passion for writing. He lives with his wife and children in North St. Paul, MN. You can learn more about him and his writing and follow his blog at www.adamnitz.com.

20352692R00190

Made in the USA
Middletown, DE
24 May 2015